Women of Washington Avenue

by

Linda Apple

Moonlight Mississippi Series, Book 1

This is a work of fiction. Names, characters, places, and incidents are either the product of the author's imagination or are used fictitiously, and any resemblance to actual persons living or dead, business establishments, events, or locales, is entirely coincidental.

Women of Washington Avenue

Cover Art by *RJ Morris*

The Wild Rose Press, Inc.
PO Box 708
Adams Basin, NY 14410-0708
Visit us at www.thewildrosepress.com

Publishing History
First Mainstream Women's Fiction Edition, 2014
Print ISBN 978-1-62830-392-6
Digital ISBN 978-1-62830-393-3

Moonlight Mississippi Series, Book 1
Published in the United States of America

The evening star glinted in the pink and purple twilight. Normally, this was the loneliest time of day for me since Ray died. But now, here with these women, it felt so right and beautiful. I held up my glass. "Here's to friends, old and new."

"Amen." Lexi stuck out her glass. "To being here for each other no matter what."

Molly Kate raised her glass. "To forever friends."

My insecurity raised its head. "Forever friends." I looked around. "That sounds so nice. I wish I'd grown up with you girls."

Lexi leaned forward and faced me. "Sugar, let me tell you something. You didn't have to grow up with us to be our forever friend." She pivoted around. "Ain't that right girls? Jema is one of us."

"She sure is." Avalee stood and held up her goblet. "To the women of Washington Avenue."

We followed Avalee's lead, clinked glasses, and drank to friendship.

Lexi opened the last bottle and refilled our glasses before joining Molly Kate on the swing. "Well, Avalee, I have to say, you could have knocked me over with a feather when Ty told me you were home."

Avalee rocked next to me. "I planned on surprising you after I left Molly's. But when I saw Ty…" Tears filled her eyes and slid down her cheeks. She took a drink and shook her head. "I know it is silly, but I had to talk to Marc, so I spent the afternoon in the cemetery."

"Not silly at all, hon." Lexi got up from the swing and went to her. Wrapping her arms around Avalee, she said, "We do what we have to do."

Dedication

To my husband, Neal Apple,
whose idea inspired this book
and who is a constant source of
encouragement and support.
I love you.

Acknowledgements

My love and gratitude goes to my husband, Neal, for the hours he spent with me on the front porch dreaming up ideas, listening to me read this book to him for hours on end and for his input. Also, heartfelt thanks to my momma, Freddie Diehl, and to my grandmother, Cladie Mae, for nurturing me as a Southern woman and for giving me beautiful memories from which to draw.

Profuse appreciation to my daughter, Olivia Apple. Her keen eye, suggestions, and comments were invaluable. Also, thanks to Jan Morrill, Pam Jones, and Ruth Weeks for the insightful help they gave me while in Red River, NM. And of course, I'll always be grateful to my mentor in writing as well as in life, Velda Brotherton.

Gratitude beyond measure goes to my editor and now friend, Ally Robertson. Finally, to Rhonda Penders and all those who have made this book possible at The Wild Rose Press, thank you for your enthusiasm, support, patience, and above all, for giving this book a chance.

Fried green tomatoes, magnolia blooms, and front porch swing blessings to you all!

Chapter 1

AVALEE
Home

When I left Mississippi, I shook the dust off my feet and vowed to *never* live there again.

Never say never.

The wind whipped through my hair as I drove my new Mercedes convertible to my childhood home in Moonlight, Mississippi. Not to visit, but to move back in with my mother. I gripped the steering wheel and called out to no one. "Avalee Preston, a fifty-five-year-old spinster moving back in with her mother."

For heaven's sake. If that wasn't pitiful, I didn't know what was.

Tension built between my shoulders and worked its way up my neck. I wasn't sure at all about this move. I could count on one hand the times I'd been home since I fled Ole Miss days before the graduation ceremonies and moved to New York City.

Manhattan had been my home for over thirty years. I'd traveled the world lecturing on floral arranging and décor. I'd also written six floral design and gardening books. How would I ever adjust to small—no—Lilliputian town living?

Oh well, no one said this had to be permanent. Still, I couldn't abandon Momma either. The family floral and garden business was in trouble, and even though I wasn't sure there was anything I could do, I had to try.

My ancestors had immigrated to Mississippi from Scotland in the late seventeen hundreds and purchased a large parcel of land to farm. But it was my great-grandfather who discovered there was money to be made by growing flowers. Over the years, his little business grew, and by the time my father had taken over, Preston Gardens shipped flowers to florists over a twelve state area and sold fresh flowers, bedding plants, and bushes from the shop close to their house.

When Momma called me distressed about the business' steady decline since Dad's passing, I wasn't surprised. He had the business mind in the family. She excelled in public relations. Numbers were not her strong suit. In all fairness, however, her lack of business sense was not the only problem. When I came home for Daddy's funeral a few years back, Moonlight was like a ghost town. Stores on the square were boarded up. Factories closed. The beautiful old homes in the historic part of town had been abandoned. Their porches sagged; the paint peeled and chipped off. The once manicured lawns were overgrown with weeds.

Even the Norton mansion stood empty after Mrs. Norton died. But Momma said the family had hired a caretaker to tend it. I hoped that was still the case.

A dull throb niggled at the base of my skull. I rolled my head from side to side, hoping it might ease the pain. It didn't. In a few minutes, I'd be in Moonlight. I made up my mind to stop at the Piggly Wiggly store to buy some Naproxen before heading to Mom's. She used those nasty headache powders. It's a wonder she still had a stomach lining.

When I crossed the town limits, I noticed a new sign had replaced the old green and white government one. It was a wood carving of a moon rising over a lake and the words

WELCOME TO MOONLIGHT MISSISSIPPI WHERE YOUR ROMANTIC DREAMS COME TRUE.

Where your romantic dreams come true? Well, how about that? When did the powers that be decide on that slogan for this forgotten little town? In any case, it wasn't true. At least not for me.

Not for Marc.

I swallowed the regret threatening to suffocate me. Even though it had been over thirty years, I could still hear the voice on the phone telling me Marc had died in a car crash. We were to be married the following week. And instead of the pain easing with time, it deepened. Not for the reason most would assume, but for a reason I had never shared.

Moonlight Lake glistened on my left and beckoned me to visit. I heeded its call and turned in. I wanted to see *our spot,* our secluded hideaway under a willow tree on the water's edge we had claimed as teens. I smiled when I saw it, relieved the tree was still there. Only now it was much larger and the curtain of leaves much denser.

Even though Mom was probably waiting for me on her porch, I couldn't resist staying a while. I parked the car, slipped out, and strolled to the tree. A breeze blew making some of its graceful branches sweep out to me as if to say, "Welcome home, Avalee." And just as sudden, the wind died causing them to drop in disappointment, as if whispering. "Where's Marc?"

I plopped down cross-legged on the grass and watched the waves lap rhythmically against the shore. The spicy scent of warm pine needles filled the air. Definitely the smell of home. Nothing in Manhattan ever smelled this fresh or this clean. A noisy blue jay scolded from his perch on a nearby pine interrupting the lake's soft voice. Annoying birds. Marc used to fling pinecones at them.

Marc.

Memories of long evenings, kissing under the willow's leafy canopy forced their way into my mind. Recollections of us entwined in an intimate embrace as we watched the moon rise and send a silvery path across the water enticing us to swim in its light. An invitation we rarely refused on those hot, humid nights. Nights we called *close* because it felt like we literally wore the air.

Amid the deafening noise from thousands of spring peepers and singing night bugs, we splashed in the tepid shallows. The deeper we swam the colder the water grew until it nearly took our breath away. But it didn't take long to warm up. I still remember the heat of his embrace, the taste of his lips, and staring in his chocolate-brown bedroom eyes.

The lake blurred. I wiped my eyes and hugged my knees. Years had passed since then, but still, it didn't seem like it. Marc and I began dating in high school. We went to college together. He was my first...and only. In our third year at Ole Miss he proposed. The date was set for June 3, 1978. It was the happiest day of my life. We planned for me to get a job after we returned from the honeymoon and for Marc to start medical school. It was all so perfect, until…

Pain drummed in the back of my head. If I didn't get to the store soon, this would turn into a full-blown migraine. I pushed against the soft grass and stood. The ground underneath me tilted, and I grasped the willow's branches to help me steady myself and wait for the sparklies to stop dancing before my eyes. Holding on to the tree's verdant arm, I took another moment to drink in the lake view. And for what had to be the millionth time since Marc's death, I whispered, "I'm sorry. So, so, sorry."

The jay hopped onto a closer branch, cocked his head, and glared at me through his black, beady eye, then began his scolding all over again.

"All right. All right. I'm leaving." Hateful bird.

Before getting in the car, I brushed the grass off my pants, then slid onto the seat and snapped the seatbelt. Just as a precaution, I checked the rearview mirror. My silly schoolgirl reminiscing probably had mascara tracks running down my cheeks, and I sure didn't want to have to explain to Momma why they were there.

The subject of love had been put to rest a long time ago. When I first moved to New York, she'd casually bring up the topic of relationships and ask if I were dating anyone. If I said yes, then she'd ask if it was serious or could it possibly be serious.

Each time I said, "No." Each time I explained how I had a career and it would not be fair to ask someone to settle for second place. Finally, I convinced her I was truly happy being single, and she let the matter drop. Bless her.

It wasn't as if I hadn't had other relationships since Marc. I just never let them go beyond the surface—or get physical. That part of me died when Marc did. To never marry was my choice. Avoiding getting physical was my safe place.

Enough of the past. I wiped the smudges from under my eyes and ran my fingers through my hair. It hung in a limp, tangled mess and was in desperate need of a highlighting touchup as soon as possible. Ugh. How I dreaded the process of finding a hairstylist. But when you have dishwater blond hair, something has to be done to perk it up.

I started the car and left the park. The best I could recall, the Piggly Wiggly used to be at the corner of Evening Shade Drive and Washington Avenue. But it might not be there any longer. The town had really changed. There were cute little shops everywhere. It had the feeling of a romantic artisan village. I wondered if this had anything to do with the new sign. No doubt I'd find out within ten minutes of arriving home. However, at the moment, all I cared about was getting to the grocery store or pharmacy.

Close to the end of Evening Shade, much to my relief, I spied the friendly pig in the red and white striped shirt waving from the store sign heralding me to stop in and shop a while. Thank the Lord. The store had been remodeled and was now a supercenter. Momma must have been in grocery store heaven when that happened.

I pulled into a parking spot and got out of the car. Heat shivered in waves from the hot asphalt. I could feel it through the soles of my shoes. The acrid odor of tar stung my nose. July was never this sweltering in New York.

A delicious blast of cool air welcomed me when

the doors slid open. Thankfully, the pharmacy was close to the front. I grabbed the pills and a bottle of water from the cooler by the checkout counter. When I tossed them on the conveyer belt the lady at the register smiled at me.

"Afternoon. Hot one today isn't it? Did you find everything okay?"

I really did not feel like a conversation. In Manhattan, sales clerks didn't make small talk. I'd forgotten this about the South. So, even though my head felt as if it were splitting in two, I forced a smile. "Yes it is. And I did. Thank you."

She glanced at my order and knit her eyebrows together. Peering at me through her wire-rim glasses she asked, "Headache?"

"Killer. It has been threatening since I turned off I-40 in Tennessee."

"Oh, so you are visiting our little town?" She ran the Naproxen and water over the scanner. "Do you want these bagged?"

"No, I'll just put them in my purse. Actually, I'm moving back home. I was born and raised here."

The woman held her hand out to me. "Well then, welcome home. I'm Jema Presley." She held up a finger. "And no, as far as I know, we are not related."

"You are a mind reader." I shook her hand. "I'm Avalee Preston."

"Not Cladie Mae's daughter by any chance?"

"The one and only. Only child that is."

Jema's radiant smile showed perfect teeth. "Then I'm your neighbor." She swept the bangs from her eyes. "Sorry, new haircut. I haven't had bangs in years, but David, my stylist, told me they would make me look younger. All they have managed to do is drive me crazy."

Jema looked to be about my age, and I could see us being friends. "I like it. Short and sassy. And we need all the sass we can muster at our age."

"Oh girl, you just wait until you pass fifty…" She wrinkled her nose. "Something."

"Believe me, I know. I've passed that line years ago."

She waved me off. "Pshhh. Go on."

The throb in my head intensified, and I pinched the base of my nose. "I think I'd better get to Mom's and lie down a while. Why don't you come by sometime soon?"

Jema's expression showed genuine concern. "Oh, your headache. You poor thing. I'm so sorry. Better take one of those pills. Here, let me." She took the bottle from my hand, opened it, broke the seal, and pulled out the cotton. "Here, the directions say you can take two to begin with." When I took the pills from her palm, she opened the water. "Wash 'em down."

I did as told. Yes, we would be friends. Good friends. I'd forgotten what genuine friendly was like. Down-home Southern friendly. "Thanks." After stuffing the bottles in my bag I turned to leave. "See you soon?"

"I'll come over after you have time to get settled in a bit. Hope you get to feeling better." She blew her bangs. "Say hey to Cladie Mae for me okay?"

"Sure thing." I waved and left the store. After getting in the car, I rubbed my neck. Marc could always massage these headaches away.

No. I wouldn't start that again. I mentally shoved

him into the recesses of my mind, took a deep breath, and blew it out before starting the car. By now, Momma was probably wearing out the sidewalk looking for me. "Here I come, Momma."

****

Just as I expected, she had waited on the porch swing with her gazed fixed on the road like a hawk watching its prey. She leaned forward when my little red car came roaring down the road. I could tell by her posture that she was unsure if it was me or not.

She was probably watching for a taxi. I hadn't owned a car in years. I didn't need a car in New York. But as soon as I turned onto the driveway of 1428 Washington Avenue, she jumped off the swing as quick as a gray squirrel and fairly flew down the steps, her arms open wide. I hoped I'd be that nimble at seventy-eight.

"Avalee, get out of that car and give your momma a hug."

All at once, I became a little girl again. I ran into her embrace. Only now I had to bend my five-foot-six frame over her five-foot-nothing body. "Momma, it is so good to see you."

"Are you hungry? Lord, I was in the garden picking peas, okra, and tomatoes at five this morning and have been cooking ever since. I've made all your favorites. Fried chicken, creamed potatoes and white gravy, fried okra, fried green tomatoes, and purple-hull peas. I would have made those baby butterbeans you like so well, but they need to fill out a little more. Oh and for dessert I made my six-layer coconut cake."

Fried anything truly was my favorite food. I'd eat just about anything as long as it was fried. The problem was staying in my size six pants. In all my years of living in Manhattan, my weight never varied more than a few pounds. I had a feeling if I wasn't careful, that would soon change.

"Wow, sounds great. What a spread. Who else is coming for supper? Molly Kate and Lexi?"

"It is just us tonight. I want you all to myself."

"All this food for two people? That's…" From the corner of my eye, I noticed Pearly Armstrong, Momma's neighbor from across the street, rise from her rocking chair and lean across her porch railing.

"Cladie? Who ya got there?"

Momma rolled her eyes. "It's Avalee. She's come home."

"Why, I'll swan." She grasped her cane and hobbled down the porch steps and shuffled across the street. "Child, it's about time you came home." When she reached us, she put her bird-like hand on my shoulder and stared at me through faded blue eyes. "Let me have a look at you." Clicking her tongue, she pronounced, "A mite thin, but Cladie here will fatten you up."

Just what I feared.

Momma didn't want company tonight. She didn't fool me with her plastered on smile. I could tell a battle raged in her mind, but she finally did what every good and decent Southern woman knows she must do. "Pearly, how about having some supper with us. I have plenty."

"Why, thank you Cladie. I've been smelling that chicken all afternoon. I don't mind if I do." She looped her arm around mine and smiled up at me. "You don't mind helping an old woman up the stairs, do you child?"

"No, ma'am. Not at all." I took Mom's hand. "Let's go eat. I'm starving." We walked up the steps into the heavenly aroma wafting from the kitchen through the screen door. It felt good to be home.

Funny thing? As soon as I walked through the door, I noticed my headache was completely gone.

Chapter 2

AVALEE
Momma

After way too much fried food washed down with several glasses of too sweet tea, I shuffled to the porch. Mrs. Armstrong and Momma followed.

"Cladie, you outdid yourself tonight. That was some mighty good eating."

"Thank you, Pearly. I'm glad you joined us." Momma lied.

Mrs. Armstrong held up the Piggly Wiggly sack. "And thank you for all of these leftovers. Why, I'll eat on them all week."

"You're welcome, Pearly. Avalee, honey, help Pearly down those steps, will you?" Could Momma have been more obvious that she wanted the elderly woman to leave? I don't think so. I took Pearly's sack and wrapped my arm around hers. When we reached the sidewalk, she winked a rheumy eye. "Thanks, sugar."

"You be careful across the street now."

"I will." She patted my cheek. "Glad you're home, Avalee. Night now."

"Me too. Night." I sauntered back to the house and eased down on the porch swing. Mom sat beside me, and together we watched Pearly hitch up her steps.

When she reached her front door, she turned and waved to us before going inside. I leaned back, unbuttoned my jeans, and moaned. "Momma, I cannot eat like this every day." Then I leaned over and kissed her cheek. "But thanks. It was delicious, as always."

"Well, it is a special occasion after all. I won't go all out like that every night." She grinned and patted my hand. Her hair, now completely white, lay in short waves across her head making her blue eyes crystalline. And even though age had stolen the fullness from her lips, her elfin grin made me smile.

The pink twilight sky glowed through the lacy mimosa leaves. Warm magnolia blossom air carried the raspy call of cicadas and tree frog song. Fireflies flashed on and off like tiny floating LED lights. I'd forgotten how much I enjoyed watching them.

"Lord have mercy, it's hot." Mom flapped her apron toward her face. "I'm so sorry for calling you home in the middle of July."

"That's all right, Mom. It all worked out. My lease was up anyway. And I can finish my book here."

"How many does this one make?"

"This will be my seventh."

"Well, I'll be. What did your father and I do to have such a smart daughter?" She shook her head. "Whatever it was, I'm glad we did. You were the first person I thought of when I got that letter from the town council. I couldn't make heads or tails of it."

"Do you still have the letter? I want to have a good understanding of exactly what they are asking before I meet with them."

"I put it in Daddy's desk. It is something about the new zoning laws and me running an agricultural business in a residential area. Foolishness. That's what. Preston Gardens has been here for generations." Momma's apron flapping accelerated. "Why, I can't shut my business down. What are they thinking? I don't need them all up in my doings. Lord, what would your father think of me if I lost his family's business?"

"You won't lose it, Momma. There is something called a Grandfather Clause. I will make a case for your staying here. Just give me some time to think. I'll come up with a plan to make them realize the value of leaving you alone." I patted her arm. "It will all work out. So what is going on here in Moonlight?"

"Well, you remember the terrible shape this town was in when your father died?"

I nodded.

"A while back, Mayor Campbell had been on vacation somewhere on the East Coast and came home with the idea to make Moonlight into a tourist village. Seems the place he visited had a layout a lot like our town. Since then, he has campaigned, raised money, and advertised all over the country trying to entice people to move to Moonlight and set up shop."

"From what I can tell, it is working."

"Mmm hmm, but I'd just as soon they leave me alone."

The night song escalated. For a while Momma and I didn't speak. I rocked the swing back and forth with the toe of my shoe since hers didn't reach the floor. The evening reminded me of all the nights Momma, Daddy, and I sat here after supper when I was a child. I'd sit on the swing with Momma, just like now. Daddy would be on the rocker smoking his pipe. In no time, my eyelids grew heavy with sleep, and I'd lay over in Mom's lap and listen to them talk in quiet voices through the buzz, chirring, and chirps in the humid night air heavy with the elixir of rose, magnolia, and gardenia scent. The next thing I knew, the sun streamed through my window waking me in my bed.

I missed Daddy. Next Thanksgiving would mark the fifth year of his passing. I remembered the afternoon he called to say he had colon cancer and how it had metastasized to his liver. Right away I began researching for the highest rated cancer treatment clinic. Then I made arrangements for him to be seen. But after a year of treatments, he decided he'd had enough chemo. I wasn't ready to give up. But he was. It took a while for him to convince me he was tired and ready to meet his maker. Finally, I understood. From that day on, we turned our attention to getting his affairs in order for Momma's sake.

When the doctors advised Momma to summon the family, I caught the first jet out of New York. Minutes after I arrived at his bedside, he passed. He had waited for me.

His funeral was the day before Thanksgiving. I had to leave for Memphis a couple days later and catch a jet to Australia where I was to give the keynote at a conference. I felt guilty, but Momma insisted I keep my engagement, pointing out how the conference chairs didn't have time to replace me, and besides, her sister Aunt Mayzel, lived just around the corner. They were the only two siblings left in the family and were very close. I knew Auntie would take good care of Momma. Even so, the guilt of leaving her in her time of need still raised its ugly head, and tonight was no exception.

The same tension that plagued me earlier began

tightening between my shoulders, and the familiar ache threatened again, reminding me of my visit with Jema at Piggly Wiggly. I reached up and massaged my neck, which actually helped this time.

"What's the matter, honey?"

"I've been fighting off a headache all day."

"I've got headache powders. Those will fix you right up." She leaned forward to stand, and I put my hand on her shoulder.

"I stopped at the grocery store and got something. I'll be all right, which reminds me, I met Jema today. She said she's your neighbor."

"At Pigg's? Yes, she's a lovely person. A widow you know. Has two lovely daughters in college."

"We didn't talk long. Tell me about her."

"She lives in the old Powers' home across the street. She and Ray moved there about fifteen years ago. I couldn't ask for a better neighbor."

"Was she at Daddy's funeral?" I recalled the loneliness I felt during the visitation and services. My best friends Molly Kate and Lexi weren't there. They were out of town visiting family for the holidays. If Jema had come, surely I would have remembered her.

"No, she was with her people in Tennessee. After Ray died, she and the girls went to her parents' every year. But now that her daughters are in college, they all come to my house for Thanksgiving."

"How long ago did her husband die?"

"Oh, I'd say it's been about ten years. A real shame too. He slipped off the dock at the hosiery factory. It was one of those humid days that made the concrete sweat. He only fell a few feet, but hit his head just so and broke his neck. He died instantly."

"How awful."

"Mmm hmm. Bless her heart. She's struggled so. Ray didn't have much in the way of social security. At least his life insurance paid off the house. The only reason Jema took that job at Pigg's was to supplement the girls' college expenses. Poor thing just squeaks by each month."

"You'd never know it by her smile. It's dazzling. And her eyes. I felt like she could look into my soul. Her expression is so...so calm. Caring."

"You'll never meet a better listener, I'll vow." Momma stood. "But she's terrible at gossip. She sees all sides. Drives me crazy. "

"Oh, Momma." I squeezed her hand. "You're a mess."

Her eyes crinkled up in a twinkly Mrs. Santa way. "How about some coffee?"

"Sounds good."

"Another piece of cake?"

"Tempting, but no. I think one piece a day is enough. More than enough."

In just a few short hours, my lifestyle had drastically changed. In Manhattan, I dodged speeding cabs and delivery trucks. Here at home, I had to dodge calories.

Soon she returned with two mugs. The fragrant steam weaved through the muggy air. Hot coffee on a hot night. Who knew the combination could work so well? While sipping from my cup, I wondered why Molly and Lexi hadn't come to see me. They just lived down the street. Were they out of town again?

In the darkness I asked, "Did you tell Lexi and Molly Kate I was coming home?"

"No, ma'am. I sure didn't."

"You didn't? Why not?"

"Like I said earlier. I wanted you all to myself for at least *one* evening."

I had to smile. True, I'd been home less than five times in the past thirty years. I felt I had good reason though: there were too many memories and I didn't want to face Marc's family. In a town this small, it was a given I'd see them. On the other hand, I wasn't a bad or negligent daughter either. During their business downtime, I flew them to visit me in the city for a few weeks. I had also taken them with me on book tours to the United Kingdom, Holland, Australia, Austria, and Germany. They saw countries that otherwise they may have never seen. Still, I understood her point.

"I'm glad you didn't. I want you all to myself, too." Momma laid her hand on my lap, and I took it up in mine. Without word, my little momma let me know how much she needed me. Right then and there I vowed to make time for many nights on the porch with just her and me.

She squeezed my hand, and I brought hers to my lips and kissed it. Yes, Lord willing, there would be many more nights just like this.

****

An unfamiliar noise woke me early the next morning. It was...birds. The white chenille blanket and the softest sheets I had slept in since childhood made me reluctant to get out of bed.

Eventually, I threw off the covers, sat on the bedside, and watched the antics of two squirrels spiraling around the pecan tree just outside my window. It felt good to be home. I really didn't realize how much

I had missed it.

I stood and stretched. Today I would surprise Molly Kate and Lexi. The forecast called for a sunny ninety-eight degrees. Sheesh. This part of home I *did not* miss.

I chose a pair of capris, a cotton tank top, and sandals. While brushing my teeth, I decided there was no use going to the trouble of make-up. In this heat it would melt off anyway. I pulled my hair into a ponytail, powdered my face, brushed on mascara, and put on a little lipstick.

Downstairs Momma had prepared a breakfast worthy of a lumberjack. Eggs, grits, biscuits smothered in sausage gravy. She looked up from the stove when I walked in. The towel thrown over her shoulder evidenced she'd been working in the garden, probably since before dawn. "Morning, baby."

"Morning. Are you having guests for breakfast?"

"Just you, me, and Felix."

"Felix? Oh, good. I can't wait to hug his neck." There were no words for how much I appreciated that man. He began working for us before I was born. I didn't know how Momma would have made it without him after Daddy died.

I sure hoped he still had a big appetite, because the only breakfast I could stomach was coffee and a muffin. Maybe steel-cut oats in the winter. "I can't eat all of this, Momma."

"Just eat what you can. Felix is going to help me shell peas and butterbeans. He can usually finish off anything I cook by noon."

The grits looked good. I hadn't had them in years. I spooned some in a small bowl, put a pat of butter on them then shook a little salt and pepper. Momma split a biscuit in half, lathered it with butter and fig preserves, and handed it to me. "You've never eaten anything *this* good in New York. I put these preserves up last week."

Carbs, carbs, carbs. But she was right. The buttery, tender biscuit with honey sweet figs was one of the most delicious things I'd eaten in a long time.

Before she could slide another thing on my plate, I rose from the table and took my dishes to the sink. "I'll be back later this afternoon to help you put up the peas and beans. This morning I want to surprise Molly Kate at her shop."

Mom padded over next to me and started some dishwater. "She's moved it since you were last home."

"Oh? Where's the shop now? Is it in walking distance?" Dumb question. Everything in Moonlight was in walking distance.

"It is on the corner of Martin Luther and Main."

"Martin Luther?"

"Martin Luther Boulevard. They renamed Spring Street. Anyway, Molly needed a bigger place with all the changes she's made. The place is really something."

"Okay then. I'm not sure what time I'll be home. I think I'll drop in on Lexi, too. Is the newspaper still in the same place?"

"Yes. Thank goodness Mayor Campbell left some of the town's cornerstones alone. I just hope they will leave Preston Gardens in place, too."

"I'll check on that while I'm in town." After a quick peck on her cheek, I left before she could tempt me with more of her breakfast for champions.

The air felt warm, but pleasantly so. I looked forward to my walk, especially after last night's supper.

The day looked promising. It would be so good to see my friends. I'd really missed them. Who knows? I may just find a reason to stay here after all.

Chapter 3

AVALEE
Ghost

I decided to take the long way to Molly Kate's bakery and strolled along Whispering Pines Road that bordered the Moonlight National Forest. The clean, pungent fragrance from the pine thicket filled me with a restful peace.

The traffic along Whispering Pines was heavier than I remembered as a girl, but it was nothing compared to the seven o'clock traffic on Eighth Street in the city.

At Martin Luther I turned right and walked toward Main. Wow. The town really had changed. More than I realized. The buildings on the square had new façades, and the old stores had been replaced by boutiques and antique and gift shops.

I spied Molly Kate's bakery. *A Taste of Heaven* flowed across the window front in beautiful script. So, she'd jumped on the renovation bandwagon and renamed her business. I liked it. The name fit. Even as a teen everything she baked was what I imagined worthy of Heaven's dining rooms.

A silver bell on the door jingled when I entered. The crowded room buzzed with folks getting pastries and...well, would you look at that. *Lattes.* Smart girl that Molly Kate. She knows how to stay current even here in Moonlight, Mississippi.

Two teenage girls worked the counter. They looked just like Molly when she was in high school. They couldn't be her daughters? Surely not. Grand-daughters maybe. My heart sank. We couldn't be that old. Could we? It just didn't feel like that many years had passed.

Molly Kate bustled through a curtain hanging behind the counter holding a tray of scones. The door jingled when another customer entered. She looked up and immediately locked eyes with me.

"Lord'a mercy, it's Avalee." She shoved the tray at one of the girls, scooted around the counter, and dashed toward me. "You're home. I can't believe it."

The crowded room fell silent, and all eyes watched as we grabbed each other in a bear hug. Molly waved her hand around the room, "Y'all can go back to talking now." Then she stepped back. "When did you get home?"

"Late yesterday."

"I had no idea you were home. Miss Cladie didn't say a word about your coming."

"No, she wanted it to be just us for an evening."

Molly nodded her head. "And she didn't want to appear rude by not inviting us over. I understand. Just like her." She folded her arms and surveyed me up and down. "You are still as cute as a bug. Do folks not age in New York?"

"Oh, we age, but we also have our secrets."

Molly Kate had always been the beautiful one in our little trio. Her jet-black hair, huge bosom, and green cat-like eyes gave many a young man whiplash. Time had been kind to her. Only hints of gray tinged her temples. Even though she'd gained weight, her ample figure was still curvy. And those eyes. Their intimidating gaze could still unnerve the most formidable deputy in the county.

"How long are you home for?"

"I've moved home. Permanently. I think."

"Really?" She clapped her hands and pulled me into another hug. "Find a place to sit. I'll bring us some coffee and scones."

Before I could say I'd already had breakfast, she'd disappeared in the crowd. A couple sitting at a table by the door stood to leave, so I weaved my way over and claimed it. The bell jingling on the door didn't stop. Customers beginning their day with coffee passed others leaving with coffee drinks and sacks of pastries. Molly's passion for baking had truly paid off.

"Here we are." Molly set our coffee and scones on the table then sat across from me. "Well, what do you think of all the changes?"

"I'm surprised to say the least. Momma told me about it last night."

"Girl, I tell you, it has saved this town. I thought I was going to have to close shop and move to Tupelo. But when Sid Campbell was elected mayor, he said he was going to reinvent Moonlight." She ripped open three sugar packets and dumped them in her coffee. "Then he came home from vacation and announced that Moonlight would be the most romantic tourist spot in the country, what with the lake and all." She buttered her scone and held it in front of her mouth. "And I have to say, they did a pretty good job." She bit the corner off and closed her eyes. "I love these things."

"They look delicious." There was no mistaking it.

The universe plotted against my waistline. I put a yellow pack of sweetener in my coffee and took a sip. "What about all these boutiques and gift shops. Who in Moonlight had the capital or inclination to open businesses like these?"

"The word is—" Molly broke off another piece of scone and dipped it in her coffee. "—that the town council purchased ads in newspapers on the east and west coasts. And they sent delegations to artsy-type cities and somehow put the word out about the new opportunities in Moonlight. Before I knew it, people were opening up businesses all over the square. That's when I realized I'd better get my rear in gear and grab this shop before someone else snatched it up." She popped the coffee-soaked scone in her mouth.

"Who is in your old place?"

"Southern Charm Antiques. A darling store. They sell furniture from antebellum estate sales. They have serving pieces and dishes. Jewelry, too. I love to prowl around in it. We have people opening businesses here from North Carolina, Tennessee, and Arkansas. We even have a couple of Yankees. I used to give them a free cookie when they said *y'all*. Now they say it all the time."

"Well, it is a catchy word."

With an impish smile she said, "Then you say it."

"What?"

"Prove to me that New York hasn't changed you. Say y'all."

Her words kinda stung. I hadn't forgotten my roots. However, in all honesty, when I first moved to the city, I had made a conscious effort to avoid saying *y'all* or *fixin to* or phrases like *cut the light off.* I pinched off a piece of scone. "Y'all sure make good pastries." And then crammed it in my mouth.

Molly Kate put her hand on my arm. "Welcome home, sugar."

The scone tasted divine. It truly was a taste of heaven, even to my full stomach. The bell jingled—again. I glanced at the door over the rim of my coffee cup. The sight of the man who stepped in made every muscle in my body freeze. *Marc? No. It couldn't be. I was there at his funeral. I saw him in his casket.*

"Avalee? Honey? What's wrong?" Molly Kate followed my stare. "Oh." Her voice softened as she reached across the table and patted my arm. "He looks just like Marc, doesn't he?"

My eyes burned. "Who is he?"

"That's Marc's brother Ty. Don't you remember him?"

"Yes. But. I mean. He's so..." My thoughts were like a train wreck. "I babysat Ty when he was four. He was only ten at the funeral. That was the last time I saw him." I blinked back tears. *He looked exactly like Marc.* The same brown puppy-dog eyes fringed with thick lashes. The same unruly brown hair. The same irrepressible smile.

He waved and strode over. "Avalee? When did you get home?" He pulled me from my seat into a hug. His delicious cologne enveloped me. I didn't recognize the brand, but it was fabulous. He stepped back. "Wow. You look great."

Dumbfounded didn't even come close to my emotional condition. Where were my words? I managed to stammer out, "It's good to see you, Ty. How are your parents?"

"Still kicking." He smiled and held his finger up. "Hey, I gotta go. Sorry, but I'm the coffee gofer today. When can we get together and catch up? Are you staying with your mom?"

"Yes, for a while anyway."

"Great, may I come by?"

My thoughts crashed together rendering me speechless again. When could he come by? Should he come by? Why does he want to come by? "Sure."

"What am I, Ty? A moldy scone?" Molly Kate arched her eyebrow.

"Sorry, MK." He bent over and kissed the top of her head. "You are *much* better than a moldy scone. Why, I'd put you right up there with fried catfish."

She slapped his incredibly cute rear. *Cute rear? Did I actually just think that?* What was wrong with me?

He winked before turning and making his way to the counter. Molly's mini-me's blushed and fell all over each other trying to be the first to serve him.

I needed to rein in my emotions. I swallowed hard and diverted my attention to small talk. "Molly, are those girls related to you?"

"Yes, they are my granddarlings. Carli's girls, Lacy and Cherrell."

"I can't believe Carli is old enough to have teenagers. She was a little thing when I saw her last."

"I know. It doesn't seem right to me either. But, then again, I still feel twenty-five. That is until I stoop to the floor to feed my cat, Gypsy, and try to stand up again." She stirred her coffee and blew the steam before taking a sip. "They're twins, sixteen. I let them help out when school is out."

"Looks like they do a good job."

"Yeah, they do until a cute guy comes in. And that fellow at the counter is definitely cute."

Ty got his order and turned to leave. When he passed us he raised his coffee tray. "See you gals later."

I waved. "He looks just like Marc." My eyes stung and I tore my gaze from him and stared down in my cup. "It's like I've seen a ghost."

Molly reached across the table and took my hand. "Honey, does it still hurt that bad? It's been over thirty-five years."

How could I explain it to her? The old adage was true. Guilt *was* the gift that kept giving. It grew like a tumor, and I desperately wanted to rid myself of that cancer, but I couldn't. I didn't have the courage. "It's just a shock to see him looking so much like his brother."

"You'll be fine, sugar. After a while, you'll get used to seeing him."

Daubing my eyes with a tissue, I attempted a smile. "Yes, I'm sure I'll be fine. It was just a shock, you know?"

"I do, sweetie. Listen, I hate to leave you like this, but I best be getting back to baking bread for the lunch crowd. Mind if I come over tonight? I'm sure Lexi will want to come over too after Ty tells her you are home."

"Are they friends?"

"They work together at the newspaper. She is a writer there. She even has her own column called 'Moonlight Madness.' It is for women over fifty and all the frustrations we deal with. It's usually pretty funny, with a cynical bite."

"Sounds like her. What does Ty do there?"

"He's their photographer." Molly Kate stood and stacked our dishes. "And his parents absolutely *hate it.* They wanted him to follow in Marc's footsteps and go to medical school. The whole thing is sort of macabre. It's as if they tried to continue Marc's life through Ty."

"Maybe because they favor so much?"

"Maybe. But Ty is a free spirit, and he followed his passion. I admire him for that." Patting my arm she said, "We'll talk more tonight. Tell Miss Cladie to set two more places for supper."

"I'm sure she already has."

"Tell her I'll bring rolls. Love you, girl."

"Love you, too."

After a little wave, she turned and headed to the kitchen. When I stood, inertia glued my shoes to the floor. I couldn't move or think. I wanted to—no—I *needed* to talk to Marc. If only symbolically. My feet found freedom, and I paced to the door, pushed it open, and hurried down Silver Light Drive to the cemetery.

Chapter 4

JEMA
Mystery

Cladie Mae's screen door slammed. I looked up from the newspaper and glanced out the window at her house across the street. Old habit. Since her husband's death, I kept a close eye on her. It was the very least thing I could do. After Ray died she was my salvation. Cladie was like my second mother.

This time every morning, she busied herself with the daily ritual of sweeping the porch whether it needed it or not. More than likely, this was her way of nonchalantly checking on her neighbors since her porch wrapped around two sides of her house. The front part faced me. The side faced Pearly, and it also gave her a good view of Molly Kate's down the road. Just can't take the mother hen out of her. I'm thankful for that. I noticed she had her rag thrown across her shoulder to mop her face. No telling how early she went to work in her garden.

Since Cladie was always up for a visit, I decided to walk over. After all, it would be a shame to sit alone on such a beautiful morning. Besides, I wanted to see how Ava was feeling. Secretly, I also hoped Cladie Mae had baked a treat. Like I needed it. Oh well, who was there to impress these days? In a word, nobody. I folded the paper and carried my cup to the sink.

When my door banged, Cladie Mae looked up from her sweeping and waved. "Get yourself over here. I'll make coffee."

"I hoped you'd offer." I trotted across the street admiring her huge azaleas. She had pink, purple, and white bushes all grouped together around her porch. At the corner of her house were the biggest elephant ears I had ever seen.

This little lady had an ever green thumb to be sure. But what said the most about my neighbor was her yard art. I could spend the day looking at her little concrete figurines, whimsical birdbaths, hummingbird feeders, and the ceramic squirrels hanging on her tree trunks. All revealed the fun spirit of this charming lady.

"You just missed Avalee. She went to Molly Kate's this morning."

"Oh poo. I was hoping to visit with her, too. How is she feeling?"

Cladie wiped her face. "Feeling?"

"She stopped by the store for some headache medicine yesterday."

"Oh, yes. She said something about that. I don't know why she won't take my powders."

"I don't think she likes those powders, Cladie Mae." I looped my arm around hers. "Do you have anything to go with the coffee?"

"I sure do. I have a whole pan full of biscuits. I'll butter them up and toast them. And I just opened a jar of fig preserves."

"Sounds yummy." I led her to the door.

"I'm glad you have an appetite. Avalee doesn't eat enough to keep a bird alive."

"Well, she's young. When she gets my age, she'll give in to her calorie phobia. I know I have. I call it *surrender eating.*"

Cladie cocked her head. "How old are you?"

"Fifty-seven." I held the door open.

"Well, she isn't *that* far behind you. She's fifty-five."

I stopped in my tracks. "You've got to be kidding me."

"No. Not kidding. She's fifty-five. I was there you know. How well I remember."

"I could have sworn she was in her forties. What's her secret?"

"Oh, I don't know. She's always had a baby face. And I don't doubt she uses some pretty expensive stuff to keep young." She slapped my bottom. "Now hurry. There's a biscuit in the kitchen with your name on it."

While Cladie Mae made the coffee, I ambled over to my favorite spot in her kitchen: a drop-leaf table with chairs on either side. Small plaster of Paris fruits and vegetables she had crafted during the winter months, when there wasn't any gardening to do, hung on the wall. Little ceramic figurines of Siamese cats sat on her windowsill above her sink. One had tiny kittens following it, each linked by a gold chain. Her same fun spirit showed inside her home as well.

"Here you are." She set my coffee and the biscuits on the table. "I put one sugar, one yellow pack, and a splash of cream in your coffee. Did I get it right?"

"Yes ma'am, you sure did."

She sat across from me and put three biscuits on my plate. "Now eat all you want. I have plenty."

I started to protest, but didn't because I knew I'd

eat every bite. She had two pots of something cooking on the stove and the fragrance of bay leaves radiated from the oven. "What's for supper?"

"Crowder peas, mashed potatoes, and a pork roast is in the oven. Want to come for supper tonight?"

"Of course." I grinned and spooned fig preserves on my bread.

"You didn't ask what was for dessert, and I know how you love sweets."

"Okay, what's for dessert?"

"Four-layer delight." She leaned over and whispered, "Lexi calls it *better than sex*."

"Better than sex? Wow. It's been a long time. I can't wait. What does it have in it? Or do I want to know?"

"Oh, honey. It's gooood. It'll make you want to stand up and sing in church. You start with a pecan shortbread crust and on that you layer a mixture of cream cheese and whipped cream, then add a layer of chocolate pudding, and top it off with more whipped cream."

"If I'm a good girl and eat all my supper, can I have two servings? Like I said, it's been a long time."

Obviously pleased, she grinned and handed me another biscuit. "Yes, ma'am. You sure can."

To save calories, I decided against the preserves. "How long is Avalee going to be with us?"

Cladie finished her coffee and set the cup down. "She's moved home."

"For good?" I surrendered and reached for the preserves.

"I believe so. I needed her to help me sort out this zoning mess and to keep me from having to close my business. She's got such a good head on her shoulders. She's a lot like her father when it comes to such things."

"Is she good friends with Molly Kate?"

"Lord, yes. They were thick as thieves growing up. Them and Lexi."

"Did they all grow up on Washington Avenue?"

"No, but close by. Back when they were little, we never worried about them walking alone several blocks to play." Cladie Mae got a far-off look in her eye. "How I miss those days." She shook her head. "Anyway, when the town started growing and new subdivisions were developed, people moved from old neighborhoods like this one. That's when Molly and Lexi bought their homes here. I heard they got good deals."

"They are wonderful neighbors. All of you are. Only I really haven't gotten to know them very well."

Cladie stood. "Well, now that Avalee is home, I have a feeling that will change." She patted my hand. "I can't believe it. I have all my girls together on the same street." Cladie met my gaze. "And I mean *all of my girls.*" She took my cup. "More coffee?"

"Please. And thank you for your encouragement. I kinda feel awkward insinuating myself in their friendship."

She slapped the air in front of her. "Pshaw. Let me tell you something. You girls will blend like soft butter and sugar. You were all meant to be friends."

"What were they like as children?"

"Well..." She thought while filling my cup and then hers. She returned the carafe to the coffeemaker and took her seat. "Avalee was the most cautious. She watched the world through her huge blue eyes without saying much. Like a sponge, she absorbed other people's pain. And she always felt like things were her fault, even though they weren't. Lexi was the one who thought up the wildest ideas. Got those girls in worlds of trouble. She was constantly in motion. A hard one to pin down. And she still is, come to think of it. Now Molly Kate? She always needed attention. She had an older and a younger sister, which put her smack dab in the middle. This made her more competitive. She worked harder for recognition than anyone I have ever known. When she was in twelfth grade, that girl pulled a stunt that finally gave her all the attention she wanted, plus some."

"What did she do?"

"She ran away with a boy she barely knew and got married."

"Shut up your mouth. Really?"

"Yes, honey, it's the Lord's truth. They ran off. Then they went back home the same day and told their parents. Of course, everyone threw a hissy fit. She told them the marriage hadn't been consummated and even though they knew it wasn't legal, their parents marched those kids' butts to the courthouse to have it annulled, just in case. The boy had somehow drawn up fake papers and such. I can't really remember all the particulars."

"Oh, my word."

"You better believe she got plenty of attention after that. More than she wanted I'd vow. She didn't like it one little bit. But even with all her doings, she has turned out to be a fine woman. I don't know a harder worker or a better grandmother."

Cladie put her hand to her heart. "Molly Kate a grandmother to teenagers. Mercy, Lord, I'm old."

"Cladie Mae." I put my hand on her arm. "You will outlive us all."

She patted my hand. "I hope not. I've got a home in Heaven and some days, I'm anxious to get there."

"Well, not anytime soon, okay? Besides, who would sit next to me at church?"

"Oh, that reminds me. Fifth Sunday supper is coming up next weekend. I need to decide what to take."

"Why, Cladie, you already know what you are taking. Your famous chicken spaghetti, of course. There would be an uprising if you dared bring anything else." I hugged her. "Now, don't you even think of leaving us for a couple of decades yet."

"Honey, if the glory train comes for me, I'm getting on. But I'm not in any bit of a hurry."

"Good. We need you here."

And we did.

After I left Cladie's, I ran through a mental checklist on my schedule as I walked home. This was my day to volunteer at the Life Source Homeless Shelter. Since it was grocery day, I would spend the next several hours sacking food from the warehouse for the homeless to pick up and take to wherever they had set up housekeeping. When I stepped onto my lawn, I noticed my drooping ferns. The weatherman warned today would be a scorcher—like every day of summer in Mississippi wasn't. I had just enough time to water before I left. While I hosed down parched plants I thought about the last biscuit I'd eaten at Cladie's. Ugh. Why couldn't I say no? My self-control was nonexistent when temptation lay before me. Therefore, to pay penance, I made up my mind to walk the four blocks in the intense morning sun instead of driving to Life Source. Then walk home in the scorching afternoon heat. The exercise would do me good.

Watering done, I tossed the hose aside and turned the spigot off. "Besides," I reasoned out loud. "If I skip lunch, I just might eat an extra helping of that better than sex stuff."

I'm hopeless.

****

The four blocks to the shelter more than paid for my gluttony. Like Oz's Wicked Witch of the West, I melted. My sweat-soaked bangs clung to my forehead like ivy on a brick wall. I found Ricki, the supervisor, in the kitchen sticking a food thermometer in the pot of soup. Bless her. She was so conscientious. The last thing our homeless patrons needed was food poisoning. Especially our HIV positive folks.

"Hi, Ricki. I'm going to get busy bagging groceries."

She looked up from the soup and nodded toward the serving line. "Would you mind serving? The kids from the Fellowship of Christian Athletes are sacking for us today."

"Sure."

"Thanks."

I went to the linen closet and found an apron. After slipping it on, I took my station at the serving line. There were two other volunteers. One served the bread and drinks. The other worked the dessert station. As people passed, I filled bowls and asked the regulars the same thing I asked every week, "How are things?"

Their answers were always the same. "Fair to middlin'. Thanks for the soup."

It all seemed so shallow to me. I knew feeding them helped. But it just seemed like they needed more. They needed...well...respect. As I scooped out ladle after ladle, I watched the familiar faces and wondered what I could do.

Lost in my thoughts, a new face caught my attention and pulled my mind back to the present. A man I'd never seen. His appearance struck me. His wavy, stringy hair wasn't anything new. Neither was his bushy beard, or the dirt under his fingernails or the layers of dirty clothes. *His eyes*. Dark and soulful. They drew me in.

I stood there, mesmerized, holding my full ladle in midair. He didn't say a word but simply glanced at his bowl and then back at me patiently waiting.

"Oh, sorry." My face burned. It had probably turned every possible shade of red. "It's just, well, I...You are new to these parts aren't you?"

He smiled. "Yes. I've come here looking for a job."

I poured the soup in his bowl, and then gave him a little extra. "Well, I hope you find one. Welcome to Moonlight, by the way."

"Thanks." He nodded and moved on.

I watched him walk to the dessert area wanting to know more about him. His name to begin with. And what kind of job was he seeking? Maybe I could help him out.

"Miss?" A lady stood with her child waiting for soup.

"Oh, I'm so sorry. Here you go."

When everyone had been served, I scanned the room hoping to see that man again, but he had left. It didn't make sense for me to be thinking like this, but I fervently hoped he wasn't passing through like so many did. There was something about him, and whatever that something was, I had to find out.

Chapter 5

JEMA
Friends

The walk home dissolved me into a wet, stinking heap. I had just enough time to hop in the shower before going to Cladie Mae's for supper. After I dried my hair, I slipped on a loose sundress and skipped the make-up except for lip gloss. After all, it was just us girls.

Since we were having pork, I chose a bottle of cabernet and hurried out the door. Molly Kate called from the sidewalk. "Hey, Jema."

"Hey, girl." I waved my bottle of wine in the air and noticed Lexi hurrying toward us with her bottle in hand. For such a short thing, she could cover distance in no time. Her red hair glowed in the sun. It suited her, fiery and exciting.

"Hi, y'all." Lexi wiggled her eyebrows and raised her bottle. "Looks like we all had the same idea. Good thing we live in walking distance."

Molly Kate chuckled. "Walking distance? With the spread Miss Cladie puts on, it's a good thing we all live in rolling distance."

Avalee called from the porch. "Come on in everyone. Momma says it is ready, and you know how she hates serving lukewarm food."

Lexi pumped her bottle. "Get your corkscrew and wine glasses ready. We have a bottle for every course."

The savory aroma of roasting pork permeated my senses. I followed my nose to the dining room to find the table laden with food. Pork roast, mashed potatoes, butterbeans, fried green tomatoes, peas, creamed corn, sliced tomatoes, and purple onions. Molly Kate set her basket of hot wheat rolls by the butter.

Lexi opened a bottle of wine, filled our glasses, and said, "A toast to Miss Cladie, the reason no one in this room is a size six."

We all cheered, "Here, here." All except Avalee. She said something like, "Oh dear."

Miss Cladie clapped her hands together. "Girls, let's give thanks and get down to business." We took our seats, gave thanks, and turned into Hoover-mouths. By the time I finished a second helping, my stomach begged me to stop. But my mouth told my stomach to shut up. Finally I had to push away. "Lordy, I can't eat another bite."

Avalee unbuttoned her pants. "I bet I've gained five pounds in less than forty-eight hours."

"Oh, hush up, Avalee." Molly Kate rose from her chair and struck a pose. "There is nothing wrong with a size sixteen. We ample figured women rock."

Lexi jumped up and popped another cork. "You got that right, girl." She refilled our glasses. "And who cares? Men don't worry about their big guts. Why should we?"

Molly flipped her hand. "You are no bigger than a flea, Miss Lexi Lowe."

"Hardly," said Lexi. "And when you are short, one pound looks like ten."

"But Lexi has a good point. The men I've known think they are fabulous. Big guts and all." I got up and started gathering dishes. "We can at least work off some of our supper by helping Cladie Mae with the dishes."

Cladie jumped up. "No girls. All of you skedaddle on out of here and go drink your hooch on the porch. I can take care of this. And when I'm finished we'll have dessert."

I groaned with the rest of the girls. But truth be known? I had no doubt I would somehow find room for dessert.

We lumbered to the porch, and I sank onto the rocking chair. The evening star glinted in the pink and purple twilight. Normally, this was the loneliest time of day for me since Ray died. But now, here with these women, it felt so right and beautiful. I held up my glass. "Here's to friends, old and new."

"Amen." Lexi stuck out her glass. "To being here for each other no matter what."

Molly Kate raised her glass. "To forever friends."

My insecurity raised its head. "Forever friends?" I looked around. "That sounds so nice. I wish I'd grown up with you girls."

Lexi leaned forward and faced me. "Sugar, let me tell you something. You didn't have to grow up with us to be our forever friend." She pivoted around. "Ain't that right girls? Jema is one of us."

"She sure is." Avalee stood and held up her goblet. "To the women of Washington Avenue."

We followed Avalee's lead, clinked glasses, and drank to friendship.

Lexi opened the last bottle and refilled our glasses

before joining Molly Kate on the swing. "Well, Avalee, I have to say, you could have knocked me over with a feather when Ty told me you were home."

Avalee rocked next to me. "I planned on surprising you after I left Molly's. But when I saw Ty..." Tears filled her eyes and slid down her cheeks. She took a drink and shook her head. "I know it is silly, but I had to talk to Marc, so I spent the afternoon in the cemetery."

"Not silly at all, hon." Lexi got up from the swing and went to her. Wrapping her arms around Avalee, she said, "We do what we have to do."

I nodded. "I visit Ray's grave, too. It helps somehow."

The sky deepened into inky blue, and sequin stars glinted against it. The air grew heavy with humidity. The crickets' and tree frogs' song became a dirge.

"All right, girls. We have to stop this right now." Molly jiggled her empty glass at Lexi.

"Now, MK, that's just tacky. Have a little heart here," Lexi said as she stood to fill glasses.

Molly Kate shook her head. "Hear me out now. I know life is hard. But we have to think on the good things." She raised her finger. "I have an idea."

Lexi stopped mid-pour and looked up. "What?"

"Listen, we all have a lot to be grateful for, right? But face it, life can be a pain, too. So let's set aside one day a month to complain." She snapped her fingers. "Whine Wednesday. We will drink wine and complain all night about the things that really irk us."

Lexi nodded. "I like that. Whine Wednesdays."

"Want to meet at my place?" I asked.

Molly Kate bobbed her head. "Love it. Whine at

Jema's. Now which Wednesday? How about the third one of the month?"

"Sounds like a plan." Lexi returned to the swing. "It's a date."

The drone of the katydids along with the throaty calls of frogs and the warm, melting effects of wine made me drowsy. I rested my head against the chair. For the longest time we all rocked in silence. Then, in the dark, Lexi's voice broke the stillness.

"I have another idea."

I lifted my head. "What?"

"Mondays suck. Right?"

"Pretty much," said Molly Kate. "So, your idea is?

"Martini Mondays. The first Monday every month, we will meet at my house to laugh. We will watch funny movies and old television shows like *I Love Lucy*. We can share funny stories and laugh until we need to wear Depends. It will give us something to look forward to each month."

"Great idea," said Molly Kate. "And if it has been an especially hard week, we can call for an extra Martini Monday."

"Sooooo," Avalee said. "Should I also check to see when AA meets?"

Lexi threw her napkin at Ava. "Oh, shut up. You love the idea, and you know it."

"I do." She sighed. "I really do. It's so good to be home with my southern sisters."

"Girls?" Miss Cladie turned on the porch light. "Dessert is dished up, and the coffee is hot. Come and get it."

We squinted at her, put our hands to our stomachs, and groaned. Then we looked from one to another, smiled, and rushed to the dining room.

Chapter 6

LEXI
Rant

After my second helping of better than sex, I staggered to the porch swing and fell onto the cushions. Thanks to Miss Cladie Mae Preston's cooking magic, I'd eaten myself into a food stupor. Why do I always forget my five-foot-three frame cannot keep up with my five-foot-six-and-beyond friends?

Avalee, Jema, and Molly Kate followed me out of the house. Ava flopped down beside me, but Jema and Molly Kate walked to the steps. Molly turned and said, "Are you coming, Lexi?"

"I'm miserable. I can't move."

Molly put her hand on her stomach. "Aren't we all? Want us to walk you part way home?"

"No. I can't budge. In fact, I'm seriously considering sleeping on this swing."

"All right, then. See you at the shop tomorrow morning?"

"Yes, and make the coffee extra strong."

"Will do. Love you girls."

Avalee waved. "You too. Night."

In the darkness, I heard Avalee snicker. I groaned. "What's so funny? I'm dying here."

"Me too, believe me."

Being with the girls at Miss Cladie's reminded me of the sleepovers we had as kids. Some nights after her parents went to bed, I'd convince them to sneak out of the house and go to the playground at the end of the street. That sparked an idea. "Hey, how about taking a stroll to the playground for old times' sake and walk some of this misery off."

"It's after midnight. Don't you have to go to work tomorrow?"

I waved her off. "Quit acting like you are over fifty." In mock surprise I put my hand to my cheek. "Oh. Wait. We *are* over fifty."

"Okay." Avalee laughed. "You made your point."

The night air had cooled, and a velvet breeze caressed my skin. As we meandered down the street, we reverted back to twelve-year-old girls giggling about the boys we used to crush on. Our conversation reminded me about what she said about Ty. "So, Ty brought back memories?"

Her sigh spoke volumes. "This whole town brings back memories. Before going to Mom's, I stopped at the lake to visit Marc's and my spot. And then at Molly Kate's, I looked up and saw Ty. It was as if Marc had walked in the bakery. I almost fainted."

"Sweetie, Marc's been gone so long. Why are you letting him dominate you from the grave?"

A defensive chord struck her voice. "What do you mean? He never dominated me."

"You never married after him, did you?"

"Well, no. But not because of him...exactly. I mean, it's not like I haven't dated. I've had a lot of relationships. But I got caught up in my career. There really wasn't time, and besides, I didn't want to be tied down. What about you? Why haven't you remarried?"

"Puleeze." I shoved my hands in my back pockets. "I'll *never* marry again. I'd say twenty-eight years of wedded bliss is enough for anyone."

"Ah, I hear bitterness. What happened?"

"I didn't like his anniversary present."

We passed the Smith's, and their beagle raced to the backyard fence barking to beat the band. Stupid dog nearly made me wet my pants. At this rate he was sure to wake the entire neighborhood.

"No, really. What happened?"

"It's true. For our twenty-eighth wedding present, Toby brought home an expensive bottle of wine and said there was something we needed to discuss. I remember thinking, 'Oh boy, he's going to take me to Europe.' We had talked about going to the United Kingdom, Ireland, Italy, France, maybe even Greece, someday. He promised me as soon as he got a partner at his medical clinic, he'd take off and we'd travel. So the year of our twenty-eighth anniversary another doctor joined him. Then a couple of months later another doctor joined. Now there were *two* docs to cover for him. I just knew he was going to produce brochures and airline tickets."

We reached the park at the end of the street and headed to the swings. I gripped the chains and lowered on the sling seat.

"So after we toasted our anniversary, he started stammering around, making no sense at all. I wondered what on earth he was so nervous about, but when I asked him what was wrong he didn't answer. He just slugged more expensive wine down and filled his glass again. By the time the bottle was empty, I guess he had enough liquid courage to finally tell me he had impregnated a woman young enough to be his daughter and wanted to know what *we* should do about it."

"We?"

"Yes, *we*. Can you believe that? Well, I gotta tell ya, for the first time in my life, I was struck speechless. And girl, a fire so hot it would singe Satan rose up in me, but I quenched it. I kept my wits about me. I didn't say a word. I got up, walked to the liquor cabinet, and chose another bottle of wine. Then I opened it, poured myself a glass, walked to Toby, and tossed it in his face."

"Oh no." Ava put her hand to her mouth and stifled a giggle. "What did he say?"

"He said he guessed he deserved that." Come to think of it, it was kinda funny. At least now it is. I started chuckling. "I went to the linen closet and got him a pillow and blanket, took it to the living room, and tossed them to him. Then said, 'You are sleeping in here tonight. I have to think on this one. We will talk in the morning.' Then I poured myself another glass and went to the bedroom."

"I'm guessing you came up with a killer plan?"

"You betcha. This called for some serious revenge. I thought all night and came up with the perfect scheme. The next morning I gave him a kiss on the cheek as usual and said, 'Don't worry about a thing, honey. It will all work out.' You should have seen his face. He was so relieved. Then he said he was late and hurried out the door saying we would talk again later in the evening. I just smiled and thought, *like hell we will.* The minute he was out of sight, I called the lawyer my husband detested because she was the county's best prosecutor and she hated doctors. I told her I was Dr. Toby Lowe's wife and I needed to talk to her *now*. She cleared her morning appointments. After I explained my situation, I asked if she could draw up the papers that day. She assured me she could. When I finished with the lawyer, I went to the bank and cleaned out our accounts. Well, I left a dollar in each one. Then I drove to Booneville and opened up an account in a local bank there."

"Lexi Lowe, you are evil."

"Honey, you haven't heard the best part." I pushed my swing back and forth. "On the way home, I stopped at Walmart and bought him a baby gift—a pack of diapers, wipes, earplugs, and condoms, in case he decided to do to her what he'd done to me, and I stuffed them in a gift bag. Then I bought new locks for the house."

Avalee laughed out loud. "Condoms? New locks? Shame on you."

"Well, when I got home I asked your momma's help, Felix, to change the locks. Then I got all of Toby's things the lawyer said he had a right to and piled them in the front yard. Then for the *pièce de résistance* I put the baby gift on top of the pile with a note saying he would soon be served with divorce papers."

Ava laid her hand on my knee, and her voice turned serious. "I know we are laughing, but it had to be a hard time for you."

The tenderness in her voice melted my snarky exterior, and I let myself feel the pain I had buried deep inside for the past four years. My throat constricted making it hard to swallow.

"How could he, Avalee? *How could he?* I did *everything* for that man. *My whole life* was all about him. I gave up my dreams, my interests, and worked like a slave to get him through school. Then I did all the things expected of a doctor's wife. Entertaining, going to every social event, working every charitable function, making sure we were in the society page. It was a good thing we didn't have children, or I would have ended up raising them alone."

At the thought of being childless, I broke down. I had wanted children, but he refused. Said there wasn't time for it. The irony of it all still left a raw place in my heart. Avalee waited patiently for me to pull myself together.

"I never had a life outside of Toby. We didn't have friends, just important acquaintances. We never went anywhere, heck, we didn't talk. I begged him to go to counseling, but he was too arrogant. Too proud. After all, what would people say about the town doctor going to marriage counseling? He was supposed to have it all together. By the last year of our marriage, he'd become a stranger whom I occasionally had sex with." I crossed my arms across my chest and stared at the stars winking in the blackness. "And all the while he was doing a girl in another town. Shoot, for all I know, he was probably tomcatting around here. Everyone wants a piece of the doctor, and I don't mean him, but what he has in his bank account."

"Did he marry the girl?"

For the first time since I'd quit smoking, I wished for a cigarette no less than nine feet long. "No. He didn't."

"Then what happened?"

"I guess you could say *justice*. Seems this girl lied to him about her age. He met her at an all majors career day at Ole Miss, where he was talking to students about opportunities in the medical field. She was there with her sister who had just enrolled. The girl told him she was a sophomore and apparently she had some real crowd pleasers under her sweater, if you get my meaning. So, my college-educated, hormone-soaked twit of a husband assumed she was a sophomore at Ole Miss and at least twenty-one. Which would have been bad enough. He turned on the charm with plenty of cash, because really? That was his only charm.

"Then out of the blue he developed an interest in Ole Miss sports. Thinking back, he was always going with the guys to football and basketball games. I should have been suspicious because he never watched the games on the television or went to one of the guys' homes to watch. It turns out he went to Oxford by himself and met her at a hotel where they played their own games. Then when she told him she was pregnant, she also admitted she misled him and informed him she was a *high school* sophomore. The kid was only fifteen."

"Oh my word. You're not serious?"

"Yep. The idiot. Her parents had him charged with statutory rape. Toby lost his license and is now in prison, flat broke. A fat, bald nobody. Serves him right."

"Goodness." Ava shook her head and silence filled the pause in our conversation. "And the baby?"

"A girl. They put her up for adoption. At least they did *one* right thing." I breathed deep and slowly blew it out. "I just don't think I will ever be able to trust a man again. The shock...the rejection...was too much. Now I'm hyper vigilant. I pick up on the smallest sign of deceit in every guy I meet."

"It is hard meeting good men at our age, that's for sure."

Reliving this despicable memory left me feeling like a limp rag. I needed sugar. The conversation had sucked all the serotonin right out of my system. "I need another piece of that better than sex stuff. I think I have a one-inch space left in my stomach. How about it?"

"On one condition. We *must start* jogging tomorrow. There isn't any more space left in the seat of these jeans and I will go naked before I buy a larger size.

"Now that I've gotta see." I hugged my friend. It was so good to have her home again.

The next morning I woke with the perfect column idea, thanks to my conversation with Avalee the night before. One I could explore for weeks—the incredible double standard some men hold over women and their complete inability to value a relationship with women over fifty. Especially if a younger woman shakes her double d's at him.

On my way to the office, I made my regular stop at Molly Kate's. Instead of ordering my usual double-shot skinny latte, I got a triple-shot full fat latte and whipped cream. I didn't give a rat's rear what men think of my expanding old woman's girth. They sure as heck didn't worry about theirs. Plus, I needed a triple-shot to get my brain working.

My editor, Vince, waved as I rushed by his door. When I lay this week's column on his desk, he may be kicking me out of his door. Ty's office was dark.

Probably on an assignment.

While my old clunker of a computer warmed up, I sipped my latte. When the caffeine finally kicked in, the ideas started coming, and I attacked the computer keys.

MOONLIGHT MADNESS

~ For Women too Old to be Young, but too Young to be Old

HYPOCRITE, THY NAME IS MAN

Readers, as you know there are certain things that drive me mad. And this fifty-something woman always has her say. Today is no exception.

The topic of this week's column is an extension of a conversation I had with my friend who is also in her fifties. Our little tête à tête *made me want to spit hellfire.*

Curious about what has me burning?

Well, I'll tell you. It is that certain group of middle-aged and beyond men who think they are too good for their middle-aged wives or women who are fifty or older. You guys know who you are. You only have eyes for young, thin women with big breasts.

And yet, you also have the uncanny ability to totally forget the reflection you see in your mirrors. You ignore your bellies that lap over your belt, your bald heads circled with a horseshoe of hair, and flabby muscles.

Can someone please explain this to me? Oh, I get you wanting girls in their twenties and thirties. After all, these gals have tight little bodies and clear, wrinkle-free faces. And of course there are those with saline-filled breasts that look like beach balls stuck on their chests with Velcro.

What I don't get is how you men actually think these women are attracted to you. Really? Why? Besides your fat stomachs, your teeth are yellow and what hair you have left is now growing out your ears and nose. And your chest? Forget it. By now your muscles are flaccid. (And that is probably not the only thing.)

Let me fill you in, guys, if these girls are paying attention to you, it isn't because you are sexy. It is what you have behind you. And no, I'm not talking about your butt. It is what is inside your wallet. Don't fool yourselves.

Why can't you men get past the outside of a woman and see what is inside their minds? Here's a newsflash for you. You are stepping over dollars to pick up dimes. Women in their fifties and sixties are very interesting. They have lived long enough to have something to talk about besides themselves, the latest fashion, shoes, purses, or Hollywood gossip. They are fun and nurturing, in other words, they think of others first. Imagine that? And they are very sexual. They are comfortable in their own skin and are not worried about getting pregnant or wanting to get pregnant. What is wrong with you pot-bellied, wrinkled, hairy-nosed men? Did you lose your good sense when you lost your hair?

So here's the deal. I would like to hear from single and divorced women over fifty. I want to know about your frustrations, complaints, fears, and insecurities with dating. Did your husband leave you for a younger woman? Do you have any advice? What about in the job market? Are you passed over for younger women?

And men, since I'm a fair-minded person, you are free to write me and defend yourself. But I'm warning you, there may be hell to pay. After all, this is MOONLIGHT MADNESS.

My fingers were numb from all the pounding, but wow, did it ever feel good to get this off my chest and onto the computer screen. And when my column went to print, that is if it made it past Vince, you better believe I'd send a copy to Toby. I sat back in my chair and took another sip of my full-fat latte.

A soft tap sounded on my office door, and Avalee stuck her head in. "Hi there. Busy?"

For pity's sakes. That woman totally destroyed the credibility of my *guys don't appreciate women over fifty* rant. Men probably salivated over her. She had a flat stomach, absolutely no wrinkles in her heart-shaped face, her blond hair was thick and wavy and her sea-blue eyes sparkled, not to mention a smile that people paid dentists thousands of dollars to get. And on top of everything else, she even had respectable boobs. Real ones. Darned her.

"Yoo hoo? Earth to Lexi."

"Oh, yes. I mean no. I'm not busy. Come on in." I motioned to the chair beside my desk. "I just finished my column. Want to read it?" Without waiting for her to answer I pushed the print button.

"Sure." She sat and crossed her long legs. What I

wouldn't give for her height. Weight looked better on tall gals. *There you go again, Lexi. You are not supposed to care. Remember? Geeze.* I threw the rest of my latte in the trash anyway.

She scanned the paper, occasionally smiling. Once she laughed out loud. When she finished she laid it down. "You can get away with this?"

"Yep. It's my madness, after all."

"Even the flaccid part?"

"Especially that. I mean, medicine for men with flat tires is blared on every television channel. Don't you get sick of seeing it on your screen?" I slapped the desk. "Think about it. Here we are in our sexual prime having to deal with men who aren't what they were in their thirties, so they take medicine to help them, for crying out loud. But these same men think they are too good for us and look for young women? Frankly, I'd like a younger man with that immediate *at your service* body part. But these young men want young women too. It's just not right."

Ava blushed. "I know what you mean. But there isn't a thirty or even forty-year-old man who would even consider a woman at our age."

"I know of a forty-two-year-old man who would. And his *member* requires no medicine."

I jerked my head up. "Ty Jackson! How long have you been eavesdropping?"

"Sorry, Lexi, but your conversation grabbed me by the ears and wouldn't let go. I mean, you had me at sexual prime."

Ava sat as if she'd been hit with a stun gun. Ty's smile faded. "You okay?"

She shook her head, then nodded. "Sorry…"

Ty knelt beside her. "It's Marc. Isn't it?"

"It's just that you look so much like him. I'll get over this. I promise."

"Hey, I still get that look from my mother sometimes. I'm used to it."

I thrust my column at him. "Here, let me know what you think."

He stood and took it. Leaning against the desk, he read the column and then handed it back to me. "As usual, you don't hold back." His smile caused tiny lines to form around his bourbon eyes.

"Well? Can't you see why I'm so frustrated?" I threw my arms up. "Heck, every woman in the United States is frustrated except for our friend here, Miss Avalee Preston who defies age. The rest of us are screwed. And not in a good way."

Ty gave a bemused smile. "Not necessarily. I like women in their fifties."

"Yeah. Right." His mollifying irritated me. I waved him off. "Go on. Get back to work."

"What? I'm serious." He picked up the copy of my column and thrust it at me. "For the very reasons you list here."

Ava watched us with a hint of a smile. Ty turned to her. "And I'd like the opportunity to prove it. How about it?"

She tilted her head. "What part do you want to prove? That you don't need *the* medicine?"

Ty tapped his jaw and feigned deep thought. "An excellent place to start." He held his hand out and took hers. "Seriously, I'd like to catch up. One adult to another. How about if I come over tonight?"

"One adult to another? As opposed to one teenager

to a child?" Her smile broadened. "I would like that."

This exchange between Avalee and Ty got a little tedious. I hated being ignored. And, she obviously forgot she had plans, so I spoke up. "She can't."

They both turned their gaze toward me.

"It's Martini Monday, Avalee. *Remember?*"

"Oh, that's right. I forgot. Sorry Ty."

"Martini Monday?" He held his palms up. "I like martinis."

This guy just wasn't giving up. "Sorry, just us girls." There was no way he was going to crash my party.

He turned his attention back to Avalee. "How about Tuesday night?" His lopsided grin could have charmed the feathers off a peacock. I've seen that look on a man before. Ty wasn't only interested in catching up. He was interested in catching. Period. Ava flushed like a smitten teenager. "All right. How about coming to supper?"

"Now you're talking. I've heard about your mother's cooking and have always wanted to put my feet under her table."

I couldn't resist. "And just where would you like to put your shoes later?"

Avalee turned hot red. "Lexi. Really?"

Ty laughed. "Yep, Lexi. You have never been one to hold back. I'll see you girls later." He waved and walked out.

The vibe in my office had definitely changed after Ty entered the scene. "Well. You two have given me my next column idea."

Ava tore her attention from the door. "What's that?"

"Older women who seduce younger men."

She snatched a paperclip off my desk and threw it at me. "You are so bad."

I laughed. But truth was? I wasn't kidding.

Chapter 7

LEXI
Martini Monday

I dumped biscuit mix into the bowl, added sausage, shredded sharp cheddar cheese, and plunged in with both hands. Greasy sausage cheese balls would go perfect with martinis. And of course fudge. I had a pan cooling on my counter.

While I squeezed the ingredients together, my thoughts went to Avalee and Ty. What if...? I shook my head. No way. But, then again, *what if* they *did* get together? Wouldn't that be a hoot? I could see why he was attracted to her. Except for the barely perceptible crow's feet around her eyes and a couple of creases across her forehead, she looked gorgeous.

My nose began to tingle. Why did that always have to happen when I was up to my elbows in goo? I rubbed the crook of my arm against it, but sneezed anyway. Good thing these things were going in a 350-degree oven.

While I rolled the mixture into walnut-sized balls, I imagined Ava getting tipsy and eating about twenty of them. Between her mother and me, my New York City friend would soon look like the rest of us. Pleasantly plump. At least that was my evil plan.

After sliding my fat and carbohydrate-laden snacks

in the oven, I checked the fudge. *Good. Nice and firm.* The aroma of warm chocolate still lingered in the air. I eyed the stove and slunk toward the pot coated with butter, sugar, and cocoa deliciousness. No time like the present to clean up the pot. I snapped up a spoon, scraped it around the sides, and licked it like a cat cleans its leg. This was my kind of kitchen duty. As usual, guilt nagged at me. So, in order to shut it up while I finished scraping the pot, I promised myself I wouldn't eat any fudge when the girls got here.

Yeah, like that is going to happen.

The fragrant aroma of sage wafted from the stove and the timer sounded. I took the pot to the sink and filled it with water before I fell into a sugar coma, slipped on the potholders, and opened the oven door. A blast of savory, moist heat warmed my face and made my mouth water. I set them on the counter to cool and slid in the other pan. There was just enough time to set up the bar and look for a funny DVD in my collection.

While I sorted through my movies, I thought about my fudge orgy in the kitchen, and remembered the *I Love Lucy* show when Lucy and Ethel worked in the candy factory. Excellent. I found it next to the Vitametavegimin episode. Yes. After a few martinis, we would all be in Lucy's shoes trying to pronounce that word. I chuckled just thinking about it.

With just minutes to spare, I set up the snack table, set out martini glasses, filled the bar sink with ice, pulled the bottle of Grey Goose from the freezer, and plunged it in the basin.

The doorbell rang, and Jema nudged the door open balancing a platter of chicken wings. "Am I too early?"

"Get yourself in here, girl." I took the tray from

her. "Especially when you are carrying a plate of wings. Martini?"

"Yes, please. I've been on my feet all day."

I poured vodka in the shaker full of ice. "Shaken or stirred?" I couldn't resist asking.

"Sugar, you can do the Charleston with it if you want. Just pour."

I poured one for Jema and one for me. I handed her a glass and clinked mine against it. "Here's to Martini Mondays."

"Martini Mondays." She took a sip and rolled her eyes. "Yum."

The cold vodka warmed my throat leaving a vaporous trail of relaxation. I took another sip and smiled. "The others better hurry, or we will be as drunk as coots before they get here."

"Not if I can help it." Molly Kate walked in with a huge dish of chocolate chip cookies. "Fresh from the oven." She set it on the table, picked up a cookie, and broke it in half. Melting chocolate threaded between the halves.

I'm doomed.

Avalee stepped in with a tray of raw veggies. *Figures.* As if she read my mind she held up her hand. "Don't worry. Momma made some dip, guaranteed to add to our derrières. I'll be right back." She went out to the wagon she'd pulled behind her and picked up a crock-pot. When she passed by me she lifted the lid.

"Oh, wow. That smells divine. What is it?"

"Sausage cheese dip." Smirking she added, "Momma didn't like my yogurt-dill dip suggestion."

Molly Kate put her hands on her hips. "Well, we can thank the good Lord for that."

I made room on the table for the dip. "Why don't you go and get your mom? Have her join us."

"No, she's busy cooking for tomorrow. Right now she's spreading her eight-layer yellow cake with chocolate icing."

"Who's coming for supper tomorrow?" Molly Kate bit into the cookie half.

"Ty Jackson. That's who." I answered while shaking the martinis.

Molly arched her eyebrows. "Ty Jackson?"

Avalee shrugged. "He wanted to catch up. We are going to talk about old times. Marc and all."

I handed Avalee and Molly Kate their glasses then lifted mine. "To the women of Washington Avenue. Knock 'em back, girls. We'll sip later."

On our second round, we filled our plates and nestled together on the couch in front of the television.

"Lord, we look like a pile of puppies," said Molly Kate. "Isn't it wonderful?"

"Sure is. Now get ready to laugh, girls." I clicked the remote to start the Lucy DVD. "We'll start with Vitametavegimin seeing how we are on our second martini." We sipped and howled for the next thirty minutes. Then I served the fudge for the chocolate factory episode. All I can say is that it's a good thing I had two bathrooms. Every few minutes one of us ran cross-legged to the toilet—another annoying thing about being over fifty.

When the show was finished I stretched. "Okay, that's all for Lucy. Now what do we have to laugh at?"

"I just happen to have something." Avalee yanked a paper from her purse. "Okay, y'all. Listen to the latest madness installment from our very own Lexi Lowe."

"No. Wait until we've had our third round." I shook, poured, and then dropped a small piece of fudge in each glass. "Prepare to be amazed."

Jema squinted at her glass. "What the...?"

"Hush up and drink." I nudged her with my elbow. "It's dessert. Think of it as a variation of a chocolate martini."

"Oooh." She stuck her finger in and worked the candy up the side, then took a small bite and chased it with a sip of vodka. "Hey, that's good."

"Would I lead you astray?" I glanced at Molly Kate who had just opened her mouth to say something. "Don't answer that."

Avalee clapped her hands together like our first grade school teacher, Mrs. Frost. "Now, y'all, pay attention."

"Wait. I have an observation to make." I couldn't resist pointing this out. "Have *y'all* noticed how southern Avalee is when she is three sheets to the wind? Those Yankees didn't ruin her after all." Plunging my finger into my Grey Goose, I pulled out the fudge and took a bite before plopping it back in the glass. Then I waggled my fingers. "Continue."

"You know what you can kiss." She cleared her throat and did her best to imitate my voice while reading my column.

At the *flaccid* reference, Molly Kate spit vodka halfway across the room. "Mercy, Lexi. I can't believe you wrote that."

"Well, it's true, and don't try and tell me you don't agree with everything in that column."

"I'm not saying I don't." She took a napkin and blotted her mouth. "After my husband died, I wanted to date again. But it was like I'd become invisible. Anytime I went out with my daughter, men made eye contact with her, spoke to her, waiters even asked *her* for *my* order. I finally managed to meet some guys. And you are *exactly right*, Lex. Some guys in their late fifties and sixties think they are players. I've found that if they are broke, they will date an older woman because they want someone to take care of them. But if they have money, then they want perfect little Barbie dolls with six inch waists and big boobs."

She finished her martini and held the tiny piece of fudge between her fingers. "I'm sticking with my cat. I'm D.O.N.E." With dramatic flourish she popped the candy in her mouth.

"Preach it, sister." I stood and high-fived her.

"I'll bet I have the best disaster date story." Jema held her glass out toward me. "No vodka, just fill it with fudge."

"Would you like coffee with your fudge," I asked.

"Yes, ma'am. Please," said Jema.

Seemed everyone else did, too, so I hurried to the kitchen to make a pot. "Don't say a word until I get back." When I returned with the coffee and fixings, we filled our cups, loaded up on cookies *and* fudge. Even Avalee. *Will wonders never cease?*

"Okay, you were saying?" I bit into a cookie, rolled my gaze to the ceiling, and closed my eyes. As the name of Molly's business says, it was a taste of heaven.

"So, as I was saying, about a year after Ray died, I met this really nice guy who started volunteering at the shelter. He asked me out to supper, and I decided why not? You know? We had a nice time and went out again. After several dates, he told me he wanted to take me to the Country Club. I had a feeling this was leading to something special, but then again, I had this weird sense about him, too. He seemed, well, secretive." She popped a piece of fudge in her mouth and moaned. "Oh my. This fudge is out of this world." She picked up another piece. "Anyway, he got us a table overlooking the lake. It was *so* romantic. He ordered for us: artichokes and drawn butter, palm salad, lobster, parmesan au gratin potatoes, and baked Alaska for dessert."

"Stop, you are making me hungry." Molly Kate reached for another cookie.

"Well, it was delicious. And the wine?" Jema waved her hand. "Nothing but the best." She leaned forward. "The bill was over two hundred dollars." With dramatic flourish she poked the fudge between her lips.

"For heaven's sakes," I said. "My husband was a doctor and he never spent that kind of money on me."

"Wait. You haven't heard anything yet. All evening I kept picking up on a weird vibe. After we finished dessert, he wouldn't even look me in the eye. I didn't know what to make of it. When the waiter left the bill, he reached for his wallet, then shrugged his shoulders and said, 'Looks like I forgot my wallet, doll. Did you bring a credit card?'"

"You've got to be kidding me?" Molly shook her head. "That's the oldest con game there is."

"He apologized over and over, but I knew I'd been had. He was too animated and at the same time, his eyes were, well, it was like there was laughter behind them. I said to myself, 'Well mister, two can play at this game.' So I gave him my biggest smile, patted his hand and said, 'Oh, you poor thing. You must be so embarrassed.' He said he was and would pay me the next day. I thought, yeah, right. Sure you will. So I suggested he order another bottle of wine. You should have seen his face. He thought he had a real sucker. And can you believe this? He raised his hand and snapped his fingers. When the waiter came to our table, he ordered a two-hundred-dollar bottle. Now the bill was over four hundred dollars. So, after the waiter poured, we toasted each other. Then I excused myself and said I needed to go to the bathroom. When I left the table I marched my butt out and called a cab. About twenty minutes later he texted me and asked if I was all right. I texted back, Yes. Never better. I'm on my way home." She fanned herself. "You should have read the hateful messages and foul language he texted."

"Bravo, Jema." I was so peeved, I ate more fudge.

"Wait. That isn't all. A couple of days later I get this call from a woman about the texts I'd sent him. It turns out he was *married.* And apparently I wasn't the only woman he'd tried to dupe. He had twenty-two other women's numbers on his phone."

"That jerk," I said. "I feel for his poor wife."

"I realized I had met her before," said Jema. "A few weeks later she came through my line at the grocery store. I realized I'd seen her before. She was the nice lady who used to work at the bookstore. When I saw her name on the check I nearly fell out. Of course, I didn't say anything to her."

"Men just don't know a good woman when they see one," said Molly Kate.

The evil twin who lives in my psyche took control of my mouth. "Well, I doubt Avalee agrees with you."

Avalee looked up. "What?"

"Ty Jackson came into my office, and I thought the poor boy was going to step on his tongue. He definitely knows a good woman when *he* sees one. In fact, I have a hunch he has the hots for her."

Avalee pointed at me. "Now Lexi..."

Molly Kate looked from me to Ava. "Ty Jackson? How old is that boy?"

"I don't know. But I do know he likes older women, and he has his eye on our Avalee."

"He does not." Ava hit me with her pillow. "And this subject is closed."

A sly smile stole over Jem's face. "Honey, surely you know that no subject is ever closed with Lexi."

"Or sacred." Molly Kate stood and stretched. "It's getting late. Time for me to stumble home."

Jema yawned. "Me too. Coming Avalee?"

"Yes." She put her hand on my shoulder. "And you behave. You know there isn't anything to Ty coming over tomorrow."

"Sure I do." And I did. There was definitely something to it.

Chapter 8

MOLLY
Confession

Note to self: *Never. Ever. Under no circumstances. Ever* drink three martinis in one night *even if* there is fudge in them. I pushed my palms against my temples and leaned against the kitchen counter. *Suck it up, girl. You should suffer, fool.*

Gypsy weaved between my feet and stared at me with emerald eyes. "Rrrowrr?"

"Time for breakfast. I know." I felt my way to the pantry and fumbled for a can of cat food. When I snapped open the lid the odor of whitefish pâtè nearly made me double over the sink and throw up the apple peels I ate when I was a baby. As fast as I could, I dumped it in Gypsy's bowl and hurried out of the room.

Ugh. The last thing I wanted to do was go to work. My head throbbed like those irritating subwoofer things in teenagers' cars. Thank heaven I had the good sense to have the girls open up the shop on time for my caffeine and carbohydrate-addicted clientele, giving me time to recover.

Speaking of addictions, a cup of extra-dark French roast sounded really good. I went back to the kitchen and put a small plastic coffee thingie in my handy-dandy-single-serve coffee pot then pushed brew. This coffee maker rocked, even if, in a few short years, these plastic tubs would overflow every landfill on the planet. I needed to get the refillable ones.

In no time at all, my coffee brewed. The robust steam from my cup soothed me as I slogged to the porch, my favorite place to start the day. When I eased onto the rocking chair, it complained with its usual pop and snap. *Sakes.* I didn't need to be reminded about last night's fudge and cookie binge.

As I sipped my drug of choice, the pounding behind my eyes eased, but the sickening sweet scent from the gardenias in the thick air made me want to throw up. A hot shower might help. But then, so would another cup of coffee. The shower would have to wait.

While nursing my second cup, I flopped in my office chair and checked email. My pulse raced a little when I noticed a message from my online friend, Colin. If the girls knew I'd gotten involved in an Internet relationship they would die, no matter how much I assured them I was being careful. I had given a fake name and said I lived in Tupelo. Everything was perfectly safe, and besides, this was my only choice as I saw it. I may be invisible in public, but not on the Internet.

I clicked on his name while my emotions did a little jig.

Dear Mary,

Sorry I haven't written in a few days, but when you see the attached picture I think—I know—you will understand. I have been adopted by an abandoned puppy.

I saw the jerk drop her out of his car and roar off. My driveway is long and I was mowing my grass, so the guy didn't know I was watching him. You should have seen the little thing. She chased after the car yipping. Then she walked back to the place where she was dumped and sat as if she were waiting for him to come back.

Poor baby. I clicked on the attachment. A darling Jack Russell pup stared back at me. Her eyes reminded me of chocolate drops. My heart melted. Not just because of that adorable puppy, but also because of this man who was compassionate toward animals. I scrolled to the next picture of Colin with the pup. I couldn't help but smile. He wasn't what one would call drop dead gorgeous, but he was really cute. He reminded me of the actor, Bill Murray. His friendly smile and gentle eyes had won me over the first time I saw his photograph. I'd often wondered if he'd sent me a real picture of himself. Now seeing him with the puppy made me confident he had. What a relief. I sent him a real photo of myself, because if he didn't like full-figured gals, then I wanted him to know I was one of them and there was no need to continue building a relationship. Obviously, it didn't matter to him. Another reason to like him. Clicking back to the email, I picked up where I'd left off.

I walked down the driveway but stopped a couple of yards away. I didn't want to scare her. There was no need to worry. She scampered right up to me in little hopping steps. Right away I knew her name was Kricket.

Can you believe that guy? But, on the other hand, I have to give him kudos for not killing her. I live on a rural dirt road and people are always dumping their unwanted animals, old tires, mattresses, you name it.

Oh well, enough of my grousing. I got a sweet girl out of the deal. Maybe one day you will meet her. But you have to meet me first. Been thinking about when that might be?

What have you been up to lately? How is the insurance biz?

Why did I tell him I was in insurance? I didn't know a thing about it. I'd told this poor man so many lies. At least I'd been truthful about the essentials, like the way I looked, my interests, and beliefs.

In three months and five days I'll be able to retire. I'm counting the minutes. I have a bucket list. First, meet you. Then I want to redo my kitchen. I really like to cook. I'm always making up new recipes. Who knows? Maybe I'll write my own cookbook.

I want to travel, too. Maybe a trip to Tupelo? I know, pushing. But really Mary, how much longer? We have been writing back and forth for several months now. I know it was a good idea to not meet at first, but lady, I am falling in love with you. I love your soul, and now I want to meet the owner of that soul. Okay, I know I'm getting mushy.

I have another question. Do you have a Facebook page? I'm thinking about setting one up myself. But that is about as far as I've gotten.

Well, Kricket is whining. I'm crate-training her, so I better let her out. Hope to

see you sooner than later.
Love,
Colin
Wow.

He's falling in love with me? And he's ready to meet me? Was I ready? I liked our agreement to write for a while before making physical or voice contact. After all the losers I'd met on these dating sites and then having to endure a meal with them, I wanted a more controlled environment. Writing. No physical or voice contact. At least while writing I could delete stupid comments. And so far, this arrangement had worked out fine.

I glanced at the clock and nearly jumped out of my robe. I had to be at the bakery in less than an hour. *Sorry Colin. I'll have to get back to you later.*

Hot water, Camay soap, and thoughts of Colin were the sure cure for a vodka and fudge hangover. When I stepped into the shower, I noticed all I had left of my Camay stash was a tiny, pink sliver. It really irked me that I couldn't find my favorite soap in stores any longer. Now I had to buy it online. I would add my soap frustration to my whine list for Wednesday.

Gypsy watched me dress, followed me while I looked for my keys, then sat by the door glaring as if to say, *it's time, woman.*

"I know you want to go out. I'm almost ready." Good grief.

As soon as I opened the door, she nearly tripped me in her haste to get out. I turned the lock and hurried to the sidewalk. In my peripheral vision, I saw Felix running toward me waving his hand.

"Miss Molly?"

Oh, Lord. "Felix, is it Miss Cladie? Is she all right?"

"Yes'm, she's fine. She just sent me to ask you to bring home two loaves of your rosemary garlic bread. She's got company coming."

It took a minute for my heart to stop hammering. When I was able to breathe again I said, "Ty Jackson. Right?"

He ran a hand through his tight salt and pepper curls. "I don't know who is coming. But she shor' is puttin' the big pot in the little un."

"You tell her I'll bring them by on my way home. By the way, Felix, what can I bring you?"

"Why, one of them cinnamon scones. You know they are my favorite."

"Will do. See you this afternoon."

"Bye now." Felix turned and ambled down the road. What a good man. He'd taken Miss Cladie under his wing when Fred died. There wasn't anything he wouldn't do for her. And if I knew that woman at all, she'd do all she could for him.

The day dragged by. I could hardly concentrate on my baking for thinking of what I wanted to write Colin. The paws on my cat clock took their sweet time to point to the twelve and the five, but finally the cat's mouth opened and the little bird on the tip of its tongue chirped five times. My obsession with cats knew no bounds.

I was about to turn the closed sign around and lock the door when Lexi rushed up and yanked it open.

"MK, I need a triple-shot before you close."

"Sorry. No time. I've got to go."

She put her hands together. "Please, please, please?

I'm fixin to take my column to Vince, and he isn't going to like it one little bit. I've got to be on my toes."

"Well, I'm going to let you in on a little secret. If it is caffeine you're after, brewed has more than espresso."

She squinted at me through her big brown eyes. "Really? Never heard that. Will you make me some?" A strand of auburn hair fell across her brow. "Please."

"Well. All right. But I've got to hurry. Miss Cladie is expecting this bread, and I'm already behind time. She's got company tonight."

"Tyler Jackson. I know." She came in and I locked the door behind her and turned the sign to *Closed.* We hurried to the back where I kept the small coffee maker for emergencies such as these. While I measured coffee in the filter, she started sniggering.

"What's so funny?"

"Oh, I was just thinking about Avalee and Ty tonight. I'd like to be a fly on the wall when he and Avalee are alone together. I'll bet the sparks will fly. He sure is one sexy guy."

"What?" I put my coffee measure down and stared at Lexi. "He's young enough to be your..."

She raised her hand. "If you say my son, I'm going to knock the fire out of you. I was twelve when he was born, and so was she."

"Well don't go putting them together." I poured water into the pot. "They both loved Marc. That's all there is to it."

"I don't think so. You weren't in my office."

"May be, but she doesn't need to go and make Ty into Marc. That would only hurt them both."

Lexi wrinkled her nose. "Well, when you put it that

way."

When the maker sputtered out the last of the coffee into the pot, I took a grande cup, filled it, and handed it to her. "Now go do battle with your old goat editor."

She grinned. "When he reads it, I feel sure he will recognize himself, and he won't appreciate it one little bit." She took a sip. "Mmm, that's good. Okay, I'm off." Crossing her fingers she said, "Hopefully, I'll convince him this column will push a lot of hot buttons and get a lot of attention. Who knows? Maybe someone from the Big Apple will notice. Wouldn't that be great?"

"Yeah. Great. Now scoot out of here. Miss Cladie is probably wringing her hands about now."

Lexi slipped out the back door while I wrapped the bread and stuck it in a sack. After setting the alarm I walked in the sultriness of late afternoon. Even though I lived just a few blocks from my shop, I wished I had driven. Heat undulated from the sidewalk billowing under my skirt. Miserable.

As soon as I reached her house, Miss Cladie met me at her door. "Bless your heart, girl. You're red as a tomato and sweating to beat the band."

"I beg your pardon, *I don't sweat*. I glisten."

"Whatever you do, get your glistening self in here and have some sweet tea."

"Yes, ma'am. I believe I will." I handed her the bread and strode to her black oscillating fan like a bee martin to a gourd. I unbuttoned the top portion of my shirt and held it open. "My momma had one of these."

"It helps move the air around a bit. On days like today, my air conditioner just isn't enough. "

"I liked sticking broom straws between the blades

to hear them click. It's a wonder I didn't lose any fingers."

Avalee jogged down the stairs like a teenager. "Hi, MK. Have you recovered from last night?"

"It took three cups of coffee and a hot shower." *And Colin.* "I finally cleared up. How about you?"

"I laid around all day. I feel fine now."

"Laid around, huh? Must be nice." I took a long drink of my iced tea.

"It really isn't. I've got to get busy or go crazy. I'm not used to all this leisure time."

Miss Cladie handed Avalee a glass of tea. "You girls go chat somewhere else, out of my way. Thank you Molly, honey, for the bread. How much do I owe you?"

"Not a thing Miss Cladie."

"I can't let you do that."

"You can send me pumpkins and mums for my porch when fall comes."

"Fair enough. And as far as I'm concerned, fall can't arrive soon enough."

"That's the truth." Avalee took my arm. "Come on. Let's go."

We settled in the living room. I took a coaster from the holder and set my tea down. In mere seconds condensation droplets had formed on the outside of my glass and puddled around the bottom. Miss Cladie was right. Fall couldn't come soon enough.

"It sure is good to have you home, Avalee. I don't believe I've seen such a sparkle in your momma's eyes in years." I took a drink and then rubbed the glass across my chest.

The grandfather clock ticked out a comforting

rhythm. Avalee looked around the room. "I know. I've been away too long. I had my reasons and felt I did the right thing." The clock sounded the half hour. When it finished, Avalee said, "But as the cliché goes, there truly is no place like home." She looked away and wiped her eyes with the back of her hand. "I need to face my demons here and get on with life."

"You mean Marc?"

She nodded, but remained silent and left me hanging. Shoot. What about Marc and demons? I had to know. I prodded a little deeper. "And you think Ty might help with these demons?"

Avalee shifted her eyes to the window. "I don't know. Maybe." She sipped her tea and sighed. "I just don't know." In an abrupt mood change, she slapped her leg and smiled at me. "Enough about me. What's up with you?"

Well. Her emotional pivot threw my little investigation right in the trashcan. But I wasn't about to give up. Besides, I had something else I wanted to investigate. Her face was the same heart-shape she had as a teen. Not a saggy jowl to be seen. And I had my suspicions.

"I'll tell you a secret if you will tell me one."

Glancing at me over her glass she murmured. "Ooooookay?"

"I know you have a secret. It is written all over your face."

"What?"

"Spill it. You've had plastic surgery, haven't you?"

"Yes. I have."

And that was all she said. She threw a look at me as if she'd made her chess move and waited for mine.

Okay, I could play this game.

"So, what did you have done?"

She shrugged. "Face lift and lipo in various places."

"Wow."

"No biggie really. In New York City it is just part of business. I had to look fresh, young, and relevant. But I wasn't competing with just women. My largest client base and biggest competitors were...are you ready for this? Gay men."

"Seriously?" In all of my fifty-six years, I couldn't remember ever having met a gay man.

"They are a very discriminating group. They keep themselves dapper, and they expect those who work for them to do the same."

"Well, Avalee, all I can say is I still love you even though you make me look like a bowl of oatmeal."

"Oh psssh." She rose from the chair. "Want some wine?"

"Sure."

While she poured she said, "Okay, I spilled. Now what's your secret?"

Oh brother. I wished I hadn't started this game. It seemed like a good idea to weasel something out of her. But now that it was my turn, I wasn't so sure. On the other hand, I really did need someone to talk to, and Ava had a level head. She wasn't a drama queen like Lexi.

"I'm interested in a guy. Very interested."

Ava handed me wine and sat. "Really? Who?"

"His name is Colin."

"How wonderful, MK. Where did you meet him?"

I hesitated. "Well, technically, I haven't met him.

Face to face, that is."

Ava pulled her leg under her and tipped her head. "What do you mean?"

Here goes. "I met him on the Internet."

She frowned. "You're kidding, right?"

"No."

Avalee jumped up like she had discovered a rattlesnake under her rear. "Are you crazy? What if he's married? What if he's a convict? What if he's a serial killer?"

"Hold on. Just hear me out." Sheeze, I expected a reaction like that out of Lexi, not Avalee.

She plopped back in the chair. "This better be good."

"So, you remember at martini Monday how I said I *managed* to meet men? Well, a few months ago, I got this wild hair while watching those dating commercials for people our age and decided to try it out. I dated a few guys, but it felt awkward going out with perfect strangers, and lemme tell ya, I met some real doozies. Anyway, because of those goons, I decided right away when Colin and I were matched up that I wanted to email back and forth like Tom Hanks and Meg Ryan did in that movie, *You've Got Mail.* So when Colin emailed me to ask me out, I wrote back and explained how I wanted to start off this relationship. No contact physically or verbally. He agreed. Seems he'd had the same experiences. So we haven't met or spoken on the phone. But, unlike the movie, we have exchanged pictures."

Avalee swirled her wine. "Well, I have to admit, you've taken a sensible approach."

"It's worked out pretty well. I've learned a lot

about him."

"Well, you may think you have. He could be lying, too. Just promise me if you decide to meet him it will be at a public place. Not at his house or anything."

"Lands sakes, Avalee. I'm not stupid."

She raised her eyebrows.

I stood and wagged my finger. "Don't say it."

Laughing she got to her feet, walked over and hugged me. "I want you to be happy. You know that, don't you?"

"I do." I handed her my glass. "Now go help your momma before that hot, tight-jeaned hunk of manhood comes for supper."

"Oh, you." She popped my bottom. "Go write that Internet serial-killer boyfriend of yours."

We hugged again. I was so thankful Avalee had come home.

****

Gypsy lay curled on the welcome mat. She glanced up at me and opened her mouth in a silent meow. I understood. It was simply too hot for conversation. "Come on inside, sweetie, and get out of this heat." In one silky move she leapt off the mat and slipped between the door and me.

While I changed clothes, I thought about Colin's email. I supposed I would have to give him an answer about meeting. But what?

On my way to the office, I mentally drafted an email. However, when I sat at my computer and put my fingers on the keyboard, my mind froze. Whatever I'd planned on writing vanished. I was a complete blank. So now what? Maybe a cold glass of chardonnay would help. In the kitchen, Gypsy rubbed against my leg while

I poured.

"Merrowl?"

So much can be said by a single cat word.

"Hungry?" She rose up on two legs and stretched her right front paw up my side.

"Okay, Mommy will get your food." I scooped fancy flaked tuna in her little fish dish and stood there a minute to admire my kitty while sipping wine. "Time to get back to Colin." Gypsy looked up and then went back to business. I topped off my glass and headed to the computer.

My mind began to relax. I decided to start with Gypsy stories, ask about Kricket, maybe tell about Avalee. Then ease into the meeting conversation. When should I suggest? Heck, I wasn't even sure if I was ready. If we did, then where? Certainly not Tupelo. Maybe I could suggest Oxford? Someplace on the square?

Gypsy jumped on the desk and spread herself on my keyboard.

"Do you mind?"

She cleaned her paw, totally unconcerned. I picked her up, carried her to the door, and dropped her on the front porch. "Out ya go."

Up the street, I noticed Ty's car in the Preston's driveway. And so it begins—again. I spoke to the night, "Please be careful, Avalee."

Back at my computer, I debated about meeting Colin. If a decision was this hard, I reasoned, then it just wasn't time. Besides, I couldn't tell him I had fallen in love with him, because I wasn't sure. I knew I admired him, but love? As bad as I hated to, I had to put him off.

Dear Colin,

Kricket is adorable. And she will be a good friend for you. There is nothing like the unconditional love of a dog. Cats? Well, they love us because we unconditionally love them. I don't think I've ever asked you, but do you like cats?

If he didn't, this relationship would have a severe setback.

I don't understand how people can just leave pets on the street assuming that they won't be run over or that someone else will take them in.

So you like to cook? Somehow, I didn't pick up on that from your other emails. I love to cook. That is why I opened a bakery

Shoot! I hit the delete button thankful for my decision to not speak on the phone. "You are in insurance Molly Kate." This deception thing was hard.

I like to bake and do it quite often, which explains my fluffy figure.

Another reminder for Colin. If he preferred skinny women, he'd better run now.

Good news! My best friend, Avalee, moved back home. We've been friends since childhood. But she moved away after college and has been in New York City for over thirty years. She's my forever-friend. Do you have any close friends?

About Facebook,

Now I had to make up another lie. I drummed my fingers on my desk while I thought. Whoever said that about tangled webs when we deceive was right. Finally an idea came to me.

I didn't set one up because of my insurance job. The last thing I want is a disgruntled client to find me and complain after hours. I get enough of that during the day.

Good. That made sense. It bothered me how I had gotten so skilled at lying. The only way out of this was to meet him and come clean. *Perhaps we should meet.*

Now, about our meeting.

I inhaled and let the air out slowly.

Let's wait a few more weeks. How about meeting in Oxford around the first of October? That seems to be midway for both of us and gives us a little more time to be sure this is the right thing to do. Let me know what you think.

I'd better close for now. Give Kricket a pat from me.

Hugs,

Mary

I hit send and swiveled in my chair to face the photo of Randy and me on our fifteenth anniversary.

"Randy, I hope you are okay with this." Unbidden, tears filled my eyes while I gazed at the photograph. "Why did you have to die? I'm still so mad at you I could stomp on your grave. Why didn't you take better care of yourself?" I hugged the picture to my chest and had my little cry. Then I kissed the picture. "I'm just kidding, honey. I wouldn't stomp your grave."

I put the picture back. The room felt so empty. So quiet. Something inside me had changed since Colin. Hugging pictures and snuggling cats was no longer good enough.

Maybe it really was time for us to meet.

Chapter 9

AVALEE
Plans

Momma's kitchen was a sauna. Her face glowed red, and glistening diamonds of sweat formed on her brow. She moved from stove to counter to fridge to sink like one of those super heroes in the cartoons I watched as a kid. Knives flashed, spoons clattered against boilers and bowls, beaters spun, pot lids vibrated from escaping steam, pans banged from the stove to the counter.

"For crying out loud, Mom. Slow down."

"I'm fine, honey." She mopped her face with her towel. "I'm in my happy place."

"Your happy place is going to send you to the ER." I scanned her kitchen in utter amazement. Even though Momma moved around the kitchen like a cat with its tail on fire, the room was perfectly clean. Not a single dirty dish anywhere. The counters were pristine. If I cooked as much as she did, my kitchen would look like Bourbon Street the morning after Mardi Gras.

"What time is Ty coming?" Momma asked as she whisked by me.

"Six."

She shot a glance at the happy apple clock that hung over the stove. "Mercy Lord, it's five-thirty already, and I haven't set the table."

"I'll do it, Momma. Don't worry."

"No, you just give him a beer when he gets here and go talk. I'll handle this." She surveyed the stove and counter. "I just hope there is enough."

My mouth dropped open. "Are you kidding me? There's enough food here to feed the entire congregation of Moonlight First Baptist." And there was, too. Pot roast with carrots, potatoes, and gravy. Creamed sweet potatoes, snap beans, fried okra, butter beans, crookneck squash, sliced tomatoes, purple onions, chow-chow, hot cornbread, Molly Kate's bread, and three desserts. "Just the roast and veggies would have been enough."

"I'm not going to have Tyler Jackson telling his momma that all I served him was pot roast.

"Well, far be it from me to spoil your reputation." I hugged her and went to the fridge for some tea. "Want me to pour you a glass?"

"Yes, that sounds good." She picked up the eight-layer cake, took it to the buffet in the dining room, and placed it between the banana pudding and the custard pie.

I gave her the tea. "I need to freshen up a little. Are you sure you don't need any help?"

"Get on outta here. There's hardly enough room in here for me."

"No room? I could have put a third of my Manhattan apartment in this kitchen."

"I remember." She picked up the pan of fried okra and poured it in the colander to drain. "No wonder you were so skinny when you came home. There wasn't any room in your kitchen to cook."

Were skinny? Oh Lord.

"Okay, I'm going to get ready." I kissed her cheek and rushed up the stairs to the mirror. Mom was right. I could barely button my jeans. *Shoot.* I chose a loose sundress and slipped it on while comforting myself by thinking it was probably just the heat that was making me swell. Pitiful, I know. But it made me feel a little better.

I splashed my face with water, then twisted my hair up in the back and secured it with a clip. There wasn't much need for make-up since I'd sweat it off anyway. I powdered my face, brushed on mascara, and glazed on lip-gloss. After slipping on flip-flops, I hurried downstairs.

Just as I hit the bottom step, Ty knocked on the door. When I opened it, I had a déjà vu moment. How many times had I jogged down these steps to open the door for Marc? *But he's gone.* I had to remind myself every time I saw his baby brother who was his spitting image.

"Hi, Ty." I swallowed as I pushed open the door. "Come on in."

"Thanks." He shoved his hands in his pockets. "You look gorgeous as usual."

You're not so bad yourself. "Oh, I bet you say that to all your babysitters."

"No, just you." He winked.

"Supper will be ready soon. Wanna beer?"

"Sure. That would be great." He tilted his head back and inhaled. "Man oh man, it smells good in here."

Momma walked in wiping her hands on her apron. "Well, if you aren't a sight for sore eyes, Tyler Jackson.

How on earth are you?"

"I'm fine, Miss Cladie. You're looking mighty fine."

"Fit as a fiddle. How's your momma?"

"As well as can be expected, I guess."

"I vow. That poor woman's been through it, hasn't she?"

"Yeah, but she's on the upswing. She'll beat this, Miss Cladie."

"I'm sure she will, bless her heart. I made enough for you to take home to your folks."

"Thank you. I know they'll appreciate that." Ty rubbed his hands together. "I've been anticipating this meal all day. It's been a while since I've had some home cooking."

Somehow, I missed something in this conversation. "What's wrong with Mrs. Jackson?"

Momma turned to me. "Emma has been fighting lung cancer, poor thing. Ty will fill you in. I'll call when supper is ready. And Ty, honey, if y'all want to sit outside, cut on the fan. It's close out there."

"Yes, ma'am, I will. It's air that you wear for sure."

I took out two Dos Equis and joined Ty on the porch swing. "Now, what's this about your momma?"

"It's those cigarettes. They finally caught up with her. I'm surprised Dad doesn't have it, too. He can't take ten steps without being out of breath."

"Oh, Tyler, I'm so sorry to hear that."

"Thanks." He took a swig of beer and then chuckled. "I don't think anyone has called me Tyler since I was in elementary school."

"Which was, ummmm, last year?"

He glanced at me and grinned, deepening the dimples in his five o'clock shadow. "I wish. Things were simpler then."

"That's the truth." I sipped my beer. "So what have you been doing these past thirty something years. College? Marriage? Kids?"

"All of the above. I graduated high school, went to the community college long enough to discover my passion, quit school, and got married. Had a couple of kids and divorced ten years later. That's my life in a nutshell."

"What is your passion?"

"Photography, much to my parents' chagrin." He took another long swallow. "Dad and Mom were hell-bent that I go to med school or get into law. But neither appealed to me. I really didn't know what I wanted to do until I took a photography class. The prof told me I had a talent for telling a story through my lens. So I did some freelance and got pretty popular."

"I'm beginning to see what you mean when you said you're nothing like your brother. He was so focused and driven academically. You have an artsy side."

"Yeah. If you think about it, Marc wanted to heal the human body. I wanted to explore the human soul." He finished his beer and set the bottle on the floor. "I'm not rich, but comfortable."

"You said you have kids?"

He nodded. "A daughter, Skye. She's twenty-two. And Glen. He's twenty. Skye's at Old Miss. Glen attends the community college. He's like his old man. Artsy."

"I'd like to meet them sometime." I held up my

bottle. "I'm out. Want another before we eat?"

"Sure." He reached down, picked up his bottle, and handed it to me.

In a few minutes, I returned and handed him a long neck. "So, why haven't you remarried?"

"Thanks." He took a long draw. "What Lexi wrote about younger women is true. At least for some. The ones I've dated are so into themselves. They want big houses with huge closets for their ridiculous collection of shoes. Some are so needy, wanting constant reassurance, and heaven forbid, if I forgot to tell them how beautiful they were, they'd pout. And I'm sorry, but when the highest level of conversation is about the latest fashion and hair styles, I'm outta there." He shook his head. "But the worst thing is most of them want kids. I'm over that."

I elbowed him. "You're pretty hard to please."

He held his head to one side and raised his hands. "Seriously. Women my age or younger are a different breed. I wasn't kidding when I said I liked older women."

"Sure you do." I tipped my beer.

All humor went out of his expression, and he studied me with dark eyes. "I mean it. And you want to hear something else strange about me?"

"What?"

"I like my ladies soft and with curves." He leaned close and whispered in my hair, "Not all angles and sharp edges."

Heat rose up my neck. The atmosphere between us had changed, hot and sultry as the air. I tried to think of something to say but couldn't.

Momma called through the screen. "Supper's on

the table. Come and get it."

Thank God for my mother.

****

The dining room table groaned under the weight of platters and bowls filled to the brim.

I shook my head. "Momma, there's hardly room for our plates."

She rested her hands on her hips and surveyed the table with a satisfied smile. "I know. Ain't it pretty? There's nothing that says *home* like a table full of food, is there? I guess you could say it's *my* art."

"Well, I, for one, am ready to put a serious dent in your work of art." Ty pulled a chair out for Momma and then for me. I'd forgotten how much I missed a southern gentleman's manners.

I tried not to stare at Ty while he piled food on his plate. With each spoonful, Momma's smile grew wider. Then out of the blue she jumped up. "I'll be right back, y'all." She pushed through the swinging door and returned within seconds holding a cereal bowl and handed it to Ty. "Here sugar. Make yourself some potlikker up in there.

"Don't mind if I do." He crumbled cornbread in the bowl and ladled butterbeans and broth over it. "I haven't had this in years." Then he dumped a spoonful of chow-chow on top. "Thank you, ma'am."

Their eyes met, and I'd swear they were falling in love.

Food. The universal aphrodisiac.

Momma watched Ty with a satisfaction I'd never seen. *I* certainly didn't give her that kind of pleasure when I ate. Ty's tea glass was empty, but Momma was so engrossed with his enjoyment of her *art* she hadn't noticed.

Amazing.

I stood. "Tea refills anyone?"

She jerked her head up. "Baby, sit down. I'll get it. Sweet tea, Ty?"

"Yes, ma'am. The sweeter the better."

While she poured he asked, "How's business, Miss Cladie?"

"Fair to middlin' I guess." She set the pitcher on the buffet. "Since that flower shop opened on the square, not many people remember me here on Washington Avenue."

"But they don't sell rosebushes and bedding plants. Right?" Ty reached for the bowl of squash.

"No, but that new Lowe's store does. And I hear they are building a Walmart near the interstate. I guess that will be the end of me."

Just then an idea flashed in my mind. "Then what we need to do is produce something they aren't going to carry. Become a boutique gardening business of sorts. Think about it. When you go to Lowe's or Walmart you see the same thing. Let's give the public plants from all over the world that would survive in our climate."

"What a great idea." Tyler looked from me to Momma. "Especially now since Moonlight is marketing itself as a unique tourist stop."

Ideas filled my mind. "With all my contacts I can find plants no one else even knows about. Beautiful plants. We can buy a few of those high-tunnel greenhouses and—"

"—High tunnel? Momma's forehead wrinkled. "Mercy sakes child. Those cost a lot of money. I can't afford that."

"You don't have to." I patted her hand. "It will be my investment."

Her eyes brightened with tears. "Baby, I can't let you do that. You need to keep your money. You've worked hard for it."

"I want to do this. After all, I'm a third generation Preston Gardens family member, aren't I?"

Ty snapped his fingers. "I know how to draw folks to Preston Gardens." He certainly had Momma's and my attention. "Why don't you have a flower market here on your property every Saturday? You know, like a farmer's market. Only you can sell unique landscaping plants."

"That's a *great* idea." Ideas bubbled up in my mind. "Not only that, we can give landscaping demonstrations and tips. Even floral arranging classes."

Momma jumped in. "And you can sell your books, do a book signing."

"I can take pictures of the plants and make them into gift cards, calendars, things like that," said Ty. "Even take shots of families visiting and give those as souvenirs."

"Lovely ideas, kids." Momma thought a minute. "But do you think every Saturday will be too much?"

"Not in high tourist season," said Ty.

Inspiration struck. "Why don't we make the first Saturday of the month the most festive? Maybe have more things for the kids, food tents. Things like that? Then the three other Saturdays can be more like a floral farmer's market. That way it won't be so much work." Another idea came. "Momma, you can bake up a storm and sell your goodies, hand out recipes."

"That's right, Miss Cladie. You can do cooking

demos, too."

"But I thought this was about flowers. How do cooking demonstrations fit in?"

"You can cook with the flowers you sell," I said.

"Eat flowers? Lord've mercy. Who eats flowers?"

"There are all kinds of edible flowers, Mom. Nasturtiums, pansies, roses."

"Roses?" Momma sat back in her chair. "Pansies?"

"Yes, they make beautiful additions to salads and desserts. Nasturtiums have a nice peppery taste. Somewhere in all my boxes I have a cookbook with several flower recipes. By the way, is there a farmers' market in Moonlight?"

"Nope." Ty pushed back and rubbed his stomach. "Plenty of home gardens, but nothing big enough to support a market."

"Well, then, on those three Saturdays we should also open it up to all the home gardeners who want to make a little extra cash. That way, Momma, you can demonstrate cooking with more than flowers."

Momma slapped her hands together. "Now you are talking." She got to her feet. "Have mercy, my head is spinning with all these ideas flying about. I need to wash some dishes and think about all of this." She stood and picked up her plate. "Now you two scoot on out of here, and I'll call you for dessert later."

Ty opened his mouth, and I stopped him. "Don't even bother. She won't let you near her kitchen." I chose a bottle of wine and a couple of glasses. "Com'on." He followed me outside and sat in a rocker. I scooted mine close to his and put a little table in front of us.

"Want me to do the honors?" He reached for the

wine.

"Sure." I handed him the bottle and goblets. After he poured, he raised his glass. "To Miss Cladie and the flower market."

I clinked my rim against his. "And new dreams." The Pinot Grigio tasted crisp and cool. I leaned my head back against the rocker and watched the evening sky deepen from light pink to rose and purple. Hummingbirds darted under the eves, sipping sugar water from the feeders. Watching the dominant male chase away all the others reminded me of an aerial ballet. Even though they were fighting, they were so graceful. The air vibrated with cicada song. I loved the rise and fall of their raspy call.

Ty's voice broke into my thoughts. "I meant what I said earlier."

"And that would be…?"

"That I preferred older women." He sipped his wine and then shifted his gaze to me. "Like you."

I looked down at my glass. I didn't know how to answer. A million things ran through my mind.

"Mind if I ask you something?"

I peered up at him. "No, what?"

"Did you ever marry?"

"No." This conversation was getting uncomfortable.

"Why not?"

I sighed. "It took a long time for me to get over the shock of Marc's sudden death. And then I had to adjust to New York." Glancing at Ty, I smiled. "As you might imagine, I was an oddity there."

He chuckled and nodded. "I bet."

"But I met Scott and he saved me. In fact, we

moved in together."

Ty frowned. "Did you love him?"

Scott's image came to mind and I smiled. "Yes. And I still do."

He contracted his brow. "Then why didn't you marry him?"

"He's gay."

The animation returned to Ty's expression. "Oh."

"Yeah. They say a gay man is a straight girl's best friend. I agree." I smiled and drank some wine. "Scott was interested in the things I was interested in. We both loved Broadway plays, fashion, decorating, and concocting strange recipes. With Scott, I always had a date without the pressure to go to bed with him." I savored my last bit of wine wishing Scott were with me in Moonlight. "He helped me through my grief and taught me the ropes of surviving in the city. First thing he did was make me join the gym he used. I didn't want to go because I hated to exercise. I thought I was in pretty good shape, and I told him so. He asked me, 'What size are you?' I said, 'A twelve.' He handed me my purse and said, 'Ava, sweetheart, if you don't get rid of that Southern fluff you will be dressing off the rack in this city, and that's not a good thing.' He walked me out the door and onto the elliptical. He didn't let up until I was a size six. Then he took me shopping and picked out my clothes. Not only that, he had his friends make over my hair and makeup. I'm surprised he didn't make me take elocution lessons to get rid of my accent. But he said he thought it was charming."

"He sounds like some of the women I've dated." Ty leaned forward and took the bottle of wine and refilled our glasses. "Always wanting to change me."

"I don't mean to make him sound shallow." I thought a minute. "You know? Scott was kind of like your professor."

"How so?"

"He was the one who recognized my talent in floral design. He introduced me to the right people, and in just a few months, I was in big demand both professionally and privately. Then someone from a publisher approached me about writing a book. One thing led to another, and then I start getting lecture invitations from all over the world. It was crazy how it all happened."

"Wow." He twisted around and stared at me a moment before asking, "Did you ever fall in love with a straight guy?"

"No, not really. I had relationships. But when my floral design business caught fire, I just didn't have time."

Ty settled back in his chair. "I guess coming home is pretty much of a letdown."

"Not at all. I can do here what I did in New York. Besides, this week has reminded me I'm truly a southern gal through and through."

He grinned at me over his glass. "I'll drink to that."

I finished my wine. Warmth enveloped my body, and I gave myself up to the cacophony of tree frogs and night bugs. The aroma of coffee wafted through the air, which meant dessert.

"So, you said you like *your* older women fluffy?"

Immediately alarms rang in my head screaming, *good Lord, Avalee. Did you just say that?* It must have been the wine. It had to be the wine.

"Lady, I don't care what size you are." His intense

gaze made me forget the alarms. He leaned forward. My lips grew hot with anticipation.

"Dessert, kids."

I jerked to look at the screen door. She wasn't standing there, thank the Lord. She had probably called from the hall. At least I hoped so.

"We better go. Momma hates to be kept waiting."

Ty lifted one corner of his mouth. "So do I. We aren't finished with this conversation."

He was right. We weren't.

Chapter 10

LEXI
Outrage

Just as I predicted, Vince got his trousers in a twist and gave me grief about my column. But after my persuasive arguments and several shots of bourbon, he finally approved my piece.

My victory was sweet, but short-lived. Nagging thoughts crowded it away. What if I went too far? Got too personal? Lost readers? Had I pushed the bar too far? But, I reminded myself that all responses, good or bad, proved people were reading my column and were moved to action. Exactly what I wanted. The absolute worst thing that could happen was if people were indifferent.

The day after it ran in the paper, I hurried to the office to see what kind of response it provoked. I could have checked at home, but I made a promise to myself when I got this column gig that my home was a sanctuary, not an office, and I wouldn't work from the house. This time my promise was hard to keep. I skipped my morning addiction at Molly's and hurried to the paper. Ty met me at the door.

"Hi, Lexi."

"Ty, hi. Listen, I'm in a hurry." I air kissed him and took the stairs instead of waiting for the elevator. I rushed to my desk, tossed my briefcase on the file cabinet, and plopped in the chair. The computer took forever to boot up. Why in the world didn't this paper get Macs for heaven's sakes?

After what seemed like forever, Gmail loaded. I couldn't believe my eyes. Over three hundred emails. "Oh, my goodness. Oh, my gosh." My heart hammered as I scrolled through the subject lines. Did I hit a nerve or what? I had to tell Vince. I pulled my laptop out of my briefcase, strode to his office, and walked right to his desk without bothering to knock. He peered at me over his glasses and laid his proofing copy down. "Well, good morning, Lexi. Come on in."

"Sorry for the intrusion, but I have something you've gotta see."

He removed his readers and sat back. "Okay, shoot."

I showed him the emails on my laptop. His face blanked. "I didn't know there were that many single women in their fifties in our small circulation."

"I haven't read them all yet. Some might be from people who know someone, or kids about their parents. Some might even be from men. Right now, all I know is that I hit a nerve."

"This is great." Vince had that *above the fold* look he sometimes got when he thought our little paper might possibly hit the big time. "I have a suggestion. While you read, organize the emails in groups, like the ones from women, kids, friends, men, like that. Then organize each group into similar experiences or issues."

"Good grief, Vince."

"No, now, hear me out. This will let us know where to focus. I might want you to write articles, do interviews."

"I can do that, but what I'd really like is to get my column syndicated."

"If this thing sprouts legs and starts sprinting, then yes. We will look into that." He stood and motioned for me to follow him. "Good job, Lexi. How about I buy you a double-shot at Molly's?"

"You've got a date. I skipped my morning cup."

"I figured as much. You are never here this early." Vince slid one brow up. "In fact, you are rarely on time."

I popped him on the arm. "Oh, stop it. That's not true."

But it was.

All morning I read my emails and did as Vince suggested, grouping them into categories. Most were from women over fifty. Some were from children about their parents.

A tap sounded at my door. Ty sauntered in and flopped on the chair.

"Busy?"

I tore my gaze from the computer. "Like a one-armed paper-hanger. What's up?"

"I need your opinion."

"Sure." Being the opinionated sort, I was always ready to weigh in with my undisputed wisdom. "Shoot."

"It's about Avalee."

Okay, now he had my complete and undivided attention. "What about Avalee?"

"I'm interested in her. Real interested."

No big surprise there.

"Do you think the age thing is going to be a

problem with her? Because it sure isn't with me."

Now I had to decide if I was going to be honest or placate him and hope it all worked out. I decided to be honest.

"Yes, I do."

He frowned and tented his fingers over his chest.

"However, age isn't your biggest obstacle."

"What is?"

"Marc."

He leaned his head back and blew air through his lips. "I might have known. It's always Marc. Even with my parents."

"You look just like him, Ty."

"So, I'll dye my hair purple and wear green contacts." He slapped his hand against the chair. "If she'd just give me a chance, she'd see I'm nothing like my brother."

"I think there is something else to it. I can't say what, but when we talk about him I get this weird vibe from her. Like something is hanging over her head."

"Do you think she still loves him?"

"No, I don't get that feeling. It's more like regret, or guilt."

He leaned forward and crossed his arms on my desk. "Do you think I'm crazy for pursuing a relationship?"

I took a long sip from my salted caramel latte. "No." Our gazes locked. "I think you are crazy if you give up."

A slow smile pushed across his face. "Thanks, Lex."

"No problem." I shooed him off. "Now go away. I've got work to do."

"You're a doll." He jumped up, leaned over, and kissed my forehead. His luscious Armani cologne caught me in its grasp.

When he disappeared out the door, I propped my head on my hands and sighed. Why couldn't something like that happen to me?

I clicked on the next email.

Dear Lexi,

The day before our daughter's wedding, I learned that my husband was having an affair with a married colleague twenty years younger than him...

That rat!

Dear Lexi,

My dad and mom were married forty years. He got a job in a university in Paris. Mom was happier than I had seen her in a long time. They bought a house and started renovating it. Six months after moving there, Dad left her and moved in with his secretary who is thirty-one. Now Mom is alone in a country where she can barely speak or understand the language in a house that is in shambles. Dad makes her payments but refuses to pay for any more renovations...

The jerk!

Dear Lexi,

My husband left on our tenth anniversary. We were supposed to meet for a romantic supper, but he never showed up. I started to panic thinking something bad had happened to him. Finally he texted me. He said he had found someone new. By the time I'd gotten home he had cleaned out his closet, taken all the electronics, and some of the furniture. The next day I called the bank, but he'd beat me to it and had cleaned out all of our accounts.

Later I found out that his new love was the wife of his bowling buddy. She is thirty. He's fifty-six.

My head started aching, and I realized it was from clenching my jaw. By the time I finished reading these emails, I'd need a stiff drink, hold the fudge. *Those poor women.* Righteous indignation burned inside me. I stood and started pacing the floor. Something had to be done. But what? I remembered a Mark Twain quote, "A drop of ink may make a million think." That was something I could do. Sound the alarm. Serve notice. Empower these women. But a million? The only way I could reach that many was by syndication.

A soft knock sounded on my door and Avalee peeped in. "Hey, Lexi."

"Hey, Avalee. Come on in. You came at just the right time. I could use some advice."

"I wondered if you'd like to go to lunch. I wanted to pick your brain, too."

"Lunch?" I glanced at the clock. Twelve-thirty? Where had the time gone? But, as if on cue, my stomach rumbled. "Sure, where do you want to go?"

"Have you been to that little tea room on Magnolia Drive?"

"No, I haven't. It just opened. I hear the orange rolls are to die for. Let's try it." I grabbed my purse.

We passed Ty's cubicle. I wanted to talk to Avalee about him, but not until a few martinis had softened her defenses. Every time she spoke about Marc, an undeniable sadness shadowed her eyes and voice. I wanted to know why and then warn her if she didn't deal with the problem, she just might miss out on what could very well be the greatest opportunity of her life. She'd been robbed of love long enough. So had I for that matter.

A thought hit me like an arrow. *She wants to talk about Ty. Of course! I'd bet my entire Elvis Presley movie collection. Probably about something that happened when he went to their house for supper.* Oh, this was going to be good.

The Magnolia Tea Room buzzed with business. I sure hoped this place wouldn't affect Molly's business. But then again, Moonlight's tourist trade had grown so fast, to fight over customers would be like two ants fighting over a dead elephant. There was plenty of business to go around.

A chubby sweet-cheeked gal, who looked as if her name should be Pitty Pat greeted us at the door. "Come on in, y'all. Welcome to the Magnolia Tea Room." She looked around. "My goodness, but we are busy today. Would y'all mind sitting over yonder in the corner?"

"Suits me," said Avalee.

"Me too." Frankly, I preferred it. Might cut some of the noise out.

We followed Pitty Pat to our table and sat. "My name is Birdie."

I liked the name I gave her better. But Birdie would do. She handed us menus that looked like fans.

"Today's special is fruited chicken salad, a croissant, roasted tomato soup, and a fruit cup with cantaloupe, strawberries, watermelon, grapes, and mandarin orange slices. Does any of this butter your bread?"

"Does mine. I'll take it." I closed my menu. "Oh, and I want one of your famous orange rolls, too."

Birdie patted the air. "Oh honey, let me tell you something. You haven't lived till you have tried those."

She pursed her lips together, squeezed her eyes shut and shrugged. With a broad smile she said, "Those orange rolls are so good your tongue will slap your brains out."

Avalee tried to hold in her giggle. Unsuccessfully, I might add. "Well then, I'll have the special, too."

Birdie scribbled on her pad. "Orange roll?"

"Of course." Avalee handed Birdie the menu.

"You girls want hot tea? Our orange pekoe is yummy with this special."

"I would." I glanced at Avalee. "How about you?"

She nodded.

"All right, y'all. I'll be back with your tea as quick as a wink."

"Well, if she isn't as cute as a bug's ear." I looked around. Whoever decorated the place had done a fabulous job. Sort of shabby chic but not outdated. None of the dishes matched. Neither did the cloth napkins or silverware. "And so is this place."

"Both are darling. I love the idea."

Birdie returned with cups, saucers, and two small teapots with tea tags hanging from under the lids. "Here y'all are. Tea should be ready to pour in a jiffy. I'll be back with your specials. Cook is taking out the orange rolls right now. They'll be good and hot for you."

"Thanks Pit—er—Birdie."

"So." Avalee poured her tea from a pot shaped like a sitting elephant, his nose being the spout. Sorta grossed me out. "You go first. What did you want to talk about?"

My teapot looked like a cupcake with a cherry on top. "I got an amazing response to my column. Even with our teensy circulation area, I got over three hundred responses."

"Wow." She lifted a white porcelain cup decorated with tiny yellow rosebuds to her lips. Blowing the steam away she asked, "How wide is your coverage?"

"We cover Union, Tishomingo, and Lee Counties." I reached in a pink glass bowl holding Melba toast packages and took one. Small pats of butter shaped like magnolia blossoms were arranged on a white dish trimmed in gold. I almost hated messing one up by spreading it on my cracker. *Almost* being the operative word. I scooped one up with my knife and spread it on the toast.

Avalee did the same. "Aren't these little magnolia butter pats cute? I wonder if they sell the molds?"

"I noticed a little gift area when we walked in. Let's check it out before we leave." If they did sell them, I had decided to buy one for Miss Cladie.

"Have you read all the emails?"

"A lot of them."

"What kinds of things do they say?"

"Some of the saddest stories I've ever heard. Most are from the women who were dumped. Several are from the children of divorced parents. I even have a few from the children who wrote about their moms leaving their dads. But from what I've read, I have to wonder if those women had good reason. I didn't get any from men." My tea needed another dollop of honey. While stirring I asked, "What I'm wondering is what direction I should take with this? How should I develop it? And how I might get it into syndication."

She thought a minute. "I, personally wouldn't know. But I do have a contact at the New York Times who might be willing to advise you."

I nearly choked on the cracker I'd just popped in

my mouth. "New York Times? Are you kidding me?"

Birdie arrived with our lunches. "Here y'all are." She set our plates in front of us, then the fruit cups and orange rolls that were as large as the saucers. Oh my goodness. Those rolls were sin on a plate, fat and fluffy, with orange glaze smeared over the top and dripping down the sides.

"They are hot out of the oven." Birdy put her hand on her breast. "If I were you, I'd put butter on them now and let it melt while you eat your lunch."

"Good idea, Birdy." I stabbed another magnolia butter pat. "I'll just do that."

Avalee grinned up at her. "My problem is forcing myself to wait until I finish lunch."

"Oh sugar." Birdy patted the air again. "Go ahead. We've got plenty more. Y'all enjoy your lunch, and if you need anything, just give me a wave."

When our waitress left, Avalee dipped the corner of her croissant into her soup. "Back to my contact? His name is Nathan Wolfe."

I nodded and shoveled a bite of chicken salad in my mouth. If taste buds could dance, mine would be doing an Irish jig.

"Well, you certainly don't seem impressed."

"Should I be?"

She hiked her eyebrows, smiled, and shook her head. "I guess not."

"Did you date him?"

"I got to know him from meeting at several social gatherings. But he wasn't my type. He was a little too much of a wise guy for me. We did become pretty good friends though." She poured more tea. "I have his card somewhere. I'll text his contact info to you."

"I don't want to seem ungrateful, but I'd prefer a woman. If he's a smart-ass, then he will probably get all self-righteous and think I'm male bashing."

"I don't think so. He likes controversial subjects."

"Of course he does. He works for the Times. Go figure."

"So, do you have any ideas about how to approach this can of worms you've opened?"

"Well, not really. That's why I'm asking you."

"What about getting a guy's perspective."

I broke my croissant in half. "What do you mean?"

"Why not have them explain why they cheated. Maybe even invite the mistresses to tell their side."

"Are you crazy?" Actually it was a fantastic idea. "I hate you."

Avalee blinked. "And just why is that?"

"Because I wish I'd thought of it first."

"Well, these are just suggestions. I feel sure Nate will have better ideas."

Time for our little chat about Ty. "Okay, enough about me. Now what did you want to talk about?"

"I have an idea I think will save Preston Gardens."

I put my fork down. "That's it?" Rats. I hoped for a juicy conversation about Ty.

Avalee glanced up. "Yeah, why?"

Somehow I needed to crawdad this conversation back. "Never mind the woman sitting across from you. She is too focused on gulping down her lunch so she can eat her orange roll. Now tell me about your idea."

"We're going to reinvent the family business. I'm thinking of putting on a weekly flower market, you know, like a farmers' market."

"Sounds like a plan. It sure would be a hit with

tourists. What day are you thinking?"

"Saturday mornings. I'm going to find plants folks can't find in the local area and then showcase them. *And* on the first Saturday of the month, we will make it a big festival, give demonstrations for cooking, flower arranging, things like that."

"The Chamber of Commerce will certainly love it."

Finally, I finished my lunch. Now for that orange roll. When I picked it up, melted butter ran over my fingers. I licked them and decided the best plan of attack would be to pull the spiral apart and eat down to the soft middle.

"I think this will drive business to Preston Gardens during the week. Momma will have an edge because she'll have something different from the big box stores."

The best answer I could manage with a mouth full of sweet dough heaven was to mumble an enthusiastic, "Um hm."

"And with my contacts, I could bring in some big names for demos." She picked up her fork and knife and *actually* cut her roll in half. She obviously had no idea of the proper procedure for eating an orange roll. "So what do you think?"

I held up my finger because I'd reached the center, a tender jewel dripping with butter and tangy orange glaze. This magical moment shouldn't be interrupted. I put it in my mouth and closed my eyes. It practically melted on my tongue. Nothing my ex-husband had ever done brought me to this kind of ecstasy or satisfaction. I opened my eyes and smiled at Avalee. "Sorry. But that was fabulous."

She sat back and smirked. "I could tell."

"Anyway, I love your idea, and you should talk to Ty about taking shots for advertising."

"We did talk, and he had some pretty wonderful suggestions." She finished her roll, but not with the same out-of-body experience as me. Poor girl.

"I'll run your idea by Vince. Maybe he can do some articles about it, and I know the Chamber will be more than happy to exploit it all over the web. You'll have such a huge crowd none of us will be able to get out of our driveways." My last remark made me think of something. "By the way, what about those zoning laws?"

"All taken care of. Just as I thought. She is grandfathered in." Ava checked her watch. "Guess we'd better go." She turned and waved to Pitty Pat.

After we paid our bill, we stopped by the gift shop. Bingo! They had the molds. I bought one for Miss Cladie and one for Molly Kate. On our way out I put my hand on Avalee's shoulder. "Don't forget to send me that guy's email."

"That guy?"

"You know, that Wolfe fellow."

She shook her head and laughed.

"I don't mind telling you, I'm kind of nervous about writing him."

"He's really nice. Don't worry."

"Right. Slamming the fraternal order of men probably isn't best way to approach him."

"He's got a devilish sense of humor. It's all good."

When I returned to the office, I spent the rest of the afternoon reading emails and growing more indignant by the minute. After work, I fumed all the way home. Good thing I walked. Driving with this much anger would be illegal. Somebody had to do something. And that somebody was me. Exposing those sorry excuses for men became my mission. I sure hoped that Nathan guy would have some good ideas, and I prayed he was as broadminded as Avalee claimed. Seconds after the thought about Nathan crossed my mind, a text from Avalee chimed with Nathan's email address.

My mouth went dry. All my bravado evaporated. I had no idea what to write this guy, where to begin. How to begin? He was a perfect stranger who lived in New York and worked at the Times for crying out loud.

Was I crazy? I calmed my nerves by telling myself he was probably some flunky. Some poor guy pounding on the keys. Just like me.

So what should I write him? Maybe start with an introduction, send a photo, and a couple of my past articles. Then humbly ask for his opinion and advice. Humbly? Ha. Like that was going to happen. Turn on my Southern girl charm? That I could do.

When I got home, I went straight to my office and turned on the computer. Tonight I had to break my promise to myself and work from the house.

After thirty minutes of start-overs, I wanted to pound my head against the screen. My words came in a mangled mash and made no sense at all. Perhaps a Coke Zero liberally laced with bourbon, enjoyed on my porch swing, would smooth things out. Couldn't hurt.

Outside, I clicked on the oscillating fan and stretched out on the swing. Would summer ever be over? Even the hummingbirds had a hard time staying airborne long enough in this hot, wet air to sip the sap from my drooping Hibiscus shrub.

Good luck little fellow.

I noticed dead ants floating in the feeder that hung in the dogwood tree. Clearly, I'd been negligent. Oh well, I needed another drink anyway. Might as well make one for my hummer friends.

Bleh. I hated washing out dead ants. While the cleaner dried, I mixed four parts water, one part sugar for the hummer, two parts bourbon, one part diet coke, one part ice, for me.

When I returned to the porch, I set my drink on the rail and strolled to the dogwood and replaced the feeder. Then I surveyed the yard. My flowers needed watering, so I turned on the hose and gave my plants a drink as well.

Okay, I knew what I was doing. Procrastinating. I really didn't want to write Mr. Wolfe. Even if he was a flunky, he was still eons ahead of me. On the other hand, what an opportunity. And by some far-fetched chance he might like my work and put in a good word for me. I might be syndicated. I could be the next, oh, I don't know...a cross between Ann Landers and Erma Bombeck.

That thought sent thrills through me and bolstered my courage. I sashayed back to the porch and sipped my drink. Maybe I could tell him my goals, my writing style. Little by little ideas came into focus. I jumped up and hurried back inside. I needed to get all of these ideas down before my mid-fifties brain went totally blank. Deep inside I knew this Wolfe guy would love my idea. Thank goodness for friends like Avalee. I hurried to my office, sat at my computer, and began typing.

Dear Mr. Wolfe,

A mutual friend, Avalee Preston, gave me

your name and contact information. She suggested that you might be willing to give me your opinion as well as advice on a project I'm contemplating.

I am a reporter and a columnist for the Moonlight Community News. It is a small publication that has a circulation that covers three counties.

Okay, I can feel you rolling your eyes. I know it isn't anything compared to the New York Times. However, I believe I have an idea for a column worthy of syndication—an advice column for women over fifty that encompasses relationships, self-worth or lack thereof, and emotional coping. My writing style is a cross between Ann Landers and Erma Bombeck.

I've attached my photo, bio, and a few of my more popular columns, including my most recent that sparked my idea.

Thank you in advance for any thoughts and advice you may have to give.

Sincerely,

Lexi Lowe

I sat back and finished my drink while I reread my email. Not bad. Not bad at all. With great flourish, I hit send. That's when the paranoid questions attacked me. What if he's bald? What if he has hair growing out his nose? What if he's...flaccid? Oh Lord. Why couldn't these questions have surfaced before I hit send?

I needed another drink.

Chapter 11

JEMA
Taking Chances

"Happy anniversary, hon." I lifted Ray's photo from the mantel and kissed it. Today would have been our thirty-sixth. I stared at his face smiling back at me and thought of all the plans we had made. Plans that dissolved in an instant with one slip on a sweaty cement dock.

Truth be known? He was probably in Heaven congratulating himself for dodging the Italian vacation he'd promised me. What a wonderful guy. Even though he hated to travel and hated the idea of international travel even more, he had promised me a trip to Florence on our fortieth anniversary. To prove his sincerity, he had grudgingly got his passport and started an Italy savings account. But he didn't have to go after all. It wouldn't have been the same going to Italy alone, so I used the money in the savings account to apply toward Amanda's and Olivia's college expenses.

I placed the photo back on the mantel. He was taken from me way too early, but I was grateful for the years we had together. I had a lot to be grateful for, two incredibly loving and talented daughters, as well as friends who were as dear to me as family.

The hall clock chimed nine interrupting my

Linda Apple

reflections. This was my day to help with lunch at the shelter. While I dressed, I wondered if that mysterious man would show up. I knew it sounded unreasonable, but I sure hoped he'd be there. Something about him stirred me. The intensity in his eyes? His gentle manner? Even though he had the same stringy hair and torn clothes as a lot of the other men, somehow he was different and Lord help me, I was attracted to him.

The half hour sounded. I checked once more in the mirror. *Oh why did I agree to bangs?* They already needed a trim. I swiped them off my glasses. As an afterthought, I daubed Chanel Chance Eau Fraiche on my wrists. Not because of him...exactly. I just liked the fragrance.

Who was I kidding?

Normally, I would have walked to the shelter but with the sun burning down and daring anyone to breathe, I didn't want to get there all sweaty.

Just in case.

I can't believe I'm being so stupid. This guy could be—and probably is—a total loser. He could be the type who preys on lonely widows who have houses. He could be a rapist, even a murderer. He…

I got in the car and switched on the ignition. While backing out I looked in my rearview mirror and rebuked my image. "For heaven's sakes, Jema. More than likely he is a nice guy down on his luck."

At least I hoped so.

Ricki had laid out everything we needed to prepare for lunch. I took an apron and hurried toward her.

"Hey. Sorry I'm late."

She sniffed the air. "Girl, you smell good. What is that?"

"Channel Chance. My new fragrance addiction. What's on the menu today?"

"Chicken salad sandwiches, potato salad, cookies, and ice cream. It's just too hot to eat anything heavier."

"Sounds good. Where do you want me?"

She pointed her knife in the direction of the counter where she had set a large pot full of boiled potatoes, a platter of eggs, and stacks of vegetables. "Potato salad needs making. I've already boiled the potatoes and eggs."

"Will do." I pulled out a cutting board. "You've gotten a lot done already. What time did you get here?"

"Oh, about seven. I couldn't sleep, so I thought I might as well get an early start while it was cool, especially since I was boiling thirty pounds of potatoes and five dozen eggs."

"You should have called me."

"I didn't mind. Besides, I had coffee and a chat with that Levi fellow."

"Levi?" The potatoes were still hot, so I started stringing celery.

"The new guy. The one with the long hair and those sexy dark eyes? I'm telling you, a girl could fall into them."

Her last statement irked me. I didn't like her talking about him like that. "What do you think about him?"

"Interesting. And I'm sure if he'd clean up and shave off his beard, it wouldn't just be his eyes that were sexy."

There she goes again. Was I jealous? Of a man I didn't know? Sakes. But it did bother me. She was newly divorced and pretty darned sexy herself. *And* she was ten years younger than me. "What did y'all talk about?"

"Me, mainly. He didn't say much about himself. When I asked questions, he dodged them." She turned toward me and put her hand on her hip. "If you ask me, he's hiding something. I don't know that I trust him."

"Could be. But on the other hand, I find it gentlemanly for him to be more interested in the person he's talking to." I chopped the celery and commenced on the onion.

"I'll allow he acts like a gentleman. But you never know about these transients. He may have eyes that could hypnotize a cobra, but he could be a real bugger, too."

My eyes watered from cutting onions, and my nose threatened to drip. I snatched a paper towel.

Ricki frowned and strode across the kitchen. She put her arm around my shoulder and pulled me into a side hug. "Honey, what's wrong?"

"Nothing." I held up the onion. "Onions always make me cry."

"Well, that's a relief. I thought for a moment you were getting all moony over that Levi fellow." As she walked back to her bowl of chicken salad, she said over her shoulder, "But I know you are smarter than that."

"You know it." While I sliced eggs, I couldn't help but wonder, *was I?*

When everything was ready, Ricki sounded the dinner bell. Men, women, and children lined up. Even though I had seen this line form countless times, my heart still hurt. How could so many people be homeless in our small community? How? Where did they stay? And why hadn't I taken the time to find out. Ricki had told me that some who came here were not homeless, but all their money went to pay the mortgage and utilities. This would probably be the only decent meal they'd eat all day, such as it was.

Until now, I had congratulated myself for feeding them. For smiling and speaking pleasant platitudes while serving them. But I wanted to do more.

While I handed sandwiches to the folks in line, I caught a glimpse of Levi. He spoke with the couple ahead of him and their little girl reached up for him. He lifted her in his arms and said something to her. I wished I could have heard what he said because she patted her little hands together and squealed, obviously delighted.

"Jema? What are you staring at with that nutty grin?" Ricki crossed her arms over her chest. "Not that Levi, I hope."

"Not really. Well, not *just* him. Have you noticed how long the line has been lately?"

"Yep. I think the word has gotten out among folks in the surrounding counties, and they've migrated to Moonlight. Sure would be nice if the counties without feeding programs pitched in. This is getting expensive, and the quality of our meals is showing it. I don't know how long the funding will last."

Ricki's comment worried me.

"That's terrible. What on earth will these people do? Lord love them, they have enough strikes against them already." I made a mental note to put this on my Whine Wednesday list.

"You got that right." She nodded at the line. "Just remember, watch yourself around that Levi fellow. He may be handsome and all, but you don't need to be getting emotionally involved. We don't know anything about him, and he obviously ain't telling."

Her warning made sense, but I couldn't help it. I felt drawn to him. When Levi's turn to be served came around, I gave him *two* sandwiches and an extra serving of potato salad. "Hope you are hungry. We don't like to waste food around here."

"Thank you. I am."

I desperately scrambled for something else to say, but couldn't think of a thing. For a moment our gazes locked. Then he broke the spell. "I appreciate the shelter feeding us like this."

Stupidly, all I could say was, "You are welcome." Before he moved away, I pointed toward the table at the end of the counter. "Don't forget the cookies and ice cream over there." He nodded. "Thank you." He walked off, and I fought to keep from staring after him.

When everyone had been served, I decided to make good on my little epiphany earlier and introduce myself to a few of the regulars. Maybe by getting to know them, I might be able to do more for them.

I picked up a pitcher of tea and walked from table to table, offering a refill and introducing myself. I sat with those who were receptive and chatted a bit. Surprisingly, most whom I spoke with were very open about their lives. I learned there was a tent village by the railroad tracks east of town. I also found out many of them had false addresses so the children could go to school without the shame of being homeless.

While I listened to their stories, my eyes felt warm and moist, but I held the tears back. It would never do to add the disgrace of pity to their situation. How I wished I had a cut up onion in my hand so I could have an excuse to cry.

As the lunch hour waned, the crowd in the room thinned, and only a few people remained at the tables. Levi sat alone in the far left corner of the room. Before I went to him, I looked around for Ricki. She was nowhere in sight. Thank goodness.

"Tea?"

He glanced up. "Yes. Thank you."

While I filled his glass, I mustered up my courage and said, "Mind if I join you for a few minutes?"

He held his hand out to the seat across from him. "Please. It would be my pleasure."

Right away I picked up on something about him. He had an accent of sorts. "I'm Jema."

His dark brown hair fell in matted curls over his brow and shoulders. "I'm Levi." He fingered a strand out of his face. "Excuse my appearance. It is hard to find a place to shower."

Lord, I'd never thought about that. Actually there were a lot of things I'd never thought about. How were these people supposed to apply for jobs if they couldn't bathe, or wash their clothes? And what about those poor children I served each week? Did the kids in their school make fun of them because of how they dressed? Did they smell bad? I'd never noticed. This time the tears came.

Levi furrowed his brow. "It's not that bad. Truly."

I waved it off. "Never mind me. I've been fighting tears all day."

"Do you need someone to talk to?"

Yes. "No, I'm fine. It's just that I've been talking to these families, and I guess I'm a bit overwhelmed with their stories." I wiped my eyes with the back of my hand. "And when you mentioned the showers, I realized how I take things like that for granted. It makes me so ashamed of myself."

"Perhaps you could turn the shame into something positive?"

"What do you mean?"

He scanned the building. "Maybe put in showers? Washers and dryers?"

"We'd love to, but there isn't any money. Ricki said just this morning how the funds are getting low."

"Seems to be a problem for a lot of us."

"It is a dilemma and yet, what do we do? It is so frustrating, and it doesn't help that most of the city's funds are earmarked for rebranding Moonlight into a tourist town. It's all so frustrating. I guess that's why I'm so weepy today. Well, it isn't the only reason." The peppershaker blurred. "Today would have been my thirty-sixth wedding anniversary."

Now why did I tell him that?

"I'm sorry. Did your husband die recently?"

"Ten years ago. But I still get a little emotional when this day comes around."

He looked away. "I understand."

Before I could ask him how he understood he turned his attention back to me.

"Are you employed here at the shelter?"

"No, I volunteer. I work at the Piggly Wiggly across the parking lot." I shook my head and let a self-deprecating chuckle escape. "Checking groceries wasn't what I saw myself doing with my life, but you do what you have to do. Even with the little insurance policy Ray left, there isn't enough money to live on, especially with two girls in college."

That's it, Jema, just spill your guts. Tell this perfect stranger all your business.

For some reason Levi had a strange effect on me. I just couldn't stop blabbering.

"In this economy, money doesn't go as far, does it?"

I shook my head, determined to keep my mouth shut.

He reached over to put his hand on my arm, but when he glanced at his fingernails he pulled it back. "I admire you for your dedication to your girls. I don't meet many who are willing to sacrifice their dreams for others."

"Oh, I didn't have many dreams. Well, except for going to Italy. Ray, he was my husband, hated to travel, but he promised to take me one day. We even had an Italy fund. But after the accident I transferred it to the college fund. I'm afraid to travel by myself."

Good grief. Was I going to have to stick tacks in my shoes and press my toes against them to shut myself up? The next thing I knew, I'd be giving him my social security number or inviting him to the house to shower while I washed his cloths.

"It can happen. I hope it will." He broke a cookie in half. "I'm looking for a job. Do you know of anyone hiring? Even if the applicant needs a shower and is wearing dirty clothes?" He grinned and popped the piece of cookie in his mouth.

"I'll check around. You are welcome to come by my place and take a shower. I could wash your clothes for you, too, if you like."

Ugh. I'm hopeless.

Levi sat back and stared at me. "I don't know what

to say. Thank you. I would appreciate that." The color rose in his face. "It is hard to accept such a kind offer, but I don't have much choice lately."

"Tell you what, I leave here in a few minutes. If you'll hang around, I'll drive you there." I filled his glass again. "Help yourself to the cookies."

Immediately doubt clouded my mind. I hurried to the kitchen to call Cladie and tell her what I'd just done. No question, she'd throw a hissy fit, but I needed her to have my back. Just in case he *was* an ax murderer.

The minute I walked into the kitchen I pulled out my iPhone and punched her number."

"Hey there, sugar."

"Hey, Cladie. I need a favor and not a lecture."

"Do what?"

"Now, just listen. I'm bringing a homeless man to my house so he can shower while I do his laundry."

"Girl, have you lost your ever lovin' mind?"

"Look, the poor guy needs a break. Just say you will come so I won't be alone."

"Missy, I'll be there, and I'm bringing my cast iron skillet with me."

"He's a nice man. You'll see. He's looking for a job, and he can't do it smelling like a pole cat."

A sigh came over the receiver. "No. I guess he can't."

"I'll call you before we leave, and you can just happen by. Okay?"

"All right, but I still want to slap some sense into you. Tell you what, I picked a bushel of purple hulls this morning. I'll bring them down and ask you if you want them. He'll never suspect a thing."

"Great idea. Thanks Cladie."

"I'll swan, Jema. What am I going to do with you?"

"Love me?"

Tenderness softened her voice. "I do, sugar. See you in a while."

My vision blurred for the umpteenth time. I was truly a blessed woman. It was about time I shared those blessings.

When I finished cleaning up the kitchen and sacking up leftovers for the families with children, I called Cladie.

"Hey girl, you on your way home?"

"Yea. We're fixing to leave in just a second."

"I got the peas in the sack. I'll head your way as soon as I see your car."

"Thanks, hon. I owe you one."

"I'll be sure and remind you of that."

I put the phone in my back pocket and thought about my next hurdle, how to get Levi in my car out of the sight of prying eyes. Namely Ricki's. Come to think of it, I hadn't seen her in a while. I called out, "Ricki? Are you still here?"

"Hey, I'm in the stockroom."

I poked my head through the doorway. "I'm gone."

"Okay, thanks. I sure appreciate your help."

"Will you get to go home soon?"

"No, I'll be in here for a while. We received some donations from a couple local churches."

"Need help?" *Please say no.*

"Naw. See you next week." She waved and went back to what she was doing.

I found Levi by the back door. I walked to him and said, "Ready?"

"I am." He held the door open for me. "I have an idea. Why don't you pick me up down the block? That way no one sees us together."

His discretion and sensitivity about the nature of the situation impressed me. At least I hoped that was his motive. What if he planned on getting in the car where no one could see him and make me drive to some remote place and kill me? *Oh Lord, what have I gotten myself into?*

By the time I met him down the block my stomach had more knots than a macramé plant hanger. He opened the door. "Are you sure you don't mind doing this?"

Was my face that transparent? "Yes. I mean no. Of course not." I shrugged "But I have to admit, it is a little uncomfortable. I don't make it a habit of offering my shower."

"I'm glad you don't. But no worries." He grinned as he sat and shut the door. "I'd be happy with the loan of a towel and a bar of soap. I could go to the lake after dark."

The very thought of the mud he'd have to wade through and the cold water made me cringe. "No. I'm all right. Really. Get in and let's go."

During the four-block drive, my courage rose as I listened to him tell me about the people he'd met since arriving at Moonlight. He spoke with such compassion. Still, I couldn't deny feeling relieved when Cladie came plodding across the street with the sack of peas in her arms.

She waved. "Hey there. I was just going to leave these peas on your porch. Lord knows I have more than enough to shell and put away. Thought you'd like some."

"I'd love some. Thanks, Cladie." Levi got out of the car and stood still as if unsure of what to do. I gestured toward him. "Cladie, this is Levi. He's preparing to do some job hunting. Levi, this is my friend Cladie Preston."

She eyed him up and down. "Do you do gardening-type work?"

"Ma'am. I'll do anything."

She twisted her mouth to the side and studied him. "It's hot work. Heavy lifting. Long hours. But I pay good and I feed good, too." Turning toward me she jerked her head his way. "And by the looks of him, he could use some good food."

Levi put his hands together and bowed. "Ms. Preston, you are an answer to my prayers." He glanced up at me and grinned before straightening. "And I like to work. This homelessness has made me feel useless."

"You're hired then. My man Felix, God love him, needs some help. He's getting on up in years, you know. Do you have any work clothes?"

"Just what I have on my back."

"Son, those won't do." She handed me the peas. "Levi, you get in the shower. Jema, come with me to find him some work clothes." She studied Levi again. "You look to be about the size of my late husband. A mite taller than he and few pounds lighter, but his clothes will cover you until you can get your own."

"Wait, Cladie Mae. Slow down." I smiled down at my good-hearted friend. "Before we go to your house, I need to show Levi where everything is first." Motioning for them to follow, I said, "Come on in."

He held the door open for us. When I passed him, I

noticed for the first time something akin to happiness in his expression.

When inside, Cladie piped up. "Now, Levi, after you have showered and put on clean clothes, I want you to go to Burt's barber shop and get a haircut. Get all that mess shaved off your face, too. I'll call ahead and tell Burt I'm good for it."

Only Cladie Mae Preston could get away with saying that. I glanced at Levi and tried to gauge how he took her mandate. He looked as stunned as I felt.

"Cladie, he might like his hair."

"Nonsense, he'll have a heat stroke trying to work under all that wool. Besides, with the machinery he'll be using, he doesn't need to get his hair caught in it and break his neck." She crossed her arms. "Now does he?"

Levi shrugged. "No worries here. I'll be glad to be rid of it." He beamed down at Cladie. "Thank you, dear lady. And when I'm cleaned up, I would like to shake your hand."

"Shake my hand? Nothing doing."

Levi's face registered surprise.

"Around here, young man, we hug."

He chuckled. "Even better."

I pointed to the stairs. "The bathroom is on the second floor at the end of the hall. You should find all you need there. We'll be back soon with something for you to wear."

Cladie chimed in. "And don't worry about the clothes you have on now. I'm going to burn them."

Well, good grief, Cladie Mae. Levi had to be embarrassed. I was embarrassed for him and, once again, came to his rescue. "But, Levi may want to keep his clothes."

He put his hand out and chuckled. "It's fine, really. I have no particular fondness for these rags."

Cladie nodded at me. "Me and Levi are going to get along just fine."

When he disappeared up the stairs, Cladie and I left for her house. On our way there, I had a moment of misgiving. What if he left with pillowcases stuffed full of my valuables? About then Cladie said, "I have a good feeling about that boy."

"You do?"

"Yes, ma'am, I do. I'm a good judge of character." She put her hand on my arm and gave me an impish look over the rim of her glasses. "And I'll bet he looks mighty fine under all that hair."

"Why, Cladie Mae. I didn't think you thought those kind of things."

She looped her arm though mine. "Lemme tell you something, I may be old, but I'm not dead, and I'm certainly not blind."

"I don't doubt that one little bit. By the way, Cladie, why did you keep all of Fred's clothes? I gave Ray's things away."

"I don't know why, but I just couldn't bear getting rid of anything. I put his clothes in the guest room closet. His shorts and socks are in the chest of drawers. On lonely days, I sit in there and stare at his church suits or his coveralls, rubbing my fingers over the material, knowing they had touched his skin. Sounds silly, but it helps."

"No. It doesn't sound silly at all. We do what we have to do."

In the guest room she took white undershirts, pale blue undershorts, and black socks from the dresser drawers. Then she moved to the closet and pulled out two pairs of khakis and four short sleeve cotton shirts. After laying them across the bed, she returned to the closet and found a pair of work-boots.

"I'm not sure if these boots will fit, but we might as well take them over just the same."

I bundled the clothes up, and as I turned to leave, Cladie said, "Just a second." She went to the dresser and picked up a small jewelry chest. When she opened the lid, a tiny ballerina popped up and began twirling to a soft tinkling tune. She pulled out a folded hundred-dollar bill and handed it to me. "If those boots don't fit, buy him some that do."

"You are an angel if ever there was one." Just then a thought occurred. "Cladie? Where is he going to sleep? I can't have him stay with me and neither can you."

She bit her lip. "I hadn't thought of that." After a few minutes of pondering, she slapped her leg. "I've got it. Fred's old shop. Felix doesn't use it anymore since we built the larger one. It's a respectable size since the benches have been cleared out, and it has a small woodstove. Even has a bathroom."

"A bathroom?"

"Yes, Fred put it in because he didn't want to dirty up the house traipsing through it during the day when he worked in the gardens. He even put in a shower to get the grime off before he came in to supper."

"That sounds perfect. I have a twin-sized bed in Olivia's room. Levi can use it. After all, she and Amanda only come home at Christmas. She can sleep in the guest room. I wonder if Felix would mind helping me move it. I have a chest of drawers and a nightstand, too."

"I'm sure he won't mind a bit. I'll ask him." She thought a moment. "You know that little bistro table and chairs on my patio? We can put those in the corner of the shed for Levi to snack on. I'm sure I have a tablecloth somewhere." She put her hands together. "Oh, I can't wait to give him the good news. Let's tell him over cake and coffee. I have a sour cream pound cake that needs to get eaten before it goes stale."

"Great idea."

We stopped in her kitchen long enough for her to pack up three large slices, and then we carried our bundles across the street. By the time Cladie and I got to my house, we had made plans that would have the old shop looking like something from *Better Homes and Gardens*.

When we walked in, I couldn't hear the water running. Oh dear. Cladie and I had totally lost track of time. He was probably waiting for something to wear. I called from the bottom step, "I'm coming up with your clothes."

No answer.

Oh no. He's gone. What did he take? I jogged up the stairs holding on to the clothes. The bathroom door was slightly ajar, and I saw him wrapped in a towel standing at the mirror fingering tangles from his hair. I cleared my throat giving him a little start.

He opened the door wider. "Oh, hello. I'm about done here."

"No, that's okay. Sorry, I didn't mean to startle you. I just wanted to give you these." I gave him the clothing. "When you get dressed, come down for coffee and some of Cladie's famous sour cream pound cake."

"Sounds good. I'll be right there. By the way, you wouldn't happen to have an elastic would you?"

"A what?"

"An elastic to hold my hair out of the way."

"Oh, a rubber band? Sure." I opened a drawer and took one out. "Here."

"Thanks."

"See you in a bit." All the way down the steps, I chided myself for thinking the worst—again. In the kitchen, Cladie had started the coffee and was carrying plates to the table. I took out the cups, creamer, and sugar and arranged them by the coffee pot.

A rhythmic thud, thud, sounded on the stairs as Levi jogged down. We both looked up when he moseyed in.

Cladie set the plates on the table with a clatter. "Mercy Lord. But don't you look nice." In a few short steps she hustled to him. "The pants are a mite short, but I can let them down. How do the boots feel?"

"They're a bit tight. But I'm grateful to have them."

She waved him off. "I was afraid of that. But I gave Jema some money, and she can take you to buy some that will fit."

He dropped his gaze and shook his head. "I can't let you do that. You've done enough already."

"Nonsense." She thought a moment. "I'll tell you what, how about me taking it out of your check."

"Done." His dark eyes held a merriment I'd never seen before.

She opened her arms. "I'll take that hug now."

He dwarfed her with his embrace. "Thank you, Ms. Preston."

"Call me Cladie." She took his hand in hers and patted it. "Now sit yourself down and have some cake while Jema shares the proposal we have for you."

"Oh?" He pulled a chair out for Cladie. "And what might that be?" He hurried to pull my chair out for me, and then he sat. "You have my full attention."

It happened again. One look into those dark eyes and my tongue couldn't form words. With his hair clean and pulled back, I noticed his hairline had receded. One thing puzzled me. His beard wasn't the same color as the hair on his head. It was a different shade, a little lighter brown, and it had some gray in it. His hair didn't.

I wondered about his age. Was he in his late fifties? Early sixties? Without his beard he might look younger.

"Cat got your tongue?" Cladie's voice cut through my musings.

"Oh, sorry." My face began to burn. I held my mug up to my lips and tried to appear nonchalant, even though I'd obviously been gawking.

While I told him our plans, he listened attentively and ate his cake. His expression never changed which unnerved me. Were we insulting him? Was he interested?

When I finished he stared in his coffee cup a few moments, then contemplated each of us before speaking.

"Ladies, I don't know what to say. Your kindness and care is overwhelming. I would be happy to accept your generous offer. But on one condition, I insist on paying rent." He laid his hand on Cladie's. "I would appreciate you deducting that from my check as well."

Knowing her like I do, he had just skyrocketed in

her good opinion. "You are a good man, Levi…" She inclined her head to the side and frowned. "I didn't catch your last name?"

Levi's face blanked. "It's...Smith."

"You are a good man, Levi Smith."

He swallowed and dipped his head. "Coming from you, Miss Cladie, that means a lot."

She turned to me. "Jema, honey, get me some paper and a pencil. I want to draw a map to the barber shop for Levi."

"This will also come out of my check. Right?"

Cladie shook her head. "If you insist." She handed him the map. "Supper is at six. Jema, why don't you come? I'll ask Felix over, too." She turned her attention back to Levi. "That way you two can get to know each other."

"I'll be there. I never miss a good meal." He hitched his pants up. "Might help me fill these out."

Seeing him pull up the khakis reminded me of Ray's belt I had found while cleaning out my closet. I must have missed it while gathering his things for the shelter after his death.

"Wait just a sec before you go." A few minutes later I returned and handed it to Levi. "This will help until Cladie makes you so fat you won't be able to fasten your pants.

Cladie swatted the air. "Oh psssh. He will work so hard it will all even out."

He slipped it on. "Good fit, eh?"

"Like a glove." Cladie shooed him. "Now scoot on outta here and get that mop cut off your head."

When he was on his way, Cladie called Bert and told him the arrangements. After she hung up, she thought a moment. "Have you noticed how different Levi talks?"

"Yes, I've noticed an accent, only I can't quite place it."

"Guess I've hired a Yankee. At least he's a polite Yankee."

"Cladie, you're a hoot." I slipped my arm around her and squeezed. "And your heart is made of pure gold. Thanks for all you have done for this man."

"No need to thank me. It's what I do." She stepped on the porch and looked at the sky. "Not a cloud in sight. I sure wish it'd rain. It's so dry the trees are bribing the dogs." With that bit of whimsical observation, she sauntered to the yard and across the street to her home.

Thirty minutes after Cladie had left, someone knocked on my door. It was Felix.

"Hi there." I always liked this gentle soul. His caramel skin hung in soft folds around his mouth. His chestnut eyes always held a smiling glint. Gray had claimed nearly all of his wooly hair and eyebrows.

"Afternoon, Jema. Miss Cladie sent me over to collect that furniture you are loaning Levi."

"Oh, my. She isn't wasting any time, is she?"

He chuckled softly. "No'm, she never does. She's been moving like a house afire since y'all left."

"Well, I guess we'd best get to it. I need to take the comforter off and gather up the bedding. How about a glass of sweet tea while you wait?"

"I believe I will. Thank ya."

After I poured Felix's tea, I hurried to Olivia's room. Several minutes later I carried the bed clothes to the kitchen. "Okay, finished. The frame is ready to be broken down." I thought about the small recliner in the corner of the guestroom. Levi might like a comfortable chair. I'd send it and the small table beside it. The lamps, too.

When Felix walked in, I pointed to the chair and table. "Let's take these, too. Call me when you are ready, and I'll help you carry them."

"All right, then." While he broke down the frame, I put the bedding in the cab of his truck. Then I returned to help him carry the furniture to the flatbed trailer. After it was all loaded I said, "Wait just a sec. Let me shut the front door and ride with you so I can help you unload all of this."

"Thank ya kindly. Sure appreciate it."

When I slid on the seat beside him, he coaxed the old truck to start. Gas fumes laced the stale cab air. I always suspected Felix of being a closet smoker. He knew Cladie would have a hissy if she caught him. As nonchalantly as I could, I rolled down the window.

"What do you think about Cladie getting you some help?" I worried that Felix might be offended. After all, he'd worked for the Preston's for years. I didn't want him to feel like he was being pushed out.

Never taking his eyes off the road, he said, "Matter of factly, I'm glad. If we do all Miss Avalee is studying on doing, I'd be hard pressed to tackle it all by myself." He glanced at me. "What's this Levi fellow like?"

"I guess you know he's homeless."

He looked back at the street and upshifted. "Yeah, I heard he was down on his luck."

"Does that bother you?"

"No. Should it?"

"Not really. But it seems to bother a lot of people."

"Guess they'd change their minds if hard luck came a-knockin' on their door."

"I suppose you're right." Felix never ceased to amaze me. Did his quiet wisdom come from years of hardship? I didn't know much about him, but I knew I wanted to be more like him. "Do you mind Levi living in the shop?"

"Not a'tall. I don't use that shop much anymore. It's too small to work on the kinda machinery we use now. The way things are heading, even that big metal building won't be enough for long." His big smile showed his gold-capped tooth. "We're big time now."

Felix drove to where Washington Avenue dead-ended on Whispering Pines Drive. He downshifted causing the old truck to groan, then turned left and drove a few yards to the shop's drive. "Here we are. Wait a second and I'll back 'er up to the door."

When we came to a stop, Felix got out and let down the truck gate. Cladie ambled out of the shop blushed red as a ripe strawberry and with the ever-present dishtowel thrown over her shoulder.

"Come in and tell me what you think." She mopped her face.

"Girl, you look like you are about to have a heat stroke." And I wasn't kidding.

"I'm fine. But it's pretty hot in there. I'll have to put a box fan in the window, or he won't get a lick of sleep."

I stepped inside. "It looks great."

"It cleaned up real nice. I swept the floors and laid out a large area rug I had stored in the attic." Crossing her arms over her chest, she surveyed the twelve-by-twelve room. "I washed the windows and tacked up these towels over them until I can get real curtains. I think this place looks pretty good."

"Looks real nice," I said. "I think he will be happy here."

Felix walked in with the mattress over his shoulder. "Where do you want this Miss Cladie?"

"Just set it against the wall over there."

"Wait, Felix. I came to help." I waved to Cladie. "I'm going to help him unload, and then I'll make the bed up."

"Thank you sugar. I'll head back to the house and get supper on."

"When I'm done here, I'll clean up and be right over."

She nodded and traipsed down the path to the house.

After Felix and I got the furniture moved in, I made up the bed, placed a doily on the nightstand, and set the lamp on it. Then I spread a cloth on the bistro table. Finally, I laid a throw over the recliner and set the other lamp on the little table beside the chair. When I finished, I stepped back and surveyed the room. It looked real homey. I wondered if he was a reader. He might like some books. If so, we could go to the used bookstore downtown.

As an afterthought, I checked the bathroom to see if anything was needed there. It had a tiny sink, a toilet, and a corner shower barely large enough for me. But it beat nothing. Cladie had towels and washcloths already in place. Toilet paper? Check. Soap? Yep. But no shampoo. He'd need toiletries and I had extra.

"Hey, Felix. I'm going to run to the house for a few more things. See you at supper?"

"I'll be there." He ran a sleeve over his sweaty brow. "Wanna ride?"

"No, I better walk since I'll be sitting at Cladie's table."

He nodded. "All right, then."

I wasn't kidding about needing the exercise. I jogged home and found some toiletries, jogged back to the shop, then back home. By the time I'd finished, I looked like a bowl of ice cream on a Mississippi blacktop. The clock chimed four. Just enough time to hop in the shower, get dressed, and hurry to Cladie's to help with supper. And, I had a suspicion Cladie would need someone to back her up while explaining Levi to Avalee.

Later on, I found my suspicion proved true. Cladie always kept her kitchen door open while she cooked to let the heat escape. When I walked up to the screen, I heard them *discussing* Levi. As a warning that I was in hearing range, I called out, "Knock, knock?"

"Come on in, Jema." Cladie's voice was tight. A rare thing.

The tension in the kitchen was thick as molasses in winter. Cladie stood at the sink furiously washing dishes, and Avalee sat on the countertop next to her. She had a white knuckled clutch on the edge. The minute I walked in, Avalee said, "Jema, do you *honestly* think it is a good idea for this homeless guy to move in so close to us?"

Without giving me a chance to answer, she slid to the floor and paced the room. "We know *absolutely nothing* about this man, and he is moving on our property."

Cladie slapped the rag on the counter. "Avalee.

Preston Gardens isn't solely your business, *yet*. I may not be a business woman, as you and your father made perfectly clear, but I am a good...no...I am a *great* judge of character. There is nothing wrong with that boy. He is more polite than any man in this town, save Felix. The only thing odd about him is his accent. And I for one am not going to hold *that* against him." She threw her hands up in the air. "For crying out loud, Avalee, we are not in your highfalutin New York City. Not every homeless man is a criminal. Not in Moonlight and, for that matter, not in New York City, either."

Avalee laid her hands on her head. "I'm not saying that, Momma."

I figured it was time for me to jump in to Cladie's defense. "Your mother trusts him and so do I." Ava turned to me and for the first time since she'd been home, she looked her age. Stress was the great equalizer I supposed. I put my hand on her shoulder. "Why don't you meet him first before you judge him? After all, don't we want the same courtesy?"

Avalee sighed. "I suppose so." She strode out of the kitchen. The china cabinet doors clicked open then clanged shut. She returned carrying three wine glasses. Then she opened the fridge and brought out a bottle of Riesling. "I propose we toast our resident mystery man. May he not kill us in our beds."

Cladie popped her with a towel. "You're a mess."

Ava poured the wine and handed us a glass. Holding her goblet up, she said, "To..." she looked at me, "What's his name?"

"Levi Smith."

"To Levi Smith."

We clinked glasses.

From the screen door, Levi said, "Well, it isn't often a man hears himself being toasted."

We all turned toward him and...Oh. My. Word. Levi could have easily passed for Colin Firth's brother. His clean-shaven face made him look *much* younger. Soft curls fell over his forehead hiding his receding hairline.

Avalee stepped back. Cladie put her hand to her throat. We all looked like largemouth bass ready to gulp bait. I found my voice first.

"You look...amazing."

"Better, eh?"

"Much." I slugged some wine. Then gestured to Ava. "This is Cladie's daughter, Avalee."

He tilted his head and gave a shy grin. "Pleased to meet you."

Her face flushed. "Nice to meet you...too. Uh, do you, I mean, would you like some wine?" Without giving him time to answer, she whirled and faced me. "Jema, come help me." Before I could answer, she grabbed my arm and pulled me through the dining room into the living room. When we were out of earshot, she gripped my shoulders and looked me directly in the eyes. "He's gorgeous."

"Well," I drawled. "He's not bad for a criminal."

She slapped my arm. "Oh, shush. Now grab a glass for Levi, and let's help Mom."

Supper conversation was interesting to say the very least. Cladie did the southern woman thing and asked Levi about his entire history. And I have to admit, Ricki was right. He skillfully dodged all personal questions. But he did it with such finesse that Cladie didn't seem ruffled by it one little bit.

The conversation soon turned to the business and what he'd be doing for Preston Gardens. I was glad to see how well Felix and Levi had hit it off. While they talked, a warm feeling stole over me. For once, something worked out for someone in Levi's situation. And if it did for him, surely it could for others.

After supper Levi approached me. "May I walk you home?"

"Yes, I'd like that."

We said our goodnights to everyone and left. All evening I hadn't been able to get a word in edgewise, and I wanted more time with him. When we reached my door I asked, "Before you leave, would you like some coffee? Wine?

"Wine sounds nice." He looked around. "The evening is fine. Would be a shame to waste it. How about us sitting out here?"

"You might think different when the mosquitoes suck all your blood out."

He chuckled. "They've been my roommates for quite a while."

"Oh." How dumb of me. "Well, then, I'll be right back. Red or white?"

"Red."

Moments later I returned with our glasses and a citronella candle. Mosquitoes had not been my roommates, and I wasn't about to be their evening snack.

"Here you are." I handed him a glass and settled on the step next to him. "So, what do you think of Cladie?"

"She's a fine lady. I like her feistiness."

"I hope you don't mind all the personal questions

she asked. I'm not sure where you are from, but that's just a southern woman's way."

"I didn't mind." He took a sip of wine and remained silent. *Darn it.*

Not being one to give up easily, I continued probing.

"Okay, then, being a southern woman myself, I want to know. Why are you so vague about yourself?"

He swirled the cabernet. "I don't mean to be vague. But I have honest reasons."

"If you don't mind me saying, those reasons feel a little scary. Are you in trouble? Running?"

He looked at me and smiled. "No, I'm not in trouble. But, yes. I am running. I can't explain why at the moment. But in future, perhaps, I may be able to explain. At least that's my hope."

"How far in the future?"

"I'm not sure." He put his hand on mine. "I know you have no reason to, but I'm asking you to trust me. At least try."

A comfortable feeling embraced me. I placed my other hand on his. "I'll try."

While we sat on the step, I noticed how nature's evening song had grown less intense even if the heat hadn't. Fall was on its way. My favorite time of year. I smiled in the dark. For the first time in a long time, I felt fully alive.

Chapter 12

MOLLY
Revelation

A rough tongue groomed my cheek and woke me from a deep sleep. Gypsy, in her less than subtle way, reminded me it was five-thirty in the morning, and she'd like her breakfast, thank you very much.

"Okay. Okay. I'm getting up. Why I didn't train you to eat just before I left for work instead of when I first woke up, I'll never know."

But of course, I did know. There were mornings I blew through the house like a Gulf Coast hurricane and my poor kitty was left to fend for herself all day. And, as all cat parents knew too well, felines had a way of showing how they did not appreciate being ignored. On occasion, I'd found a memo to that effect in my bedroom slippers.

I emptied a can of chicken morsels with egg sauce in her bowl before I made coffee and checked my emails. While I sipped my dark roast, I waited for the computer to boot, then clicked on my email account. Twenty-four of them and not a single one from Colin. *Shoot.* What was going on? He seemed fine with my suggestion to wait until October. Afterwards our emails had been as regular as ever. But now it was the last week of September, and I hadn't heard from him yet.

What was up with that? He'd never gone longer than a couple of days without emailing me. Was he having second thoughts about our meeting?

Frankly, it surprised me how much his not writing bothered me. If only I could whine about it to the girls tonight at Whine Wednesday. But none of them had any idea about him. Well, Avalee did. I couldn't imagine having her response times three. But I needed to talk to someone. Perhaps if I waited until our third glass of wine? Maybe I'd be in a better frame of mind when they pummeled me with all their warnings and verbiage about Internet dating. At least after their initial shock and warnings, I could talk about him.

"Mrrow?" Gypsy jumped in my lap and bumped my nose. The stench of cat food wasn't the most pleasant odor to smell before six a.m., but her nose kiss was a balm to my disappointed soul. I snuggled her up in my arms and stroked her head. She kneaded her paws against my breasts. Her purrs grew more appreciative with each scratch behind her ears and rubs under her neck. Then, she was done. Quick as a wink she jumped to the floor and went to her spot on the sofa where she began her routine, cleaning her paws, legs, and ruff. She stopped long enough to give me a half-eyed stare.

Cats. You gotta love them. I got her message. *Get over it and get on with life.* "Good advice, Gyps." I turned off the computer and headed to the shower.

At work I made miniature four-cheese scones for our Whine Wednesday meeting later in the evening. Of course, when they came fresh out of the oven I had to taste them to make sure they were just right. And if I say so myself, they were pretty darned tasty. *Take that Magnolia, whatever your name is.* It still nettled me to hear Lexi go on and on about those darned orange rolls. I had my suspicions of why that tea room's baker frequented my shop so many times before they opened and why he kept asking me questions about my pastries and buying several of each. Trying to figure out my recipes, no doubt. Even so, I wasn't about to lower myself and do the same by copying them.

Another whine topic. I could start with the recipe-stealing bakery and work my way up to Colin. Unless I lost my nerve. I dreaded the drama, which was sure to happen if I told the girls about him.

At five I closed up shop and hurried home. I had just enough time to feed Gypsy, change, and go to Jema's. The late afternoon air had strong hints of fall. I breathed deep and looked forward to kicking up a rainbow of gold, red, and orange leaves on my walk to work.

The moment I turned the key in the lock I glanced through the living room window and saw Gypsy bolt off the couch. She met me at the door, her green eyes round with anticipation, then slipped past me into the yard. If I didn't know better, I'd swear she had a date with a gentleman friend. However, I had taken care of that.

When I finished changing and freshening up, I called for Gypsy to come back inside and eat. She didn't heed me, and since I didn't have time to wait, her highness would just have to wait for supper. I checked my basket. Wine, scones, whine list. Yep, all there.

Jema was sweeping her porch when I walked up. I noticed she'd rearranged the rockers to face each other with a small table in the middle.

"Hey MK." She pointed to the chairs. "I thought

we might want to drown our sorrows outside."

"Well, you know me. Outside is my favorite room in any house. I brought scones and cabernet."

She blew her bangs away from her glasses and grinned at me. I got the feeling she had absolutely nothing to whine about. Oh well, that left more time for me.

"Perfect. Come on in. I made chocolate truffles. The cab will be lovely with it."

Jema positively glowed. I couldn't stand not knowing why.

"Okay, what's up? What's with the silly grin on your face? Spill."

"Oh, I don't know. Just happy I guess."

"Happy? About what? That dopey smile of yours says a whole lot more. I swear your teeth are about to blind me."

She waved me off. "Oh psssh. Why shouldn't I be happy? After all, since Avalee came home, you and Lexi have become more than neighbors. I have three dear friends. Sisters really."

Not one to back off, I pressed on. "But at our last Whine date you had plenty to say, and we were friends then, too."

She propped her broom against the doorframe and took the scones from me. "Molly Kate Fairchild, you are impossible. I'm just happy. That's all. Now pour us a glass of wine."

"All right. But mark my words, I *will* get to the bottom of this before the evening is over."

Jema looked down at me over her glasses. "No doubt."

"Oooooh, so there *is* a reason."

"Could be. But we will save it for another time."

Darn. I hated not being in the know, and she had clearly out maneuvered me. "Where's the corkscrew. Maybe wine will loosen your lips."

"Don't count on it." She opened the screen door. "I set everything up in the living room. It's on the table."

Jema's living and dining area was a large open space. She had set a darling table. The plates were stacked on one end and the wine glasses were lined up. A pink Depression glass bowl held the bar equipment. At the other end she had four caricatures of the cartoon Maxine the Crabby Lady mounted on cardboard stands. Each of our names were paired with one of the caricatures. Lexi's was Maxine complaining about men. Mine was about cooking. Jema's was about irritating customers, but Avalee's took the prize. It was the one of Maxine walking out the door and her saying her butt jiggle was her way of saying goodbye. Knowing Avalee's obsession with her weight, she'd die when she saw it. I never knew Jema had such an ornery streak.

"Is Avalee here yet?" Lexi stormed through the door with a bottle of red and two of white. "Didn't bring food. I don't plan on eating anyway. Where do I put these?"

I motioned. "In here."

She put her Syrah beside mine and plunged the whites in the ice bucket.

"That's a lot of wine, Lex." I picked up the corkscrew. "Bad week?"

"The worst. Where is Avalee? I'm so mad I could bust." Lexi yanked a bottle out of the ice. "I'd like to take this bottle, walk to New York, and clobber Mr. Nathan, big-shot jackass, Wolfe over the head."

Jema and I asked at the same time, "*Who*?"

Avalee waltzed in and set down a plate of cheese and crackers. "Who's got your panties in a knot, Lexi?" She noticed her name over Maxine's cartoon. "Funny, Jema."

Lexi pulled the cork from the bottle. "I'll talk about it after my first glass."

"I set up the porch for us to whine outside," said Jema. "How about it?"

"I'm about to rant big time." Lexi filled her glass. "I'd rather not do it for all the neighbors to see, if that is okay with everyone."

"All right, Lex. Sounds like we'd better get started before you self-combust." Jema opened the Chardonnay and poured.

We filled our plates and went to the sectional sofa. Frankly, I was glad to see Lexi so fired up. It gave me time to work up my courage to mention Colin. "Let 'er rip, Lexi."

"Well, y'all know I wrote Avalee's *friend* for advice and sent some examples? Well, I finally heard from him today. He certainly took long enough, and frankly I wished he hadn't bothered." She lifted the goblet to her lips and drank deep. Then she produced a folded sheet of paper. "Here, ladies, is his inspired, *professional* reply." After another drink, she cleared her throat and began to read in her most sarcastic voice.

Dear Ms. Lowe,

In regards to your email, I have read your examples and some of the responses you received. What I have to say is probably not something you expect or want to hear. But I must say it all the same and remember, you asked for my opinion and advice.

To begin with, it is hard for me to be impressed with so few responses. However, with such a small circulation I'm sure it seemed significant to you. But in all honesty, it isn't.

Secondly, while the emails from these poor women are distressing, might I remind you that there are two sides to every story? Frankly, you sound like a frustrated, bitter female who hasn't been bedded in quite some time.

Finally, what good is a column like this? If you stop and honestly think about it, while the column does offer women a place to vent, in a very short time your readers will tire of it and consider it insipid.

My advice is this; if you truly care about these women, then do something to help them. Get other points of view. Men for example. Maybe even the mistresses. Start a dialogue. Make helpful (not bitter) observations.

Of course, I realize this may not be possible in your current frame of mind. My advice? Get laid.

Sincerely,

Nathan Wolfe

Oh sweet Lord. I nearly choked on my wine. Avalee pressed her lips together and stared at Lexi owl-eyed. Jema covered her mouth with her free hand. Fits of laughter demanding to be set free electrified the air.

Lexi put the paper down and glared at us. "What?"

Jema pressed her lips with her fingers until the tips

turned white. Her shoulders shook. Ava blew her cheeks out. What the heck? I threw my head back and let 'er rip. I hadn't laughed that hard in years. Jema and Avalee followed suit and howled. I fell on the floor and held my stomach. Tears rolled into my ears.

Lexi jumped up, stomped to the table and refilled her glass. "I'm certainly glad I'm such good entertainment this evening." She swallowed more wine.

Avalee caught her breath. "Sorry, Lexi. But that *was so* funny."

With a thump she set her glass down and folded her arms. "Well, I don't see a *thing* funny about it. He trashed my column and made me sound like a shrew. The jerk."

"You have to know him." Ava wiped her eyes. "He's really a nice man. His sense of humor is really dry. That's all. And really, he does have good advice. In fact, it sounds a lot like what I told you, if you will remember...and admit."

"Oh pffft, Avalee." Lexi snatched a piece of cheese.

Jema blew her nose, then chimed in. "He really does, Lexi."

"Even I can see what he is saying." I picked up the scone plate and passed it around.

"For instance?" Lexi strode back to the couch and dropped on the cushions. "Enlighten me."

"Well," I said. "After a while it *would* get tedious reading all those sad stories. All those problems with no real solutions. Sounds like a recipe for reader frustration." I flipped my hand at Lexi. "Look at yourself, for example. You're frustrated."

Lexi sat cross-legged on the sofa and stared off the

way she always did when the wheels turned in her head.

Avalee examined her scone. "All I can say is now I understand the email Nathan sent me today."

Lexi yanked her head around. "What? What email?"

"Oh, you don't want to hear." Avalee pinched a piece off the pastry and popped it in her mouth.

"What? What did the imbecile say?"

"Before I tell you, I have to know. Did you send him a picture?" She peeked over her wine glass.

"Well, yes. What does that have to do with anything?"

"That explains it then." She took a sip

"Oh, for heaven's sake, Avalee, would you spit it out already? Explains what?"

Ava looked at the ceiling. "Well." After a few moments she leveled her gaze at Lexi. "He said if you needed a volunteer to help you with his last suggestion, he'd be happy to oblige."

Okay, that time I did choke and then fell into another fit of laughter. Jema, bless her heart, tried to not laugh, but she couldn't hold her giggles in any better than I could. Soon she erupted.

Lexi's face grew red. "Why, that arrogant ass." She strode back to the wine. "And I'll thank y'all to get a grip."

"He's always been attracted to short red-heads." Avalee stood. "And he is, after all, a celebrity."

Lexi frowned. "I've never heard of him."

I thought a moment. "Nathan Wolfe. The name does sound familiar."

Jema touched her finger to her chin. "Come to think of it. It does."

"Jema? Is your computer on?" Avalee asked.

"Yeah."

We tromped to her office. Avalee sat in the chair and brought up the image of one distinguished, very handsome man. He looked to be our age, but his jawline was still defined and strong. More proof Mother Nature liked her sons best. Women get wrinkles and men get character lines. His blue eyes had a direct expression like a man who knows you are wrong but listens to you anyway before he corrects you. His thick black hair formed a widow's peak high on his forehead, and gray tinged his temples. *And I knew exactly who he was.* "Oh my word. That's the guy I see sometimes on CNN and FOX."

Jema stared at the image, her mouth opened then shut. She shook her head. "I can't believe it."

Lexi's face was crimson. "Avalee, I ought to ring your neck. Why didn't you tell me he was a celebrity?"

"Well, I guess I didn't think about it. He's just a friend to me."

"Girl, you ought to go after this one." Jema lifted her glass to her lips. "He's a looker. And probably rich. Marry him and take us all to Italy."

Lexi studied her fingernail. "Not interested."

"Mmmm, mmmm, mmmm. Give him my email address Avalee." I turned to Lexi. "You are nuts, lady."

Lexi left the office and drawled over her shoulder, "He's okay."

I followed her. "Okay?" I opened the Syrah while she attacked the truffles.

"All right. All right." Lexi slapped the table. "He's freakin gorgeous, apparently a celebrity, AND I want to throw myself in front of a dump truck. Are you happy now?" She flopped down on the floor and put her face in her hands. "I'm so embarrassed."

"Now, hon, don't be." Avalee sat beside her. "I've known Nate for quite a while, and you are *exactly* what he needs. Someone who will stand up to him."

"Here, here!" Jema raised her fist in the air. "The South shall rise again."

"Yeah." I reached down and pulled Lexi to her feet. "Go get 'em, sister!"

Lexi looked from one of us to the other, her smile slowly built. "Well, I just might accept y'all's challenge." She lifted her glass. "To the South!"

We all joined in. "To the South."

Jema clapped her hands. "Okay, girls, refresh your drinks and snacks."

Plates and goblets refilled, we snuggled down for the next whine. Jema looked around. "Who's next?"

"I don't have anything except," Avalee wrinkled her nose. "I've gained eight pounds. I feel like I'm on a runaway train and can't stop."

"Well, I think you look a lot better." I couldn't help it. She did look better. However, my timing for spouting this opinion was terrible because all eyes were on me. I felt like a bug surrounded by chickens.

Jema said, "What about you, Molly Kate?"

"I may have a couple of things."

No one said a word. They just stared and waited. Talk about feeling put on the spot.

"Well, for one thing I'm sick of hearing about those orange rolls at that magnolia place—Lexi."

Lexi spoke up. "Nice try, MK, but by the color in your face, I think that little whine was just a warm up. Now tell us what is really on your mind."

Oh for crying out loud. Might as well get it over with. I finished my wine first.

"Okay, I'm gonna tell y'all something, but *save* me the hysterics, okay?"

"Whoa," said Lexi. "This is gonna be big."

I got up and refilled my glass.

Jema put her hand to her breast. "Well, mercy sakes, Molly Kate. What on earth?"

Avalee watched with a smug smile.

After a deep breath, I said, "I'm interested—*very interested*—in a man. His name is Colin. And I met him on an…" I rushed on, "*Internetdatingsite.*"

The room fell silent. In all my life, I've only been in one tornado. The sky took on a greenish cast, and the air was eerily still. Like there was no oxygen in the atmosphere. That's the way it felt in the room. My friends looked at me like a tree full of owls.

And then the tornado hit.

Lexi leaned forward. "Are you crazy?" She vaulted to her feet. "You are out of your ever-lovin' mind." She glared at Jema and Avalee. "Someone get me a rope. We need to tie this girl up till she comes to her senses."

Thank goodness Avalee came to my defense. "Now settle down, Lex. It isn't always so bad."

Lexi crossed her arms and sniffed. "Then you are crazy, too."

I noticed Jema sitting stone silent. Her happy glow had faded. *What was that all about? Did she have a secret like mine?* She stood and walked to the wine bucket. "Now, Lexi, let's hear her out."

"All right, then." Lexi plucked up another truffle. "Shoot."

"So, remember at our first Martini Monday I said

I'd managed to meet some men? And y'all know those dating commercials? The ones that show all those twenty- and thirty-something kids looking for love? Well, I never paid much attention to them because I'm too old. But you know, I'm young enough for a relationship, too. Then, one night a commercial came on for people fifty and over. I don't mind sayin, I paid attention to that one and thought, why not? So I checked it out. The free side had way too many men, so I signed up for the subscriber side. I figured the better guys would be there anyway.

"I made up a username, and when they wanted an email address, I created a new email address with a fake name. I wrote my profile saying I was an insurance salesperson who lived in Tupelo. Then I had to write my interests, what I'm looking for, stuff like that. The site asked that I send a picture, so I found the absolute worst picture of myself that I had and sent it. I figured if that didn't scare a prospective suitor away, I had a keeper."

Lexi smirked over her wine. "Or someone whose mug is worse than your picture."

Jema leaned forward. "And a keeper contacted you?"

"Yep. And just so you girls know, I'm being careful. Usually you set up a place to meet. Before Colin, I followed protocol and all the guys were disaster dates. I couldn't get out of the restaurant fast enough. And since I didn't want to go through that again, I told Colin I wasn't ready for a date just yet. I explained about my previous experiences and suggested we know each other through email first. He agreed to my terms. So for the past several months we've been writing back and forth."

Jema held a truffle to her mouth. "Several months? He's patient. I'll give him that. Where does he live?"

"He said he has a farm in Sardis."

"Have y'all talked on the phone?" She bit into the candy.

"No. I think we both feel more in control writing. That way if we say something stupid we can delete it."

Avalee eyed the last truffle, but then turned away. "So what's there to whine about?"

"Well, just when everything seemed to be going good, even talking about meeting, he suddenly quit writing. I haven't heard from him in a week. What am I supposed to think about that? He doesn't want to meet me? He hit the road? And the sad thing is...now I'm realizing how much I care."

"That sucks." Lexi crawled to me and put her arm around my shoulders. "Honey, if he had any idea what he was missing, he'd be here right now."

That did it. I couldn't hold back my tears any longer. Jema and Avalee came over and joined in a group hug.

Lord, I loved these girls.

****

By the time I got home, I felt fabulous. Friends, wine, and freedom to whine left me all warm and peaceful. Also very tipsy. Gypsy jumped from behind a bush and followed me inside, all the while giving me a good meowing for not feeding her.

"Too bad Gyps. Remember this before you run out the door next time."

She stared me down with urgent jade eyes and switched her tail. And since I speak fluent cat, I heard her message loud and clear, "Shut up and open the can."

I did as I was told.

The second I had the can emptied she buried her face in the bowl. Must have been some night. You know? No human dominates me. I am usually in control. But my cat? Another story all together.

Gypsy finished her supper in two shakes and strolled to her carpeted hidey-hole, slipped in, and began washing her paws. Good idea. Only I preferred a hot bubble bath.

When I passed my office and saw my computer, a twinge of sadness stung me. I wondered if he'd written. If he hadn't, my mood would nosedive. Maybe he had? Not knowing would drive me crazy, so either way my frame of mine was ruined. I sat and pulled up my email.

He had!

My breath caught in my throat and my heart began to pound with anticipation. But, then again, what if this was a *dear Mary* letter? I swallowed and opened it.

Hi Mary,

First off...please don't be angry with me. The Internet service in the entire area went down and the cable company has been digging for days to figure out what happened. I've been worried about what you must have been thinking all this time. I couldn't even go to a coffee shop or bookstore. They are affected, too. This morning I packed my laptop and drove to Senatobia. So here I am in a coffee shop finally able to write.

This week of not hearing from you has made me more sure than ever that I want you in my life. I'm tired of waiting. Let's meet this Saturday. You said October and that is the first weekend. You suggested Oxford? I'm cool with that. We could meet at Bouré on the square. I hear they have great shrimp po'boys. Around 11:00?

    Please say you will meet me.

Love,

Colin

Giddy wouldn't begin to describe how I felt while reading his email. I wanted to call the girls and tell them the good news. But it would have to wait. I hit reply and started typing.

Dear Colin,

    Yes. It is time to meet. I've been perfectly miserable this week, and I've come to the same realization. I want you in my life, too. I just got home from an evening with my friends, and I tattled on you for not writing. They plied me with wine and sympathy, but nothing can compare to your email, dearest. My sleep will be sweet tonight. I can hardly wait until Saturday.

Until then.

Your Mary

I hit send, sighed, and left to run a hot bath.

At four o'clock the next morning my eyes flew open. *Oh, Lord. What did I do?* Foggy memories of what I wrote Colin the night before drove me from my warm bed and into the dark office. I stumbled to the computer and turned it on. The stupid thing took what seemed to be hours to load. I tapped my finger on the desk. *Come on, come on.*

Finally my emails popped up and I saw Colin's reply. All it said was, *Fantastic! It's a date. Colin.*

I scrolled to what I had written and reread.

I've been perfectly miserable? Want you in my life? Tattled on you for not writing? Dearest? Sweet Sleep? YOUR MARY? Merciful heavens. My cheeks were on fire. How could I ever face him? I sounded like a love-struck twelve-year-old girl.

Self? Never, ever, never, write an email under the influence of copious amounts of wine. Never!

While making coffee, another alarming thought shot through my mind. Saturday? Today was Thursday. I had nothing to wear. My hair needed dying. When I parted it, the white roots made me look like a skunk. My nails were atrocious.

Two days? Molly Kate? Really? You are stupid, stupid, stupid.

The coffee barely made it in my cup before I was drinking it and pacing the kitchen floor. Avalee would know what to do. I'd call her the minute I got to the shop. While pouring my second cup, I glanced at the clock. Quarter till five. Maybe if I finished the baking early I could leave in time to get my hair and nails done. That is if I could get in to see David at Township Salon. He'd gotten so popular that ladies drove from other states to sit in his chair. I didn't blame them. He was that good.

While blow drying my hair, I wondered what I'd do if I couldn't get an appointment? Then an idea came to me. I took my mascara and applied it to my part. It looked okay if I could keep it off my scalp.

My streak problem was sorta fixed, and I could do my own nails. Now I was left with only one problem—

my closet. It was hopeless. No doubt about it, I had to go shopping. I hated, loathed, and despised shopping.

I breathed in deep and held it in for a few seconds before blowing the breath out. My nerves were as wild as a June bug on a string. I'd be a total mess by Saturday.

As soon as it turned eight, I called Avalee.

"Hello?"

"Avalee? It's me, Molly Kate. I need help. You've gotta help me."

"What? What's wrong?"

"He wrote me. I need help."

"Who? Colin?"

"Yes. He wants to meet Saturday, and I don't have a thing to wear."

"Girl, I ought to slap you into next week. You scared me to death."

"I'm sorry, but I hate to shop, and I have no idea what the style is now. You always look so fabulous and I want to look good for him. I thought we could go to Tupelo today."

"Well, you are in luck. I need to go there anyway and pick up some things for the greenhouse."

"Great? What time?"

"Eleven?"

"Works for me. I'll call my granddaughters and see if they can come in to work my shift. They are out of school today because of a teacher in-service."

"Takes two to replace you, huh?"

"Actually, it takes more. But they are all the family I have to impose on, and I'm going to have to bribe them big time. They probably had plans to sleep in. I'll be at your house a little before eleven."

"Okay, see you then."

At ten-thirty I left the shop and headed home. Before going to Avalee's, I stopped at the house to let Gypsy out and change. I stared at my clothes stymied. I couldn't even choose something to wear shopping for heaven's sake. Going to the bakery six days a week had robbed me of what little fashion sense I had. Thank the Lord for Avalee who always looked like she stepped out of Marie Clare magazine, even when she mowed the lawn.

The October air still felt warm, but at least it moved. The humidity was losing its hold. I could actually walk the two blocks to Avalee's without breaking into a sweat. Cladie rocked on her porch, waving a Moonlight Baptist Church fan back and forth with the same easy motion of her rocker. "Morning, sugar. You're off work early today."

"Yes, ma'am. I'm going to Tupelo with Avalee. How are you today?"

"Fair to middlin'. Can't complain." With the fan she motioned to the door. "Go on in and help yourself to some coffee. There's some fresh zucchini bread, too, if you are of a mind to try it. I'll swan I don't think those zucchini vines will ever die, and I can't bring myself to pull them up."

"Thanks Miss Cladie, but I've been snacking all morning. Mind if I take some home?"

"Honey, take all you want. I have squash the size of baseball bats. Take those, too, and make zucchini scones or something."

"I might just do that."

Avalee pushed the screen door open and joined us. "Ready to do this?"

"As ready as I'll ever be." I waved to Miss Cladie. "Bye, now."

She flipped her fan at us. "Bye, y'all. Have fun."

We hopped in Avalee's candy apple red convertible. Now this would be a fun ride. She tied a scarf around her hair, revved the little Mercedes up, and off we flew down Washington Avenue. *Why did I even bother fixing my hair?*

Avalee glanced at me and said, "I have just the place to take you, Molly."

"Where?"

"Dress Barn."

"Dress Barn?" Are you kidding me? Is it for heifer-sized women?"

"No, silly." Ava laughed. "It has some darling clothes."

"Sounds tacky."

"We can start there and then go to the Mall. There are some cute shops downtown, too."

Forty-five minutes later we pulled into Tupelo. She took off her scarf and looked perfect. Wished I'd had the good sense to wear a scarf. I needed to find a mirror somewhere to coax my hair to lie down and play nice.

Avalee pointed at me and chuckled. "Girl, you look like you stuck your finger in an electric socket."

"I was afraid of that."

"No problem." She popped open the glove compartment and pulled out a mister of water, a brush, and hairspray. "I'm always prepared."

"Bless you, sister." I pulled down the visor mirror and fixed my hair the best I could. "That's going to have to do. I'm famished. Let's have lunch first."

"Cracker Barrel sound good?"

"Love it. Let's go."

After we were seated, we looked over the menu. Avalee ordered a grilled chicken salad. No surprise there. But then she ordered sweet tea. Finally, her resolve was cracking. I ordered sweet tea, and the veggie plate with fried okra, turnip greens, pinto beans, dumplings, and corn muffins with apple butter on the side. For some reason they quit serving muffins and biscuits while people waited for their food, so I spoke up. "And would you bring our muffins while we wait?"

"Yes, ma'am. Sure thing." The waiter left and returned with the teas and the muffins. I took one, split it open, and buttered it. Ava didn't follow my lead. She just sipped her tea, darned her. I guessed dessert was out of the question, too, and I dearly loved their lemon icebox pie. What the heck. I might just have a slice anyway.

The waiter brought our orders, and we got to business. Ava stabbed her salad. "Now, what were you thinking about wearing Saturday?"

"I don't know. That's the problem. That's why I need you. Capris or jeans seem too casual. Skirts and dresses seem too dressy." I crumbled a muffin on top of my greens.

"Well, a sundress isn't too dressy, and you have great legs."

"I do have great legs. I have great boobs, too. It's just the stomach and butt part that aren't so great."

"Oh, psssh, there are ways to fix body flaws."

"Liposuction?"

"Well, that's one solution. Albeit expensive and I don't think you can have it done before Saturday." She stuffed a forkful of lettuce in her mouth.

For the rest of our meal she made suggestions. I started getting hopeful we'd find just the right outfit.

When we finished, I pushed my plate away and decided against the pie. "Okay, I'm in your hands. Work your miracles."

She signaled the waiter. I envisioned her in one of those fancy New York restaurants, and the green-eyed monster rose inside me. I'd give my right arm to go to one of Bobby Flay's places."

For the next couple of hours, we went from store to store. My feet hurt, and I wished I'd eaten the pie. Finally, after all the places we'd been, I found something at that Barn place. The saleslady was so nice. She even wrote my name on the dressing room door. I finally settled on a white sundress with red polka dots. It had a scoop neck, and the hem was just below my knees. It also came with a red crocheted jacket for camouflaging my batwings. Both my cleavage and calves were highlighted. The rest of me was smoothed out with a three-percent spandex body suit I found there, too. I already had the perfect red strappy sandals to go with it.

"What about accessories?" The saleslady held up a red bead cluster necklace with earrings and a bracelet to match.

I turned to Avalee. "Do you think it is too much?"

The saleslady smiled. "As we always say around here, 'Go big or go home.'"

"I think they look fabulous." Avalee took the necklace and fastened it on me. I held the earrings to my ears and studied my reflection, turning to the right and left.

I handed them to the salesclerk. "I'll take these,

too."

"Watch out, Colin." Avalee fluffed my hair. "He may think he is sacking up kittens, but he's about to get a hold of a wildcat."

"That's right, honey." I made a claw motion. "Grrr."

Saturday morning my alarm blared at 6 a.m. I don't know why I even bothered to set it. I didn't sleep two hours together. My eyes probably looked like I'd been in a boxing match and lost.

Gypsy lay curled on the bedspread against the curve of my back. "Sorry to disturb your Saturday morning sleep-in girl, but Momma is getting up."

She opened one eye, then straightened into a straight stretch, opened her mouth in a wide yawn, and stuck out her rough, pink tongue in a long curl. When she could reach no further she bundled back into a ball and stared at me through slit lids mumbling, "Mrrr," before tucking her head under one paw and falling back to sleep. Watching her, I wished I could be that relaxed instead of feeling like ants were crawling through my veins.

I dragged myself from under the covers and trudged to the bathroom, hoping a hot shower would relax me. When I looked in the mirror I was relieved to see my eyes weren't abnormally puffy. But that skunk streak. Yuck. Just as I predicted, David didn't have an opening. Guess I'd have to try my mascara trick.

After my shower, I blew my hair dry and slipped on my robe. Every cell in my body begged for coffee.

While putting the coffee thingie in the maker, I heard a commotion on my front porch. *Great.* Who on earth would be at my door at this time in the morning?

The bell rang. I ignored it hoping whomever it was would go away. No such luck. It rang again and then someone rattled the doorknob.

Well, that's scary.

I peeked out the window. There stood Avalee, Jema, and Lexi with bags hanging off each of their arms.

What in the world?

As soon as I released the latch the girls stumbled in. Lexi shot me her Cheshire cat smile. "Surprise! I had this great idea." She waved toward Jema and Avalee "Meet the Molly Kate makeover team."

Jema and Avalee bowed low.

Lexi held up a box. "I'm taking care of your roots with this handy, dandy, root touch up stuff."

Jema held up a manicure set and a bottle of *Cha Ching Cherry* polish. "And I'm doing your nails."

Avalee chimed in. "And I brought the best moisturizers and makeup money can buy. We are here to make you a complete vision for your Internet, psychopath, dog-loving boyfriend."

Lexi pointed to the chair. "MK, sit down." She pointed at the girls. "Y'all set your stuff up. This won't take ten minutes. And Avalee? Why don't you pull out Molly's dress and make sure it isn't wrinkled." Scrunching up her nose while whirling a cape around my shoulders she added, "And make sure it doesn't have cat hair all over it."

I opened my mouth to stand up for my poor Gypsy, but Lexi bent down and pecked me on the cheek. "No offense, MK." Then she went to work on my skunk line.

In no time she had me bent over the sink rinsing

my hair and wrapping it in the towel. Then Jema went to work on my nails while Avalee smeared moisturizer on my face. Then she took the tweezers and attacked my eyebrows.

I jerked back. "Ouch, Avalee. That hurts."

"Oh hush up. Beauty is painful."

Jema started working on my toes. Her soft fingers sent tickle alarms all over me. I tried to yank my foot back, but she only grasped it harder.

"Hold still, now."

"But it tickles."

She glanced up at me and grinned. "Beauty tickles, too."

Lexi blew my hair out and started hot ironing it. While my curls cooled Avalee went to work on my face. She lined my eyes, brushed on eye shadow, curled my lashes and combed on mascara, sponged on foundation, puffed on powder, swept on blush, lined my lips, and slicked on lipstick.

When she finished, Lexi combed, teased, and sprayed my hair. I couldn't wait to see what kind of miracle they had performed. "Got a mirror, Lexi?"

"You can't look. Not yet." She took my hand and led me to the bedroom. "Come on and get dressed."

Avalee handed me my spandex body shaper. "Now put this on."

"Y'all will have to leave while I do this."

Lexi piped up. "Uh, uh. Nothing doing. You'll cheat and peek."

"No I won't." They just crossed their arms and stared at me. "Okay, okay. Then turn your backs. I'm not about to entertain you by wrestling this thing on."

They faced the wall, and I squeezed and stuffed my

body in the darned thing. "Okay, you can turn around now."

"Wow," said Jema. "I gotta have me one of those."

Avalee took my dress from the hanger and helped me slip it on. I put on my sandals, the shrug, and jewelry.

They stepped back. Lexi made a circling motion over her head with her finger. "Turn around and let us have a look."

I held out my arms and made a full circle. "Well? Can I look now?"

Judging by their wide eyes and slack jaws, they must have done better than they expected. At least I hoped that was why.

"You look incredible." Avalee took me to the mirror. "What do you think?"

I couldn't believe the reflection staring back at me. I was—well—pretty.

"Oh, my, Lord." My eyes moistened, but I didn't dare blink and ruin my makeup."

"Somebody get a tissue quick," yelled Lexi. "Now MK, don't you go messing up your makeup, you hear?"

"You girls must have channeled Michelangelo. I look fabulous." My eyebrows arched perfectly, and my eyes looked like Gypsy's. The way Ava lined my lips gave me a full, seductive pucker. And I would *never* have chosen that shade of red for my lips and nails. But it looked fabulous. "Avalee? How did you make my face look so thin?"

"Just a couple of makeup tricks I learned along the way. I used two colors of blush." She stepped back to appraise her work. "You look just like the vixen you were in high school."

"Now for the finishing touch." Jema brought her Chanel and spritzed my neck and wrists. "And, one for your heart." She sprayed the air and pushed me through the perfumed mist.

Avalee glanced at the clock. "What time do you leave?"

"Nine."

Lexi grabbed my purse and shoved it in my hands. "Then you better get a move on or you'll be late."

"But Gypsy hasn't—"

Lexi rolled her eyes. "Don't worry about your mangy old cat. I'll feed her."

Once again, I bit my tongue. Lexi simply didn't like cats, so it was pointless to come to Gypsy's defense. "Okay. Thanks." I breathed in and let it go. "Well, here goes."

They all followed me to my car. I got in and rolled down the window. "Keep your fingers crossed."

"I'll do more than that," said Jema. "I'm going to go fall on my knees."

"Thank you, Jema. I need all the help I can get." I waved while backing out. They blew kisses. God love them. What would I do without those girls? Everything was perfect except for that niggling thought in the back of my mind. *Am I doing the right thing?*

By the time I reached New Albany, the doubts in my head had reached a full-pitched fit. They screamed, "You are absolutely nuts. What do you think you are doing? You are too old to be acting like this. And you are fooling yourself if you think he's going to be attracted to a tub of lard like you. Turn around before you make the biggest mistake in your life."

At the next gas station I pulled off the highway

onto the parking lot and leaned over the steering wheel chiding myself for being such an idiot.

That's it. I'm going home.

I threw the car in reverse and headed back to Moonlight. While speeding down highway seventy-one I drafted an email in my mind to explain to Colin why I didn't show up.

Dear Colin, I'm so sorry for not showing up for our appointment but something came up at the bakery, I mean office.

Okay, that's lame.

Dear Colin, I woke up this morning with strange pains in my chest and was rushed to the emergency room.

Well, if I'm going to lie, I might as well go all out. Of course I could tell the truth.

Dear Colin, I chickened out.

Chickened out? I slammed on the breaks. I'd never been afraid of anything in my life. And I didn't intend to start now. I checked in the rearview mirror to see if I'd just caused a twelve-car pileup and caught a glimpse of my reflection. I did look fabulous and all because of my friends.

I'm not old, and no matter what size I am, I'm a desirable woman.

It annoyed me how I had almost bowed to the media's definition of what a person was supposed to look like. Who was and wasn't desirable.

I turned the car back toward Oxford, all the while repeating a mantra, "I'm fabulous. All two hundred and twenty five pounds of me. And I'm interesting. *And* I'm smart. I built my own business. Take that, you Hollywood, fashion, and advertising idiots."

My foot turned to lead, and my car gobbled up the white dashes on the road as I made up the lost time. With each mile, my confidence grew. This woman had a lot to offer, and as far as I was concerned, Colin was one lucky man.

With the *I am woman hear me roar* thoughts, I almost missed the Oxford exit. I jerked the car onto the lane and skidded to the shoulder.

For pity sakes, MK. Get a grip.

The nearer I got to the meeting place, the faster my heart beat. When I reached the square, the lovely gardens with orange, red, and yellow mums distracted me from the returning niggle of worry. Just the thing I needed to calm down. I circled around the square and spied a car backing out of a parking spot in front of *Bouré*.

A good sign? I pulled in and checked my makeup before getting out. In my mind I heard Lexi say, "Go get him, girl." And that is exactly what I intended to do.

I strode through the door and glanced around the room. A gentle-looking man with a thin wisp of hair across his head looked up.

Colin.

I waved and walked to him. He looked as relieved as I felt. His countenance reminded me of my husband's expression when he arrived home from a long business trip.

He stood. "Hello, Mary."

"Hi, Colin." He reached for my hand. The moment we touched I felt as if I was the one who had come home.

We sat across from each other at the table. "I can't believe we are finally meeting."

"Me either. You are more beautiful than I thought."

Okay, he's a keeper. He recognized a goddess when he saw one. I smiled and admired his face. His picture hadn't done him justice. But it was his voice that made my knees weak. It reminded me of warm honey, deep, sweet, and gentle.

"How was your trip from Tupelo?"

"Good." Panic slammed me. I just knew I'd get caught in a lie. I had to tell him the truth—and soon, but I couldn't muster the courage. "How about yours?"

"Same here." He studied my face. "I know this sounds funny, but I feel like I know you."

"Yeah, I'm getting the same feeling."

Colin looked at his hands. "I have a confession to make."

My excitement plunged. *Okay, here it comes. He's married. I'm sure of it. This was too good to be true.*

"My name isn't Colin. I gave a fake name."

I understood. I had done the same thing. Perhaps I should confess too. Instead I asked. "Okay, what is your name then?"

"Stan Montgomery."

"Oh. My. Lord."

Chapter 13

AVALEE
The Secret

What day is this?
Since leaving New York, I had asked myself that question every single morning. My days flowed from one into another and much to my surprise I liked it. Tyrannical urgency had given way to slow and steady. Things got done without self-imposed panic. My book was nearly finished, the business plan was coming along nicely, and Preston Gardens finally had a fresh, new focus. Dad would have been so proud. A pang of sadness washed over me. I missed him.

Mom called upstairs, "Avalee? The coffee is on. I'm getting ready for church."

"Thanks, Mom." I supposed I should go with her, but this morning I really wanted to stay home and have coffee with Jesus on the front porch. "I'll be down in a minute." Kicking the chenille bedspread off, I stood, stretched, and then peeked out the window to check the weather.

Molly Kate's car wasn't in the driveway?

Ugh, Molly Kate? Please don't tell me you spent the night with a total stranger. But, on the other hand, what if she hadn't? Oh Lord, what if he had hurt her? Or worse? I could just kill her for doing this. That is, if she wasn't already dead.

I grabbed my cell and stabbed in her number.

"Hello?" Her voice sounded husky with sleep.

"Molly Kate! Where in heaven's name are you?"

"What?" She yawned in my ear. "Wait a minute." The rustle of sheets, the soft padding of slippers, and the door clicking confirmed my suspicions.

"You slept with him, didn't you?"

"Calm down Avalee. And quit acting like my mother. I'm fifty-six, for heaven's sake. And no. I didn't sleep with him."

"Where are you then?"

"I'm at his house, but in my own room."

"Uh huh, then why did I hear you get out of bed and walk out?"

"You'd never make a private investigator."

A toilet flushed. "Oh."

"Sorry, but you deserved that. Anyway, we had a few drinks, and he didn't want me to drive. I'll be home this afternoon."

The swarm of stinging bees eased in my chest. "Well, what happened? What's he like?"

"I'll tell all you gals when we get together tomorrow night for Martini Monday. That way I don't have to keep repeating it. And you won't believe in a million years what I have to tell you."

A soft smack sounded over the phone. Molly Kate's voice went up an octave. "Oh, you're up." Another smack.

For crying out loud. The last thing I wanted to hear was them making out.

Then she said, "Hey, I've got to go now. I'll see you later."

"But—" She hung up. She *actually* hung up on me. *Right in my ear.* Well, of all the nerve. And what was I not going to believe? Arrrrgh, darn you, Molly Kate.

Momma stepped in my room. "You going to church?"

"No, ma'am. Not this morning. I will next week, okay? I think I'll meet with Jesus on the porch swing."

"I've had many a discussion with him on the porch." She furrowed her brow. "Honey, are you feeling all right?"

"Yes, ma'am. Why? "

"You look a little flushed."

Small wonder seeing how Molly Kate nearly scared the life out of me. "I'm fine. You go on. Is there anything you want me to start for lunch?"

"No. I've got lemon chicken cooking in the crockpot. I cooked the vegetables yesterday. All I need to do is heat them up when I get home and fry the potatoes and onions."

I followed her down the stairs to the kitchen. "Would you like me to drive you to church?"

"No, it's too pretty a day. I think I'll walk."

"Okay. Say a prayer for me."

"I will, but while you are having your visit on the porch, put in a good word for me, too."

"As if I need to. You are one of God's favorites."

"Honey, he loves us all the same." She slung her purse on her arm, kissed my cheek, and left.

I sipped my coffee and watched through the window as Momma sauntered down the sidewalk. No telling who she'd invite to lunch. Perhaps it was better for me to stay home so I could start heating the food before she returned. After I refilled my cup, I headed to the porch. It wouldn't do to keep Jesus waiting.

I loved my peaceful time of solitude with God. It always gave me clarity. The cool, crisp fall morning made my senses sing as I watched a lone hummingbird dart back and forth sipping from the feeder. Preparing for the long flight to his winter home no doubt. I sure would miss those little guys.

An hour passed, and my stomach began to grumble. The ol' tummy was getting a little too used to the new ways of eating and had grown quite demanding. I decided to tame it with just one piece of toast and make it wait until lunch. I stood to go back into the house, but stopped when I saw Ty pulling in our driveway. He waved and jumped out. I noticed again how his grin pushed in deep dimples. Marc didn't have dimples. Or at least I didn't remember them. I held the door open.

"Come on in. What brings you out so early?"

"I thought you might like to join me for a bike ride along the lake. This is a beautiful day for an outing."

"Sounds fun. But I'm having some toast first. Want some?"

"Toast? At Miss Cladie's? What is this world coming to?"

Just then I remembered one of his favorite childhood treats. "Okay then, how about toasted pound cake?

"Say, now you're talking."

"Pour yourself some coffee. It'll be ready in a jiffy."

I sliced the cake in generous pieces, slathered them with butter and slid them in the toaster oven. Soon the rich aroma of butter and vanilla filled the room. When the slices were brown and crunchy, I pulled them out and put them on plates, two for Ty, one for me. I could easily have eaten all three.

"Here you are."

He leaned his head over the plate and took a long sniff. "Man that smells good. It's been awhile since I've had this."

Images of him eating toasted pound cake as a nine-year-old boy flashed in my mind. My attraction to him seemed wrong on so many levels. But have mercy, he was one fine-looking man now.

I cut off the corner of my piece with the edge of my fork. "Been a while for me, too. Scott wouldn't let me eat anything like this."

"Your gay roommate?"

"Yeah. I sure miss him." I popped the bite of cake in my mouth. The toasty sweetness bathed in butter transported me to a happy place. Ty must have been in his happy place, too, because he never looked up from his plate until he finished.

"Man, that was good." He caught my gaze with his impossibly sexy eyes. "Now how about that bike ride?"

"I'm going to need it after this breakfast."

"Then get your helmet and let's go. Where's your bike?"

"Hanging on the rack in the garage."

"I'll get it." He looked at my jeans. "You better change. Bike chains eat up pants like those."

"Okay. Be back in a sec." I jogged upstairs and put on a pair of capris. I found my helmet and skipped downstairs to join Ty. *Skipping downstairs? At my age?* What was it about Ty that made me act like a starry-eyed sixteen-year-old? Other than the fact he was drop-dead gorgeous *and* twelve years younger than me.

I really needed to walk this dog back to reality and resolved to do just that. But when I stepped outside and he beamed his smile at me, my resolved melted like sugar in hot tea.

We pedaled down Washington Avenue and turned left on Main Street. On Sundays, downtown Moonlight was like a ghost town. It still seemed strange to me. New York City didn't close for anything. However, as people moved to Moonlight and started businesses, it wouldn't be long until our little town would be open every day of the week. That thought made me a little sad.

When we reached Magnolia Drive, we turned right and pedaled up the incline to the park entrance. My legs burned from the strain against the hill. I hadn't seen the inside of a gym for nearly two months, and I felt it. Darn it all. It took months to get in shape and weeks to lose it. *Mental note to self, find a gym.*

The minute we passed through the stone and timber gate, I had a moment of panic and silently begged that he not go to Marc's and my secret place. To my relief, he turned onto the bike trail and rode past the large willow. Shafts of morning light glinted between the forest's leafy canopy, sending golden coins on our path. The humidity had finally lost its grip, and we enjoyed a balmy seventy degrees. The breeze delivered a potpourri of fragrances: pungent pine, spicy wildflowers, and musty dried leaves. If this bouquet was a cologne, it would be called *autumn.*

Sumac bushes had turned bright red. Patches of purple coneflowers, lilac bellflowers, pink asters, and brown-eyed Susans waved on either side of the trail.

Scott always said, "It's great to be alive," no matter the circumstance, good or bad. Today, I wanted to shout his mantra. It was indeed great to be alive.

Ty pulled up to a tree beside a swinging bridge, and I stopped beside him, thankful for the break. My legs were on fire. He hung his helmet on the handlebars. "Isn't this fantastic?" He pointed to the water thirty feet below. "That's Moon Creek." Then he jogged about a third of the way across, turned, and signaled for me to do the same.

Throwing my hands up I shouted, "There is absolutely no way. I hate heights. I wouldn't even look out my apartment window when I lived in Manhattan."

"Oh, don't be such a baby." He jogged back, swooped me up, and broke into a gallop back to the middle.

I screamed and threw my arms around his neck, hanging on for dear life. Just a tiny peek over the edge made my heart do the jitterbug. "Have you lost your mind?" I buried my face in his chest. His muscles were taut and hard. He tightened his hold, and even though I knew my infatuation with him was hopeless, it felt so wonderful. His aftershave made me want to perch my chin on his shoulder and stay there even if we were dangling over Niagara Falls.

When he set me down, I clutched the ropes. "Don't you dare make this thing move."

Now, why did I say that?

A glint shown in his eyes, and he started rocking it from side to side. My hands locked into a death-grip. "If I could let go, I'd strangle you."

He laughed and held out his hand. "Take a hold."

"I can't." My wrists ached from clenching for dear

life.

His brows lowered. "You're serious aren't you? I'm sorry." He eased toward me and put his hand on mine. "Here, let me help." With tenderness he lifted the fingers of my right hand and entwined them with his. With his other arm he circled my waist and pulled me toward him. I released the grasp of my other hand and held on to his waist.

He bent his face close to mine. "Better?"

My practical self said, "resist his lips being so close." My woman self wanted to stuff a sock in my practical self's mouth. To be honest, I could have stayed on that swinging bridge all day and night, as long as Ty held me. I managed to mumble, "Yes. Much."

"You want to sit here and enjoy the scenery for a while before striking out again?"

I nodded.

He started to move his arm from my waist, but stopped. "You okay?"

"I'm fine." *Sorta.*

After he helped me to firmly ensconce my rear on the bridge, he shrugged off his backpack. "I brought some water and trail mix. Want some?"

"Water would be great."

"Here." He handed me a bottle *and* a package of the mix. While we snacked I began to relax, even though I was suspended in the air by this rope and board contraption. The crystal water tripped over small rocks and swirled around large boulders on its way to the lake. The ripples reflected the sun creating thousands of dancing jewels on the water's surface.

"It's so beautiful here, Ty. I didn't know anything

about this place."

"I probably shouldn't tell you this, but this bridge has been here since my grandpa was a boy. When I was a kid, he used to bring me here."

"Did he bring Marc here?"

Ty watched the water. "I don't really remember."

Stupid, stupid, stupid. Of course he doesn't. When Marc and I started college, Ty was only in first or second grade.

I felt Ty studying me. "Don't go there, Avalee."

"Where?" As if I didn't know.

Without a word he turned to me and took my face in his hands, then lowered his lips on mine. The warmth of his kiss, the gentleness of his touch, silenced all the protests rising in my mind. I leaned into him giving him permission to taste to his heart's content. I couldn't help it. For the first time in a long time, I remembered what it felt like to be a woman—a desirable woman. When he pulled back, I caught my breath, embarrassed at my yearning.

He studied me before saying, "There are few things I am sure of, but I am sure of one thing."

"What's that?"

"We are supposed to be together."

"But Ty—"

"Don't give me that age thing." He took me in his arms and kissed me again, long and lingering.

As much as I didn't want to, I pushed back and opened my mouth to protest, but he took advantage and kissed me again, deeper and more intense.

My practical fifty-five-year-old self disappeared and my thirty-something self was reborn.

An hour before dinnertime, Ty and I returned to the

house. We put up our bikes, and I hurried to the kitchen to warm up the food. Every time I thought of Ty's kisses on that beautiful bridge my cheeks flushed. Hopefully the heat from the stove would fool my mother's eagle eye.

Ty eased behind me and started kissing my neck. "Ty, stop. Momma could walk in any second." I turned and he kissed me square on the mouth. Through silly, little girl giggles, I protested again. "Now, stop that. Want some tea?"

He put on his best little boy pout and said, "I guess so." He inhaled. "What do I smell? Whatever it is, it's awesome."

"Lemon and garlic chicken. Want to stay for lunch?"

"Are you kidding? Sure I do."

"Then you'll have to help." I pulled out bowl after bowl of food from the fridge and handed it to him to put on the counter. Then I handed him the potato peeler and a knife. "You peel and cube potatoes, and I'll chop onions so Mom can fry them as soon as she gets home.

"Wow, this is a lot of food. Who else is coming for lunch?"

"Well, let's see. It is Sunday, so Mom will ask everyone she sees on the way home from church. So I'm guessing you need to cube the whole five-pound sack of potatoes."

"You're kidding. Seriously?"

I angled my head and lifted the corner of my mouth in a smirk. "The whole thing."

"Okay. Whatever you say."

By the time Mom got home, all the veggies were in the warming trays and the potatoes were ready to fry.

When she saw this, she clapped her hands together. "Why, bless your hearts. Thank you." Without bothering to change, she donned her bib-apron and pulled out two thirteen inch skillets, glugged oil in both, added bacon drippings for flavor, and turned the burners on. In no time the mouth-watering aroma of frying onions and potatoes wafted through the house. While she worked she said, "I'm sure glad y'all made up all these potatoes. I invited Felix, Jemma, and Levi to lunch."

I glanced at Ty. "Where did you see them, Mom?"

"Oh, Felix was by the shed. Jema and Levi were sitting on her porch." She put her hand on Ty's arm. "And you are staying for lunch too, you hear?"

Nodding at Ty, I gave him my *I told you so* look.

He grinned. "Miss Cladie, you couldn't run me off if you wanted to."

Momma handed us plates and utensils. "Good. Now y'all go set the table, and I'll get the food dipped up."

Like good children, we obeyed. When Felix, Jema, and Levi arrived, we assembled together and enjoyed the time-honored love of food and conversation. Felix reached for more mashed potatoes and said, "Miss Cladie, I saw this catalog with a hydroponic set up. They had tomatoes and cucumbers growing in buckets and lettuce on a table-like thing. And you don't use dirt. Just water with the nutrients mixed right in. I'm thinking that you and Miss Avalee ought to look into it."

"What a great idea, Felix." I turned to Mom. "We could buy a large polycarbonate greenhouse. I've toured through a lot of them. I hear they are great for growing year around."

Momma pulled a potato roll apart and smeared it with fig preserves. "I don't know. Those things are expensive, and truth be told, I like having a break from the garden. Besides, what would we grow?"

Jema jumped in the conversation. "I'd love to have vine-ripe tomatoes in January instead of those cardboard tasting things. And I'll bet the produce manager at the store would jump at the chance to buy your veggies."

"You mean Walter at Pigg's?" Momma bit into the roll and thought a minute. She pointed her finger at Jema, then at me. "Y'all might be on to something."

Levi spoke up. "And Miss Cladie, since you have Felix and me to do the work, you could still have that break."

"I talked to Mom and Felix the other day about growing edible flowers."

Jema stopped her fork in front of her mouth and looked at me. "Edible flowers?"

"Yes. They are the thing on the west coast and in New York. Chefs put them on salads and use them as garnish, bakers candy them and decorate with them, and bartenders use them in their specialty drinks."

A spark shown in Levi's eyes. "But is there a market for all of this in Moonlight? This needs to be considered before investing in expensive hydroponic systems."

Levi surprised me. I guess I supposed he was uneducated since he was homeless. A pathetic, ignorant and prejudiced supposition on my part, I'll admit. Obviously he had business sense.

Ty piped up. "We could develop an Internet

business."

"That would work." Levi looked at me. "You say there is a good market?"

"Yes. Just look online."

Momma clapped her hands together. "Well then, let's do it." She pushed away from the table. "But for now, let's have dessert. How many for eight-layer-butter cake with chocolate frosting?"

The guys waved their hands.

I stood. "I'll help you, Momma." I had other motives besides being helpful. I wanted to slice my own piece. Momma's cooking had made it darned near impossible to snap my jeans, and I absolutely refused to buy a larger pair.

In the kitchen, she cut five huge wedges and was about to cut another.

"Wait." I held up my hand. "I'll cut my own piece." I took the knife and sliced off a piece.

"Lord've mercy, Avalee. You sliced it so thin it will disintegrate before you get back to the table."

"It's just right." Still, with a longing eye, I coveted everyone else's slices and sighed.

****

Monday morning I woke at daybreak. I don't think I've ever looked so forward to a Monday in my entire life. The day absolutely crawled. I was dying to know what happened between Molly Kate and Colin. She didn't get home until late Sunday night after I'd gone to bed and left before sunrise to get the baking done. One thing for sure, not a single one of us would be late tonight for Martini Monday. I grabbed the cheese balls Mom had made, a box of crackers, and a bottle of citrus flavored gin.

"I'm gone, Mom. Sure you don't want to join us?"

Momma called from the den, "No, I'm watching *Wheel*. Tell me all about it when you get home. Wake me up if I'm asleep, okay?"

That's my mother. She was a faithful fan of *Wheel of Fortune*. I don't think she had missed an episode since it began as an afternoon game show. Sometimes she recorded them, but sooner or later, she watched every one.

"Okay. I'm gone."

I put my goodies in my trusty little wagon and hurried to Lexi's. When I reached her screen door, I tried knocking, but music blared on her CD player and drowned me out. "Hey, Lex. Some help please."

Her feet pounded toward the door, and in a flash she threw open the screen. Her eyes were wide with anticipation. "Have you heard anything yet?" She took one of my trays.

"Nope. Take my word for it. MK will stretch this thing out as long as she can. I'm sure of it."

"Not if I can help it. Put those cheese balls by the chicken wings. I picked them up on the way home."

While we hung around the snack table, Jema tapped on the door.

"Knock, knock." A sack hung from each arm and she held a tray of California rolls. With her foot she cracked the door ajar, then bumped it wide open with her hip. "Is Molly Kate here yet? Has she told you anything?"

"No and no." I took her tray and the sack containing the vodka. "What's in the other bag?"

"Wasabi and soy sauce. We have a sushi chef in the deli now. Those California rolls are to die for." She looked at the table. "Did anyone make anything sweet?"

"I did." Molly Kate sashayed in the room.

We stampeded her.

"Whoa, girls. I know you want to hear about my date with *Colin*." Her smile confirmed my prediction. The hateful thing was going to drag this story out. "But you will just have to wait."

She set the platters on the table and took off the foil. "Turtle cheesecake bites and chocolate chunk brownies."

If she thought for one minute this would placate us she was wrong. Well, mostly wrong.

Lexi whipped up the martinis and practically threw them in our hands. We rushed to the living room and flopped on the nearest pieces of furniture.

"Okay spill," said Lexi. "Or I may have to hurt you."

Molly sipped her gin martini, nibbled a bit of olive, and said, "Okay. But girls, you won't believe it. I've learned truth is truly stranger than fiction."

We all leaned forward. A slight irritation tinged Lexi's voice. "Try us. What?"

"Well, we met at *Bouré*. I recognized him right away. And he recognized me, which was surprising, considering I sent him the most awful photographs and then y'all made me look like a glamour model."

She took another sip and held up a finger. "Right off he confessed he'd been lying to me about who he was all the time."

Lexi jumped up. "I knew it. I just knew it. He's married, isn't he?"

Molly wore her maddening *I have a secret and I'm*

enjoying this look. "Hold on and I'll tell you. And don't forget, I've done some lying myself."

Lexi stirred her drink with her finger. "That's different." She sucked the vodka off her fake nail.

"The answer to your question is no. He isn't married. He's a widower like me."

"Then what did he lie about?" asked Jema.

"His name. It isn't Colin. It's..." She looked at Lexi and me. "Are you ready for this?"

I couldn't stand it. "For crying out loud. What?"

A smile crept over her face. "His name is Stan Montgomery."

Stunned silence filled the space between Molly, Lexi, and me. Jema sat there clueless.

Lexi bellowed out, "STAN? *The* Stan Montgomery? The one you married in high school?"

Now Jema's expression was just as astonished. Apparently Momma had filled her in.

My voice pitched. "How on earth could you not have known that?"

"People age." Molly smirked. "Except for you Avalee."

"Cladie Mae told me something about your marrying," said Jema. "But I want to hear the whole story."

Molly held up her glass. "I'll explain after a refill."

Never in the history of bartending had four martinis been mixed faster. We all settled in and anticipated Molly's retelling of the long ago marriage. She snuggled against the couch pillows. "You see, I'm the middle child in our family. I have an older sister and a younger sister. Before my little sister was born, in my child-mind, things were great. My older sister got plenty of attention as the oldest child and me as the baby. But when my little sister came along, I was stuck in the middle. It was as if I'd been demoted. At least that was how I felt. So, in order to be noticed, I became an overachiever. I was on the honor roll and the captain of the cheering squad, but nothing ever seemed to lift the middle child veil off me. So, in high school, I got this great idea to get my parents' attention. I decided to run away and get married."

"To Stan?" asked Jema.

"Yep. The idea came from a conversation I had with this nerdy boy named Stan. We had study hall and science together. He was always a good listener and understood my frustration. He was pretty frustrated, too. The poor guy couldn't get the attention of a girl even if he waved a hundred dollar bill. He wasn't bad looking, just a bit too quiet and waaaay too intelligent. And what made matters worse; he didn't have an athletic bone in his body."

Lexi made a face. "Truer words were never spoken."

"Anyway, one day we came up with this idea to run away together. For the next several weeks we made our plans. Being the genius he was, he came up with a fake marriage permit and where we could go to find a clueless justice of the peace."

Jema walked to the snack table and got a couple of California rolls. "Did you go in the middle of the night? Wake the poor JP up?"

"No. We went on a school day so the office would be sure to call our parents. And when our parents found out we had skipped, they would be at home burning up the telephone lines looking for us. It all went beautifully. I told the JP this sob story about me being pregnant and our parents kicking us out of the house. Stan gave him the license and letters of permission from our parents. Stan told the JP our parents were so ashamed of us and they didn't care what we did. Y'all would have been proud of my acting skills. When Stan said that, I burst out crying." Molly Kate chuckled. "That poor justice is probably still talking about those poor kids and their horrible parents."

"Did y'all..." Jema flushed. "Honeymoon?"

"Heavens no." Molly dipped her roll in the wasabi sauce. "We never intended to stay married. We went straight to my house and told my parents and braced for the fallout." She put the roll in her mouth. Instantly her eyes started watering. "Wow. If my nose is ever stuffed up, I'm eating this wasabi stuff."

Jema handed her a tissue. "Miss Cladie said your trick worked, and you got plenty of attention."

Molly wiped her eyes and blew her nose. "It worked all right. The first question Dad asked was if we had consummated our marriage. I didn't know what he was talking about, and Stan whispered it in my ear. I can still remember how hot my face got. I blurted out 'Of course not. We didn't have time.'"

Lexi threw back her head and laughed. "What a hoot."

"It was." Molly Kate's eyes danced with merriment. "Our dads didn't waste any time making sure our illegal marriage was annulled. And from that day on, I got plenty of attention. More than I wanted. On the other hand, Stan was the big man on campus. After all, he'd seduced the captain of the cheerleading team. The jocks were sure we'd had sex. We didn't see much of each other after our little escapade since the school staff and our parents watched us like cats watch mice."

Lexi finished her martini. "Well, now that I think about it. It does make sense why you two didn't recognize each other after all these years. You really didn't know each other very well."

"Precisely," said Molly Kate. "Who knew we would be so compatible? We had a great weekend."

Lexi's eyebrows went straight to her hairline. "Did you have sex?"

"No." Molly took a cheesecake bite. "It's too early for that. We want to get to know each other first. I don't want everything we do to become a means to an end—the bed. Unfortunately, I know by experience how easy that is. Not going there anymore."

I thought I knew Marc too, only to find out I really didn't. My voice swelled with sorrow and guilt. "I believe that."

Molly Kate nodded at me and got another cheesecake. "We spent the weekend at his house talking. Getting reacquainted. He's a retired pharmacist and loves to cook. He has a real nice home in the country. Sort of a gentleman's farm with a few cows, a dozen or so chickens, and some goats." She peered at me. "And he has a beautiful vegetable garden."

"Well, he sounds okay, I guess. Maybe even pretty good." I gave in and reached for a brownie. "But just in case, we've got your back."

****

It was around eleven when I left Lexi's. Jema walked with me. When I was younger, I felt safe walking alone on the streets of Moonlight after dark.

But Moonlight was growing up and embracing vacationing strangers. I felt better having someone with me. When we reached her house we hugged, and I crossed the street and sauntered home.

Momma was asleep, and I didn't have the heart to wake her. Besides, Molly Kate's bit of news would make good coffee talk. Even though it was late, I wasn't the slightest bit sleepy. I sat on the swing and thought over the past few weeks. Jema and Levi. Molly Kate and Stan. And if I knew Nathan at all, I could predict an interesting relationship just might develop between him and Lexi. And then there was Ty. I knew the *real reason* why our relationship could never work. It wasn't because of the age difference. My being older didn't matter a smidge to Ty. He'd thoroughly convinced me he considered my age a plus. The problem was the secret I'd buried deep inside years ago, and the guilt from that secret killed every relationship I'd ever tried to enter. I knew it would happen with Ty, too. Especially Ty.

I laid my head back and let my tears flow. It was time to be honest with him before this relationship went any further. I needed to finally confess what I'd hidden all these years. But how? How would I ever be able to find the courage to tell him I was the one responsible for his brother's death?

Chapter 14

JEMA
Questions

A cold November breeze fluttered through the brown leaves still clinging to the trees outside my window. I loved the changing seasons. Autumn always made me feel reborn after a sweltering summer. I enjoyed October's pleasant seventy degrees. Now I looked forward to winter. This morning's frosty air felt delicious and reminded me the holiday season had begun. For the first time in years, I looked forward to them. And I knew why. Levi Smith.

In a few days the first annual Moonlight Fall Festival would be held. It was the brainchild of our mayor to raise money for the revitalization project. Those who wanted to sell their crafts and wares could rent booth space around the town square. The monies from the rental went to the project. There would also be a revitalization donation box at each booth. Of course the money made through sales would be the vendor's to keep. Several church and civic groups knew of Lifesource's increased financial needs. Therefore, as a way to help, they rented booth spaces and pledged to donate all the proceeds from their sales to the shelter. Bless them.

Ricki and I also rented a spot. She volunteered to

bake pies and cookies since those items are always in demand this time of year. Since I loved crafts, I decided to find a holiday themed knick-knack for my contribution. While trying to figure out what to do, I went to my favorite Internet idea place, Pinterest, and found just the thing—a pumpkin with silk flowers arranged around the stem area and topped off with a raffia bow. Cladie said I could rob her pumpkin patch, calling it her contribution. She even volunteered Levi to help me. Bless her.

Even though I'd be rummaging around in a pumpkin patch, I worried over what to wear. Of course, if Levi weren't around, I'd wear grubbies. Since he was, I wanted to look nice. Maybe even kinda sexy. Silly? Sure. Adolescent. Absolutely. But I didn't care.

I chose slim jeans and a long-sleeved black tee shirt with a scooped neck. When I finished dressing, I stood in front of the mirror. Not bad.

I may not have Molly Kate's confidence, but I felt I looked pretty good. After a quick makeup check, I left and tromped to the side of the house to get the wheelbarrow. The cold air nipped my neck and ears making me wish I'd worn a jacket, but that would have ruined the effect of my ensemble. Again, ridiculous. And again, I didn't care.

My plan was to get several small to medium-sized pumpkins, as well as two large ones. One would be for my porch, the other for Cladie's. We both loved decorating for fall and between us, we always held the proud distinction of making our end of Washington Avenue the gaudiest.

I passed the new high tunnel, poly-whatever-you call-it greenhouse where Levi and Felix worked. Avalee hadn't wasted a minute in purchasing one after our talk over supper several weeks back. Even better, Levi hadn't missed a night at my house since then either. It's funny. He never talked about himself or his past and yet, I felt like I knew him. But I really didn't know him at all. That used to bother me, but not anymore. My intuition told me he was a good man.

On the other hand, while he didn't talk about himself, he had a way of getting me to tell everything about myself. I kept saying things I never intended to say. He knew practically everything about me except my weight. *That* bit of information I would keep to myself. *I think. I hope.*

When I came close to the greenhouse Levi met me. "Need some help?"

"Sure. I'll never pass up an offer like that." I noticed he had rolled up his shirtsleeves. "But you'd better put on a jacket." By now I wished I hadn't been so vain and put one on myself.

"It is rather chilly. I think I will. It's so warm in the greenhouse, I forget how cold it is outside." He trotted back inside and returned, pulling on a red flannel jacket and tossing a blue flannel one to me. "Noticed you forgot yours."

Like I said, a good man.

He eyed the wheelbarrow. "Looks like you are planning on quite a haul. Mind if I push?"

"Not at all." I relinquished my hold on the handles.

"And what do you plan on doing with all of these pumpkins?"

"I have a craft idea to raise money for the shelter at the Fall Festival."

"Oh you do, eh? How 'bout some help?"

"Gathering pumpkins, or the craft?"

"Both."

"I'd like that. How are you with a glue gun?"

"A what?"

"A glue gun." I swiped my hand across the air. "Oh, never mind. I'll show you tonight. Supper at my place first? Then we can work."

"I'll be there."

We stopped in the middle of the patch. Bright orange pumpkins of all sizes and shapes lay among wilted, yellow vines.

Levi set the barrow down. "What size are you needing?"

Scanning the field around me, I spied the perfect pumpkin. Moving a few feet forward, I took my knife, cut it from the vine, and held it up. "Just like this one."

"The size of a soccer ball, then?"

"I guess. Never paid attention really."

"It is. Trust me."

I found another pumpkin a little larger, the size of a basketball and cut it free. "And this size would do, too."

"For sure." He turned and wandered through the patch gathering pumpkins. In no time I had all I needed. Before we left, I chose Cladie's and my pumpkins. Levi hefted them on top of the others and pushed the load home for me. When we reached the garage, he took my hand. "See you around six?"

"Yes. And come hungry."

"I already am."

By the look in his eyes, I had the distinct feeling he wasn't referring entirely to food. Our relationship was moving forward at an astonishing rate. Was I being foolish? Or maybe after being invisible, as Molly so aptly put it, I was enjoying being seen. Not only seen, but admired. Truthfully? I was as hungry as he was.

Oh, stop analyzing everything, Jema.

I watched him walk back to the greenhouse. Things would just have to fall where they may. For now, my plans were to indulge myself while I could.

At straight-up six, Levi tapped on my door before walking inside. "Something smells good."

"Hey there. Supper is almost ready. Why don't you pour us some wine?"

"What are we having?"

"Curry chicken, rice, and veggies."

He thought a moment. "Riesling would be good with that, then. Do you have any?"

"I do. In the fridge. And don't get alarmed when you see how many bottles of wine are in there. They're left over from our last Whine Wednesday."

"Maybe you girls can have the next one at my place, eh?"

"You'd kick us all out after thirty minutes of our griping."

"I'd just drink more wine." While he poured, I wondered how he knew Riesling paired with curry chicken. All I knew was red went with red meat and white went with white meat. The mystery about Levi continued to deepen, and tonight I was determined to get some answers. For heaven's sakes, I was falling in love with this man, and I knew nothing about him.

Emotions swirled so loudly in my head I didn't hear him walk up behind me. When I felt the heat of his breath on my neck and the soft brush of his kiss I turned to face him.

He handed me the wine. "Here you are."

"That was nice."

"What? The wine?"

I set my glass down and wrapped my arms around him. "No, this." On tippy-toe, I lifted my lips to his.

He placed his glass next to mine and picked me up in his arms as if I were a child. At first our kisses were gentle as we explored, but soon we were both lost in the intensity of our craving. Everything melted away. Time and space? Gone.

I ran my hand up the back of his head and tangled my fingers in his hair as he carried me to the couch. Our kisses grew ravenous. In our ardor all kinds of thoughts ran through my mind. Was he going to make love to me? Was I ready to take that step? Did I have on my granny panties?

I knew I should stop this, but I couldn't. Wouldn't. When he laid me on the couch, I pulled him on top of me. His body's desire pushed hard against me. And then, as sudden as our passion flared, he stopped and rolled to the floor.

What just happened?

He sat with his back against the couch and sucked in a deep breath. I didn't know what to think. Insecurity flared inside me.

"Levi? Did I do something wrong?"

He locked me in his gaze and smiled. "No." He blew out a breath and shook his head. "No, you did too much right."

I rose up on one elbow. "Then what? Why did you pull away?"

"Jema, a long time ago, I learned the hard way how relationships built on passion have foundations made of toothpicks." He stroked my face with his finger. "You are so lovely. So interesting. I want to know you, not just your body. And I can't help it, I'm a man. If we make love now it will cloud my mind to everything else. I want to get to know the real you, your heart, your personality, your interests. I want to know what you love and hate, what makes you laugh. When I know these things, then I want to know your body."

Well. That's different.

I'd never heard any man say *anything* like that. And you know? I liked it.

"Thank you for being stronger than me." I leaned over and kissed his cheek.

"Stronger, eh?" He ran his fingers through his hair. "Let's not make this a habit or it may have to be you who is strong."

I got off the couch, still shaky with desire. "I can't promise anything. But I'll try."

He stood and drew me close. "Jema, you are unlike anyone I've ever known. And I've known a lot of people. I hope you realize how incredibly special you are."

"I'm just a southern woman." I kissed his nose. "A southern gal who's famished."

We sat down to eat and chatted while eating, but all through our meal my mind wandered back to the couch. My visceral reaction to Levi's kisses still surprised me, and I had to smile to myself. This old girl still had it.

When we finished eating and cleaned up the dishes, I put the pumpkins and crafty stuff on the kitchen island. Then I introduced Levi to the glue gun. It took a while for him to get the hang of squeezing the trigger and applying flowers to the hot glue. I hate to admit it, but I was way too entertained watching him jump every time his thumb made contact with molten glue. His gentlemanly manners gave way to murmured expletives.

"You get a boo boo?" I tried to hide my smile.

"Boo boo? More like a skin graft. This thing is vicious." He smirked at me. "Go ahead and laugh. I know you want to."

A few giggles escaped before I reeled them back in. "Need some ice?"

"No, I'm fine. It may come in handy one day not to have fingerprints."

In a couple of hours we finished crowning all the pumpkins with silk mums, leaves, dried pods, and raffia bows.

Levi leaned back to admire our work. "These are nice, eh?"

"Lovely. I'll bet they'll be gone within an hour." I stood and stretched. "How about some coffee?"

"I'd like that."

While I pulled out cups and plates, he cut a couple slices of apple pie. The feeling of home glowed in the room and in my heart.

He handed me pie, and I gave him coffee. We strolled to the living room and sat on the infamous couch which still made my heart beat a little faster. However, a comfortable silence soon settled between us. Sitting there with Levi reminded me of long-ago evenings with Ray. Comfortable. No weird or awkward feelings drove us to fill the air with words.

I cradled my mug with both hands and held it close to my chest. This would have been a good night to build a fire.

Levi glanced at me. "Cold?"

"A little."

He put his arm around me and drew me close. "It is getting chilly. Makes me think about all my homeless friends. Camping wasn't so bad when the nights were warm." His voice dropped. "But with winter coming, it will be hard on them. I worry about the children."

"I can't imagine." The thought of cold little ones made my throat constrict. "Maybe we can set up cots at the shelter. I'll talk to Ricki." I glanced at the pumpkins. "I hope we make enough money to buy washers and dryers. Maybe even install a few showers."

"That would be nice. I remember wanting nothing more than a hot shower and clean clothes. I haven't taken feeling clean for granted since Miss Cladie hired me. Bathing off in a public restroom is awkward at best." He stared at his cup with a gaze so intense I dared not interrupt his thoughts. Lord, what I would have given to be able to read his mind. I wanted to know everything about Levi Smith.

****

The day of the festival arrived, and I arrived early to our assigned spot in order to help Ricki set up our booth.

"Morning, Jema."

"Morning. Wait until you see the pumpkins Levi and I made."

"Levi huh?"

"Oh, stop it. He works for Cladie Mae now."

"Uh huh. And you still know nothing about him." She shook her head. "Anyway, here are my contributions." Several boxes brimmed with pies and cookies wrapped with clear cellophane and tied up with gold, orange, red, and brown ribbons. She also had a huge bowl of candy.

"Are you selling the candy, too?" I picked up a peanut butter cup and unwrapped it.

"No. This was left over at the shelter after Halloween, so I thought I'd bring it for the kiddos at the festival to fill their pockets. I sure don't want it around me anymore."

"I know the parents will appreciate your generosity. Especially when the kids are pinging off the walls at bedtime." I picked up another piece.

Grinning, she shrugged. "Not my problem. Besides, if you keep nibbling, there won't be any left for the kids anyway."

I tossed the wrapper in the trash. "Keep reminding me, okay? I seemed to have misplaced my self-control when I turned fifty. That was seven years ago, and I still haven't found it."

Levi pushed a wheelbarrow loaded with decorated pumpkins to the booth. "What's not our problem?" He set it down and brushed his hands against his jeans.

"The sugar rush we are about to give the children at the festival." I resisted another piece of candy.

He snapped his fingers. "Oh, by the way, Miss Cladie called and said she sent Felix with a load of mums for you to sell. He left them at Lifesource. How about riding back there with me so we can load them up and bring them here?"

"Sure thing." I waved to Ricki. "Be right back."

She folded her arms, stuck out one foot leaned back on the other. Without saying a word, she spoke volumes.

At the shelter, an autumnal rainbow of mums filled two parking places. Between these mums and our decorated pumpkins, I had no doubts we would be the first to sell out.

"Wow, these are beautiful. I want some for my house."

Levi grinned. "Felix told me Miss Cladie said you would and for you to come by the nursery and get what you wanted."

"She's such a dear."

We picked up an armload and carried them to the truck. He set his load on the bed and turned back to get more, but he came to a sudden stop. His face blanched.

"Levi? What's wrong? Are you sick?"

He shook his head. "No. But I just remembered something I needed to do. Would you mind finishing? I'll walk." He tossed me the keys and spun around. Without waiting for me to answer, he jogged down the sidewalk and disappeared between neighboring houses.

I stared after him a few seconds, bewildered. When I turned back around to the truck, I saw something I'd never seen before in Moonlight. A black stretch limousine. It crept along the street to our parking lot and pulled in.

What on earth?

A stocky man, dressed in a suit stepped out and surveyed the building. His shock of white hair contrasted against his tanned skin. He pulled his dark sunglasses off and tossed them on the limo seat.

With a high and mighty attitude, he strolled over and glared at me. Even though it wasn't polite to size him up before speaking to him, I did just that. I didn't like the man. Not at all.

He pointed his stubby finger at me. "You there. I need some information."

Not a *please would you help me* or even a *hello.* How rude. "About?"

"I'm looking for Matthew Abrams. He's been kidnapped, and I have reason to think the person or persons responsible are somewhere around this area."

A kidnapper? In Moonlight? Not possible. My stomach turned to stone. My voice felt unsteady, so I swallowed before I answered. "I don't know anyone in this town by that name."

"I have a photo." The stranger reached inside his jacket and let go with a string of curse words while he patted all his pockets. "Look, I've misplaced Mr. Abram's picture. But he's six-two, around two hundred pounds, maybe two-twenty. Salt and pepper hair?"

"No. Sorry."

"Have you noticed anyone new in the area?"

"Sir, you are at a homeless shelter. There are a lot of transients."

My interrogator grunted, then handed me a card. "If you see someone fitting that description, give me a call." He turned to leave but swung back around. "And if one of your *transients,* as you call 'em, acts suspicious, like he or she is hiding something, I want to talk to that person, too."

He pivoted, returned to the limo, and got in. After he slipped on his sunglasses, he tipped his chin at the driver and they drove away.

My mind whirled with disturbing uncertainties and fear as I finished loading the truck. While I drove back to the booth, nagging thoughts kept buzzing around my head like an annoying fly. Why did Levi act so strange? And that man—who was he? Detectives didn't ride around in limos. What bothered me the most was his last statement before he left. "If one of your *transients* as you call them acts suspicious, like he or she is hiding something..."

As much as I tried to push them away, my doubts about Levi resurfaced with a vengeance.

Chapter 15

LEXI
Saving Face?

As much as I hated to admit it, Nathan Wolfe was right. Every day more and more emails poured in from women complaining and whining. I even began to sympathize with some of their husbands. My problem now was how on earth I could use his suggestion and still save face?

I scrolled through my archived emails and reread my reply to him hoping it wasn't as bad as I remembered.

Dear Mr. Wolfe,

Well, if you are not the master of decorum and rationale. Oh, wait, you aren't. No, you are the very type of man I wrote about in my column. I find you insipid. And your insinuation regarding my sexual life is laughable.

Laughable? Unfortunately, it was more than laughable. It was the absolute truth. Darned him for being right—again. I propped my face in my hands and continued reading through squinted eyes.

So take care of yourself and find that eager twenty-something who only has sex with you because of the more important people she will meet while hanging on your arm.

One other note, I read one of your articles. You really need to learn the proper use of commas. Or is your editor a dolt? (That's southern for idiot in case you didn't know)

Sincerely,

Lexi Lowe

Good heavens. It wasn't as bad as I remembered. It was worse. When would I ever learn to keep my mouth shut and my fingers still? On the other hand, since he probably didn't read my column anyway...probably? Who was I fooling? There was no chance in hell he had read my column. I decided to follow his advice. No face saving necessary. I loosened my shoulders, held my head high, and began typing.

MOONLIGHT MADNESS ~ For Women too Old to be Young but too Young to be Old and it Drives us Mad!

Okay girls, after hundreds of emails from you, let me just say, I hear ya! I'll allow there are some pretty sick cookies out there. Sounds like most of those fellows haven't got the good sense God gave a goose.

On the other hand, griping about these jerks doesn't do much to help us, does it? What we need to do is take a hard look at our circumstances and determine if there is anything we could or should do to improve ourselves.

Yes, ladies. Even when we have been wronged, and I include myself because I've been in some of your shoes, there is always room for an honest look within.

Recently, I received advice from a very unlikely person who writes for the New York Times (are you impressed?). This person suggested my readers not just tell their story, but also how they got through their pain.

By sharing our journey to healing we help each other. Pretty good idea, right?

So, how about it? Tell us the steps you took to rebuild your lives. Another thing. I want to hear from men who have left their wives for younger women. I want to know why it is okay for you to let yourself go but expect your wives to look like models. Maybe I'm wrong about this. I've been wrong a few times. Very few, mind you.

Heck, while I'm at it, how about all of you mistresses? Let me hear from you, too. Why have sex with married men? Maybe you didn't know he was married? Perhaps you did? If so, why did you do it? What was there to gain? The betrayed women of America want to know. We really do. Perhaps we will learn something about ourselves. And while it may be painful, it will help us when we risk a relationship again.

So how about it? Do you men and mistresses have the rocks in your pocket to answer this column? I guess I'll have to wait and see.

Until then, the Madness continues.

I sat back in my chair and blew out a long breath. *Well, Mr. Wolfe. We will see if your suggestion works.* I never liked it when any of my columns bombed. But this time I secretly hoped for flat out failure so I could shove it in his face. That is, if I ever got the chance. Which I wouldn't. But it was still nice to think about.

My stomach grumbled, and I looked up at the clock. One. Wow. I'd written through lunch. That rarely happened. Chicken salad and an orange roll from the Magnolia Tearoom sounded divine, but I didn't want to face Molly's wrath. So I decided to go to her place and see what was on the soup menu for the day. After sending the column to Vince, I snatched my purse and hurried out before he cornered me with a lecture on typos and how much unnecessary work I caused him.

Cold wind slapped my face the second I stepped outside. Soup at Molly's was a good decision after all. Even so, I still wished she'd cave and copy the tearoom's orange roll recipe.

The chalkboard sign by her door had the soup of the day as Chicken Pot Pie. Warm, yummy, comfort food for a chilly day. *Yes ma'am, I'll take it.*

The bell jingled against the glass when I walked through the doorway. The aromas of bread baking, coffee brewing, savory roasting chicken, and sautéed vegetables cradled my freezing senses. As usual the place was packed and a cacophony of voices competed with Ol' Blue Eyes who crooned over the sound system. It looked as if I'd have to get my order to go, but a couple stood to leave. Thank goodness. I wasn't ready to do battle with Vince over my column just yet.

I plopped my purse in the chair and turned to push my way to the counter and place my order when Molly hurried over with a rag in hand.

"Thank you, Mother Nature, for this blessed cold day." She grasped the dirty dishes with one hand and wiped the table with the other. "What'll you have?"

"Table service? That's a first. I'll have the soup of course. Have you eaten?"

"No, so I think I'll join you. Be back in a jiff." Molly watched me through alert eyes. "And I have a surprise for you."

"What?"

"Never you mind."

Well, *that* gave me something to think about. It had to be about Stan. I'd bet my bottom dollar they were engaged. That'd explain the sparkle. Molly's getting married. What a hoot! And she thought I wouldn't have it figured out by the time she got back with our lunch. I spied her coming from the kitchen with a tray holding our soup and something else.

With a flourish Molly slapped a saucer in front of me. On it was a huge, fluffy, orange roll. "Surprise."

"Well, I'll be."

Plopping down across from me, she leaned over. "And just wait until you taste it."

"Wait? Me? Never." It was hard for me to follow my own rules for the proper consumption of an orange roll, but I held fast. I peeled off the outside crunchy layer and took a bite. Tangy orange flavor burst in my mouth. "Oh my Lord in heaven, Molly Kate." Euphoria. I savored the sweet morsel.

Molly's gaze held fast as she watched me eat. "Just wait till you get to the center."

Normally, this process could not be rushed, but this time I made an exception. Unrolling to the center, I held up the tender pastry soaked with butter and orange icing and popped it in my mouth. Bliss exploded on my taste buds making me salivate and my jaws ache. It was sooooo good. I couldn't help but think about Nathan Wolfe's suggestion in his email about getting laid. This was far better than any sex I have ever had. Of course, I wouldn't tell him that, because I knew what his answer would be.

"Now you've gone and done it, Molly girl. I've eaten dessert before lunch. I'll want dessert again."

"I know, so that is why I brought you another one. I just couldn't wait to see what you thought." She waited. "Well? What do you think?"

"Magnolia's cannot hold a candle to yours. Theirs tastes like vending machine pastries compared to this."

Molly slapped the table with both hands. "Yes, ma'am. That's what I'm talkin' about." She slid a bowl of chicken potpie soup across the table.

"I had my granddaughter buy a half dozen. Then Stan and I ate every one trying to break down their recipe and improve on it."

"Stan? He was here? Why didn't you say anything? He bakes?"

"No, I went to his place. I didn't say anything because I didn't want you girls having a conniption. And yes, he's a fabulous cook."

"So, what's up with him not coming here? You hiding him? Is he that ugly?" Steam rose from the soup in my spoon. I blew it and eased it into my mouth. Oh. My. Goodness. Good thing the soup was hot, or I'd be lapping it out of the bowl like a starving dog.

"No. He's not ugly. I think he's cute. He'll be at my house next week for Thanksgiving. Would you like to join us?"

"I thought you'd never ask." I gave up being careful and burned my tongue. "What can I bring?"

"Martini makings?"

"That I've got." I slurped up the last of my soup and eyed the orange roll. My stomach cried, "No!" but my mouth said, "Go for it."

Molly stood. "I want coffee with my roll. How about you."

"Sounds great."

Well, well, well, we finally get to meet Stan. He had no idea Molly Kate came with three friends in the package. And if he dared hurt her, he'd have *all* of us on him like wet leaves. As far as we could help it, she wouldn't wind up like the women in those pitiful emails that filled my box.

Call me paranoid, but I had a suspicion he wanted to ditch his farm, move to the city, and suck off her. After all, Molly was a successful businesswoman.

I decided to call a secret meeting with Avalee and Jema. There was no way on God's green earth I was going to let Molly Kate be crushed. Mr. Stan Montgomery was in for the interrogation of his life.

After lunch I strolled back to work in no hurry to see Vince. Just as I expected, when I passed his office he called, "Lexi? Come in here."

"All right." I fell into the chair in front of him with a cup of hazelnut coffee fixed the way he like it. "Here ya go. Figured you might need it."

He took it and said, "New York Times? Someone from the New York Times read your column? Thanks for the coffee by the way."

Well, that wasn't the reaction I expected, but hey, I'd take it. "Nathan Wolfe."

"Nat…" He jumped up and braced himself on the desk. "No. Nathan Wolfe? Are you serious?"

"Oh, he's nothing special. Just a reporter."

"Are you kidding me? Do you watch CNN? FOX? MSNBC? Even the BBC for crying out loud?"

"Nope."

"He's an investigative correspondent. I see him interviewed on television all the time. All over the freakin' world."

He would die if he knew what I'd written to his *news rock star.* His ecstatic ramblings hit my ears like the waw-waw-voice of Charlie Brown's teacher until he said, "I'm going to call him right now."

Like an alarmed white-tailed deer, I jumped up and seized his hand. "No." Nailing him with the most ferocious look I could muster I demanded, "Do not call him."

Vince sank back into his chair and tented his fingers. "Why not? What did you do, Lexi? Hmmm?"

Lord, I needed a drink. "Let's just say we have a little dispute going on at the moment."

"Dispute?"

Casting around for a way to put a positive light on it I blurted out, "He wanted to sleep with me, and I refused."

"Sleep with you?" His frown formed a little crisscross on his brow. "Really?"

His incredulous look flew all over me. "What? You wouldn't want to have sex with me?"

His face flushed merlot. I stood and walked to the door. Before leaving I turned and smiled. "Thought so."

As soon as I got home that evening I went to the all the news websites and searched Nathan Wolfe. After that Whine Wednesday when the girls told me Nathan was a reporter and was sometimes on those twenty-four hour talking head shows, I figured he was fairly well known. But I felt confident, at least I hoped—I prayed—he wasn't the rock star Vince blathered on about.

I was wrong. Nathan Wolfe *owned* the Internet. *Oh no, oh no, oh no, this whole thing is getting out of hand.* I picked up the phone and dialed Avalee.

"Hello?"

"Avalee? I'm going to kill you. *Do you hear me?* Kill you."

"Lexi? What on earth are you talking about?"

"Nathan Wolfe."

"What about him?"

"I made an absolute fool of myself with someone who everyone in the world knows about except me."

"You found out about him a long time ago. Why are you so upset now?"

"I don't watch the news. Not even since you showed us his picture. I had NO IDEA he was a *news god*. And here I have insulted him in every way possible."

"Good. He needs humbling."

"But not by me. I've made a complete idiot of myself."

"Don't worry about it. Like I said, he has a wicked sense of humor."

"Whatever. I'm going to make a strong martini. Wanna join me?"

"Be over in a sec."

I snatched the Goose out of the freezer and shook up a couple. The doorbell rang and Avalee walked in with a disturbing smile. "What?"

"Let's finish our martinis before I tell you."

"No. What? Tell me now."

"Nathan is coming to Moonlight."

I took a slug. "When?"

"Next Monday."

I finished my drink and strode to the bar and made another.

Chapter 16

MOLLY
Plans

Planning a Thanksgiving meal had never been so hard. I had no idea what Stan liked. I remembered my first Thanksgiving as Randy's new wife. I was nervous then, too, but at least I knew his favorite foods.

Gypsy jumped onto the windowsill by my kitchen table and waited expectantly for a rubdown. I ran my fingers through her silky, black fur. "Well, girl. What do you think? Traditional? Or something crazy and unexpected?" She blinked, lowered on the sill folding her paws under her and purred. "Just as I thought. Traditional."

First I needed a list. I picked up my pen and jotted down the names of all who would be here. Stan, me, Carli and Jeff, Lacey and Cherrell, and Lexi. Maybe one year his sons and their families would join us.

"Just listen to me, Gypsy." I stroked her back. "Here I am already planning a future with Stan, and he hasn't even asked me to marry him."

The thought of marrying at my age sent a little thrill through me. Planning a wedding would be such fun now that I'm old enough to have some sense. I felt a silly smile spread on my face.

Then the voice of reason surfaced, and my smile

faded. *What if he did ask? Would he sell the farm and move here? Would he expect me to sell my business and leave Moonlight?* I loved my home. I loved Moonlight. I built my business from a catering service to a successful bakery/restaurant. Surely he wouldn't expect me to move. Then again, he could be thinking I wouldn't expect that of him. All the dancing hearts and fluttering butterflies disappeared from my mind. Reality set in.

The phone rang and jerked me to the present. Gypsy lifted her head and stared as if to say, "Well? Are you going to get that? The ringing is disturbing my nap." So as her dutiful staff member, I answered. The screen showed Lexi's name.

"Hi Lex. What's up?"

"Hey. Listen, me and the girls want to have a little get together when Stan comes. You know, welcome him back, catch up and all of that. When will he be here?"

"This afternoon."

"How about tomorrow evening then?"

"How nice. Tomorrow it is. What can I bring?"

"Stan. Nothing else. The girls and I will handle everything."

Something in her voice...

"Why am I feeling uncomfortable right now?"

"Oh, go pet your cat. You'll feel better. Bye now." The line went dead. I reached over and scratched behind Gypsy's ear. But I didn't feel better.

As the time drew nearer for Stan to arrive, I could hardly contain my nerves. He simply had to rekindle some fond feelings for his old hometown and for this house. I just didn't think I could leave it.

A car door slammed, and I hurried to the window. Stan pulled a suitcase from the trunk. I checked my reflection in the living room mirror one more time before opening the door.

"Hi Stan, need any help?" I walked to the porch steps.

He grinned at me while shutting the trunk. "Nope. I got it." In no time he closed the distance between us. "Man, it's good to see you again." He took me in is arms and laid one on me.

*Lord have mercy, what if Miss Cladie sees, or Lexi, or, or...oh my...*I wrapped my arms around him and gave in to the moment. After our lovely lip-lock, I pushed back and said, "Goodness, what a greeting."

Stan picked up his suitcase and held the door open for me, "Just missed you, that's all."

Gypsy moseyed over and gave him a sniff, lifted her paw, and jerked back. Stan laughed. "Yes, Gypsy, that's dog you smell. Her name is Kricket."

Without meowing a word, she turned tail and trotted out. "I can see she's not impressed." He lifted his eyebrow. "I'm not making a good first impression, I'm afraid. Good thing I left Krik with friends."

"Oh, don't worry about her. She'll make you staff soon enough. Come on. You probably want to freshen up." I led him up the stairs to the guest room. "Here's your room. The bathroom is through the door on the left."

"Looks great." He threw his suitcase on the bed, sat down, and pulled me onto his lap. "Molly Kate, I must confess I'm crazy about you." He gazed at me with his aqua eyes then leaned over and brushed his lips across mine. The tickle felt electric. I wanted more, and honey,

I took it. Believe me, Stan gave it right back. What seemed like hours later, we came up for air.

"Whoa. Whew." I stood. "Wasn't expecting that."

He took my hands in his. "Did I tell you how much I've been missing you?"

"And I've missed you, too." I caressed his face. "A lot." Taking him by the hand, I pulled him toward the door. "How about a drink?"

"Sounds good. But first..." He enveloped me, and once again we were lost in an urgent fog of desire. At this rate, supper would never be finished. Which was all right by me.

When we finally made it to the kitchen, Stan insisted on helping. I had to admit, it felt good having a man cooking with me. Sipping wine, peeling potatoes, stealing a kiss when I passed by. I'd forgotten how amazing small talk could be and the simple pleasure of laughing together. I loved having someone around who could say more than meow.

After eating, we left the dishes and sat on the floor in front of the fire. I leaned against him and relished the heat of his body. It had been a long time since I'd felt this content.

Stan kissed behind my ear and said, "Supper was delicious." The warmth from his breath sent chills though me.

"Not bad for a chubby old woman. Huh?"

"You are beautiful, Miz Molly Kate Fairchild. I wouldn't change a thing."

"Not even my size eighteen pants?"

"Well." Stan leaned close. "The only thing I would change is they would be on the floor." He kissed me and then whispered, "I love every inch of you."

"Love?"

"Yes. Love." He kissed me again and said, "How about more wine?"

I nodded and started to stand. He put his hand out. "No, I'll get it. You've worked hard enough. Enjoy the fire."

"Thank you." *Ah-mazing*. Someone waiting on me for a change. Gypsy jumped in my lap and bumped my nose with hers. "Well, Miss Priss. What do you think?" She curled into a ball on my lap, turned on her purr, and proceeded to clean her paws.

Stan padded back into the living room and handed me a flute of champagne.

I took the glass. "Goodness, where did this come from?"

"I brought it to celebrate."

"Celebrate? What?"

"Us." He eased beside me and caressed Gypsy's throat. Her purr decibel increased dramatically. I noticed something glittering on his forefinger. I picked his hand up and looked. A diamond solitaire. A *huge* diamond solitaire. I met his eyes in wonderment.

"Molly Kate, I don't want to live one more hour without you." He slid the ring off and took my hand. "Would you consent to be my wife...again?"

There were so many questions, so many things to think about, work out, so many possible problems... "Yes. Yes!"

He slid the ring on the fourth finger of my left hand and then kissed me. We toasted each other, tippled our champagne, and then he kissed me again. Disgusted, Gypsy charged off into the kitchen.

"I love you, Molly Kate. We were meant to be

together. Our coming together again is nothing short of divine intervention."

"I love you, too." Admiring his gentle expression and soft smile, I said, "Isn't it funny? We are finishing what we started." Then, at the worst possible time, the practical Molly emerged. I sat back. "But how? How are we going to make this work? Sell the farm? I can't ask you to do that. I can't sell the bakery."

He put his finger to my lips. "I'll do whatever it takes. We will work something out." He set his glass down. "But whatever we do, you must know I am not the type of man who expects his wife to be the wage earner or only provider in the family. I am well-capable of taking care of you."

Stan Montgomery will never know how much I appreciated his statement. I pulled him close and murmured, "You are every girl's dream and to think, you are all mine. Stan Montgomery, you are my prince."

"And you, dear lady, are my princess."

And you know what? I felt like one.

The next morning, for the first time in years, I didn't wake to a rough tongue on my cheek, but to the aroma of coffee and a soft kiss. I rose up and tried to focus.

"Morning Glory."

"Aw, Stan. How sweet." I gratefully took the coffee wishing I could have at least combed my hair. "Take a good look now. This face and body is what you will be waking up to every morning."

"Baby, we are going to have to have an agreement starting right now."

I blew the steam from my cup and took a sip.

"What's that?"

"You are going to have to stop talking about my lady that way. You are not fat, ugly, or undesirable in any way. I am not the kind of man who is suckered by sight. I fall in love with what will last, and that is who you are on the inside. And darling, I hit the jackpot. You are beautiful, and you have a beautiful soul." He patted his belly. "I just hope you feel the same way about this fat, old, bald man."

"I only have one thing to say."

"What?"

"Stan Montgomery, will you marry me?"

He took my coffee cup from me. "Are green tomatoes fried?" He leaned over to kiss me, but I threw my hand over my mouth.

"Nope. Morning breath! I have to lay down the law about kissing before toothpaste." I rolled off the other side of the bed and rushed to the bathroom to brush my teeth.

Stan laughed. "Noted. When you are done, get dressed. I have breakfast ready."

Breakfast? I squeezed a generous amount of toothpaste on my brush. *Eat your heart out ladies. And won't you be surprised tonight?* It was then the little devil on my shoulder whispered an idea in my ear. I laughed out loud spraying soapy specks all over the mirror. I rinsed my mouth and hurried to collect my kiss and tell Stan my idea.

He sat at the table reading the paper, with none other than her highness nestled on his lap.

"Well, well. If that don't beat all."

Stan glanced up from his paper. "What can I say? Women just cannot resist me." He lifted Gypsy and settled her on the windowsill. Then walked over and wrapped his arms around me. "Now may I kiss you?"

I didn't give him a chance, pulling him toward me, I made his wait worthwhile. When we finally broke free, he blew out a breath. "Man, how soon can we get married?"

"Oh, I think I can have everything planned in a few weeks. Are you game?"

"Oh I am. Believe me, I am." He lifted the calendar off the wall, flipped the page to December and ran his finger across it. "How about the 14th?"

"Excellent. I'll call in the troops." And then my idea for devilment came to mind. "Speaking of the troops. I have to warn you, tonight you will get the grilling of your life."

"Oh, really?"

"Yes, by Lexi mainly. She is on an *all men are scum* rant."

Gypsy sat by the door and stared at us. "Mrrreow?"

"Yes, ma'am." I went to the door and opened it for her to go out. The sun shown bright in the topaz sky, and the air felt deliciously cold. "Stan, it's such a gorgeous day. How about us taking a walk around the town square? I want you to see how it has changed and show you my shop. And while we are walking, I'll tell you about the little trick I want to pull on the girls."

"I like the sound of that." He helped me shrug on my coat. "Partners in crime again, right?"

"Absolutely."

We walked along Main Street and Martin Luther King Boulevard. I pointed out my shop. "On the way home, we'll stop in, and I'll give you the best scone you've ever put in your mouth. And you'll get to meet my granddarlings, too."

"Do I need to be worried about them hating me?"

"Naw, they'll love you. Everyone will love you."

"As long as you love me, I'm a happy man."

I squeezed his hand three times. "That will be our signal. I. Love. You." He squeezed my hand four times. I glanced up at him. "What did that mean?"

"I. Love. You. Too." He lifted my hand to his lips.

We passed the court house and crossed Magnolia Drive. When we came to the entrance of Moonlight Lake, Stan nudged me to the left onto Leslie Lane. "Where are we going?"

"I wanted to see the old Norton place. I remember when I was a boy wishing I lived there."

"Me too. I used to hide in the azalea bushes and watch Mrs. Norton's tea parties."

We neared the corner of Leslie Lane and Nightingale and the elegant antebellum came into view. Beautiful as always. The two-story house had four columns across the front reaching from the ground to the roof. The entry was a double door with a cut glass circle-top window above it and cut glass sidelights. The second story door was exactly the same, and it opened onto a balcony. The first floor had an east and west wing with columns supporting the wrap around covered porch that spanned the front and sides of the mansion.

Behind the west end was a sunroom leading into another two-story building. The back yard had a beautiful courtyard with a wrought iron gate. On the other side of the gate was a large pool with a pool house at the far end. The place was spectacular. The grounds were breathtaking. It made my green thumbs itch.

I caught a glimpse of some kind of sign partially

hidden by one of the rosebushes. A realty sign? I blurted out, "Look. It's for sale." Turning to Stan in disbelief I said, "I didn't think the Nortons would ever let this place out of the family. I wonder what happened."

Stan bobbed his eyebrows. "I've never seen inside. Have you?"

"Why, no. I haven't."

"Want to?"

"Of course I do."

He checked the number listed on the sign. "Well, well, Lela Blodgett. Haven't seen her in a while, thank goodness."

"She hasn't changed one iota."

"Great." He punched in the number. "Hello? This is Stan Montgomery. Yes. *The Stan.* I'm moving back to town and saw the Norton place is for sale. I'd like to see it. When? Now if possible. Okay, I'll wait. See you in a few." He turned to me. "Prepare yourself."

In no time, Lela came roaring down the street in her black Kia. Before she even got one foot out of the car, she had already started yapping, "Why Molly Kate, shame on you. You didn't say a word about Stan being in town." She tossed her bleached-blond hair and looked Stan up and down.

Never cared much for Lela.

Someone needed to teach her how to apply eye shadow and what shades to choose. The shocking blue eye color she used made the wrinkles on her lids look like the tide was rolling in. But worst of all her thick black Cleopatra eyeliner. Tacky, tacky, tacky, for a woman pushing sixty.

Lela clicked her tongue. "My, my, don't you look

fine? So you want to see this house huh?" She stroked Stan's arm. "Honnnneeeey, you must be one successful fella. Are you single?" She put out her well-manicured hand. "Just teasing."

I'll bet you are.

When Stan could get a word in, he said, "Nice to see you too, Lela. And no, I'm not single."

I bumped his side with my elbow. If he said a word, the whole town would know about us before I could get to the sidewalk. And I wanted Carli to hear about us from me.

Lela pursed wrinkled red lips. "Awwww, that's too bad." She leaned over at me. "Isn't it Molly Kate? Unless…?"

I feigned disinterest. "Yeah. Too bad." Nice try Lela.

"Oh well, let's go in and have a gander."

Forty-five minutes later we walked out the front door. I had never seen such a house. Six bedrooms, six and a half bathrooms, a library, a dining room, two living areas, a sunroom, and a kitchen large as the entire bottom floor of my home. And the two-story building attached to the sunroom was another house entirely. It had a large kitchen, living room, three bedrooms, an office, two and a half bathrooms, and a greenhouse porch. Lela said Mr. Norton had built it for his parents.

Then there was the pool house. It had a kitchenette, bathroom, bedroom, and living area. And all of this for a tidy sum of just over a million dollars.

When Lela finally left, Stan and I sat on the front porch rockers. He reached over and took my hand. "Like it?"

"Like? I love it."

"Then, how about it?"

"How about what?"

"Let's buy it."

Did I hear him right?

"Buy it? Are you kidding me? How? It's over a million dollars. And even if we could afford it, what ever would we do with all that room?"

Weaving his fingers with mine, he hesitated before saying, "Now I don't want this to sound wrong, but honey, I don't want to move into *your* house and live off the income of *your* business."

He stood and held his arms out wide. "Look at the place. While walking through town, I thought about how it is turning into a tourist get-away." Excitement filled his voice. "Wouldn't this make a great B&B? Just think, I could run it. You keep the bakery and supply the baked items for our guests. And I can pursue my cooking passion while I run the business. We could live in the house off the west wing and make new memories there. Our memories. What do you think?"

"I love the idea. But how could we ever afford it?"

"I already have most of it. When I sold my chain of pharmacies, I invested. And I can sell the farm. I have developers breathing down my neck all the time. I'm sure I'll get enough to pay cash for this place."

"What about my home?"

"Now that's something you'll have to decide." He took both my hands in his. "I will support you in whatever you want to do."

I stared at the towering magnolia trees in the yard and remembered how excited Randy and I were when the Washington Avenue house came up for sale. A lot like today. We fell in love with the house. Only it took us years to pay it off. We brought our newborn daughter home to that house and raised her there. It is where my granddaughters had spent their growing up years visiting Noni and Poppa. Randy had died there.

At that moment, I understood what Stan was saying. Washington Avenue was mine and Randy's house. Our history, our life, our memories. I gazed into Stan's kind eyes. He was my future. This house on the corner of Leslie Lane and Nightingale was our future. I could see me living here, decorating for the seasons, hosting guests, and building new memories. Of course Carli wouldn't like me selling the house and moving.

Out of the blue, an idea came to me. I could give the Washington Avenue house to her. Like an early inheritance.

"I want to run something by you first."

"Shoot."

"What do you think about me giving my house to my daughter? It is where she grew up, where her dad died. It holds all her childhood memories. The twins as well."

"I think that is an inspired idea."

"You don't mind? I mean, I won't make much of a financial contribution to the Norton house."

"You are bringing the heart into it. And believe me, at a B&B, we will work our tails off, but have fun doing it." He hugged me close and said, "From now on, this is the Montgomery house."

I held him tight and squealed. "I can't believe this."

"Come on, Miss Molly. Let's go buy a house."

We made it home in time to freshen up before leaving for Lexi's. We had our plan all set. I chuckled all the way there. This would never do. I had to get a grip, or our little charade would be birddogged out in less than a second. I bit my lip while we walked up the porch steps and knocked on the door. It swung open and Lexi pushed on the screen door.

"Come in, ya'll. It's so good to see you again, Stan." She stuck out her hand. "Remember me? I'm Lexi. One of Molly Kate's oldest friends."

"How could I forget? You were one hot ticket then." He eye-balled her with lecherous appraisal. "Even hotter now. I always liked redheads."

Lexi slapped a glare at me. I just shrugged, and we walked inside. My insides ached holding the laughter at bay. "And you remember Avalee, right?"

Stan let out a long, low whistle. "Helllloooo, baby." He turned to me. "She sure didn't let herself go like you did." He took Avalee's hand. "You are one sexy lady." Avalee jerked her hand from Stan's and narrowed her eyes before turning a questioning look at me. Again I just lifted my shoulders and let them fall.

"And this is Jema."

"Hellllooooo, gorgeous. You must have not gone to school with us, otherwise I'd sure remember you." He grinned and stepped away from me. "Molly, I'm not so sure about us any longer."

Lexi stomped her foot. "That's it." She stabbed her finger toward the door. "There's the door. Get out of my house, you—"

Stan put out his hands. "What? Just because I appreciate beautiful, sexy women?"

I couldn't stand it. I burst into giggles. Stan joined me, and we laughed until tears ran down our faces. When I could breathe, I held up my left hand with the blinding solitaire. "Gotcha."

Lexi, Avalee, and Jema stared at the stone and then at Stan. He wiped his eyes. "Sorry girls, but Molly put me up to it." He placed his arm around me and held me close. "This lady is the most beautiful woman in the world as far as I am concerned, and I'm going to spend the rest of my life worshiping at her feet."

"Well," said Lexi. "After I slug you both, I'll make you a martini. Geeze Louise." When she returned with our drinks, she looked at the ring again. "For a stone that size, you are forgiven."

Jema nudged in for a look. "When? Have you chosen a date? And where? Have you decided on a honeymoon spot?" She clasped her hands under her chin. "Oh, go to Italy, to Florence. I've always wanted to go there."

"We do have a date." I held my hands up. "Now brace yourselves. December 14th."

Avalee opened her eyes wide. "This December 14th? Girl, you've got to be kidding me."

"Nope. And you haven't heard it all," I said. "He bought me a new house."

Lexi frowned. "But you have a house."

"I'm giving it to Carli. Stan and I want to start fresh together."

"But, you *are* staying here in Moonlight. Right?" said Jema.

"Yep. Our new house is just across town." I smiled up at Stan. "He bought the Norton place for me today.

A glass shattered. Lexi stood stock still, her hand poised as if she still held it. When she found her voice she said, "Well, Stan, I guess you pass inspection."

Avalee clapped her hands. "We have a wedding to plan. And what better place than the new Montgomery

Mansion? I'll take care of the flowers, and Ty will take pictures."

Lexi joined in. "I'll handle all the announcements, invites, things like that."

Jema raised her hand. "And I'm sure Cladie Mae is going to want to cook for you, so I'll help her."

Stan grinned. "And I'll stay out of the way."

"I have another request." I took my friend's hands. "Even though Stan isn't going to have anyone stand with him, I want you all to stand with me. It only seems right."

Lexi smirked. "Just don't make us wear stupid-looking dresses. Okay?"

"Don't worry, Lex. I'll make sure they have plunging necklines."

Jema mocked horror. "You can't do that, it would be too expensive."

Lexi tilted her head. "Expensive?"

"Yeah," said Jema. "I'll need to get a boob job."

I waved her off. "Pffft. Yours look just fine. In fact, we all do. We are goddesses."

Stan laughed. "And I'm honored to be in your temple."

In the past couple of days, my life had been transported into a fairy tale where everything was happily ever after. What could possibly go wrong?

Chapter 17

AVALEE
Visitors

Monday morning Jema knocked on the door and called, "Anybody home?"

"I'm in the kitchen."

She lumbered inside, loaded down with empty bowls and casserole dishes. In each one was a piece of candy. "My momma taught me to never return an empty dish. This is the best I could do."

"Oh, you silly." I unburdened her from her load. "Coffee?"

"Yes, thanks. I've only had one pot."

We sat at the table under the laughing tomatoes, smiling carrots, grinning celery, and smirking onions.

Jema looked around the room. "I see everything is back in order since our Thanksgiving feast. As usual, the meal was delicious. I'm still stuffed."

I sipped my coffee. "Well, Momma said it was the first time she'd cooked Thanksgiving dinner with such little thought. Molly Kate's wedding has trumped everything, seeing how it's only a few weeks away."

Jema stared dreamily over her cup. "I know. Isn't it romantic?"

"Sure is. I'm calling in a lot of favors from New York City, including the services of my dear friend

Scott. He's flying in tomorrow. I can't wait to see him. Except I dread him seeing me."

"Whatever for?"

"He'll be horrified to see how much weight I've gained."

She waved me off. "Oh pashaw. You look exactly the same. Only better."

"Ten pounds better." I stood to refill my cup. "Oh well, when he tastes Momma's cooking, he'll remember how good it was when she cooked for us in New York. Hopefully he'll give me some grace."

I leaned against the counter. "But you haven't heard anything yet. Guess who else is coming."

"Who?"

"Nathan Wolfe. He's coming today."

Jema's lips parted in a sly smile. "Lexi is going to die."

"I know. But it gets better. He emailed and said he couldn't find a room in a hotel anywhere within a fifty mile radius of this—well, I won't repeat what he called our little town—because everything was full for the holidays. So I invited him to stay here. The problem is I offered before I knew about the wedding. I'm afraid he'll have to be on his own."

"I guess we could see if Lexi will entertain him." Jema giggled.

"Wouldn't that be interesting?"

"Very." She frowned and cocked her head. "Why is he coming?"

"He's investigating something." I held out the pot. "More?"

"Definitely."

"Seems there is a missing millionaire, or

billionaire, can't remember. Something about his being kidnapped, I think. Anyway, someone has picked up on a paper trail close to here."

"Oh." Jema studied her cup. "Do you know this man's name?"

"Nathan said it was, oh shoot. I can't remember. Matthew something."

Her face paled. "Matthew Abrams?"

I returned to the table and sat. "Yes. That's it. Jemms? What's wrong?"

Her eyes glistened. "Nothing."

"Yes, there is, what is it?"

"Really. I'm fine. Thanks for the coffee." She stood. "I have to go."

Pushing the chair back, I got up and reached out to her. "Jema?"

Shaking her head, she hurried out the door.

Well, great. One more thing to worry about. Wedding flowers, fireworks between Nathan and Lexi, Scott's chastening, and now Jema. What in the world was wrong with her? The phone rang and scared the bejezus out of me.

"Hello?"

"Where in this hayseed place am I?"

"It's good to talk to you too, Nate."

"Sorry. How are you?"

"Crazy. Didn't you get a GPS?"

"Yes, but I don't know how to use the darned thing. I take taxis, remember?"

"You are such a diva." *Lexi was going to eat this man for lunch.* "What was the last town you passed?"

"Tup something."

"Tupelo."

"Sounds right."

"You are almost here then. Just turn north on the Natchez Trace. That's the easiest way when you don't know where you are going. Then take the Moonlight exit. And *do not* go over the speed limit. There is no tolerance. The police will nail your rear."

"I can just imagine. I'm getting Bubba vibes all over the place. It'll be awhile before I get there. I think I'll stop for breakfast at one of the local cafés."

"Be sure and get grits." I snickered.

"Why do I suddenly feel alarmed?"

"No need to be alarmed. They're good. Really. With a lot of butter, salt, and pepper."

"Maybe, but I'm not promising anything. Now, if I take about forty-five minutes for breakfast, how long will it take to drive to Moonlight?"

"About an hour."

"Then I'll see you in a couple of hours. That gives me time to get lost a few times."

"You really need to learn how to operate a GPS."

"I do. Just didn't think I needed it."

"Yeah, right."

"I'll sign off for now. But keep your phone on and close."

"All right. See you in a few. I'll have hot coffee ready and just so you know, saying no to my Momma when she offers you food is the ultimate insult."

"Shouldn't be a problem. I'll eat a light breakfast. Skip the grits."

"Good. Be careful."

"Bye, beautiful."

"Bye."

Momma walked in on the last of my conversation.

"Who was that?'

"Nathan Wolfe."

"Oh my goodness, is he nearly here? I don't have a thing ready."

"Really, Mom? We can hardly shut the refrigerator door. And someone has to eat all this cake and pie to make room for all the cooking you are going to be doing for the wedding."

"I can't serve a guest leftovers. Especially one from New York."

"Don't worry about it Mom. He's here on business. He'll probably eat out most of the time. And when Scott comes tomorrow—"

"—Oh Lordy, I forgot about him. I need to make a list. Honey, run to Pigg's for me, will you?"

"Momma, relax. There is plenty. And while I'm thinking about it, do you remember how he was always on my case about my weight?"

She nodded. "Yes, I do."

"I want you to do your best and put a few pounds on Scott just for meanness."

"Well, when I visited, he didn't hold back on anything I cooked. Best I can remember, he ate everything."

"I know. And since his guard will be down. We can empty out the freezer. Fry chicken, fry catfish, and feed skinny Scott. Okay?"

"Oooooh." A conspirator gleam glinted in her eyes. She clicked her tongue. "Gotcha."

The little yellow bird on the Swiss chalet clock cheeped nine o'clock. I had just enough time to meet Ty and Molly Kate at her new house to talk about decoration plans. Ty's job was to take pictures of all the areas where she wanted flowers so I could custom design the arrangements for that space.

"I'm gone, Mom. I'm meeting Ty and Molly at the mansion. I'll be back in about an hour." I clutched my purse and ran out the door.

The Norton place, or should I say the Montgomery place, was beautiful any season of the year. Even in winter. The white columned lady stood gracefully on her generous acreage. Winter had stripped the lush greenery from the old oak trees, exhibiting their twisted branches like fine sculptures. The blooms were gone from the crepe myrtles, azaleas, and rose bushes leaving lacy stems and shoots. Grandiose magnolia trees stood around her like evergreen sentinels. Their leaves and pods would make beautiful arrangements and lavish garlands.

Molly stepped on the porch and called out, "Well? What do you think?"

"I think I'm positively green with envy. That's what I think."

"Well, don't be. We are turning this into a business. A B&B." She hugged herself and shivered. "It's getting chilly. Get yourself inside, and I'll tell you all about it. Ty is already here."

I wandered up the gentle slope of the brick walkway toward the double mahogany front doors. This walk and entrance needed something to make a fabulous statement. I wanted a picture.

"Wait. Before I come in, would you tell Ty I need him and to bring his camera?"

She nodded and went inside. Soon Ty jogged out.

"Hi, babe."

With just two words he threw my mind spinning in

another direction. I needed to focus.

"Morning. Would you mind taking pictures of the walk, the front of the house, and the door?"

"Do I get a kiss?"

"What? No. We are working now."

"Now?" He winked. "That means there will be a later."

I gave him my most serious glare. "Get to work."

He stuck out his lip. "Yes, ma'am."

While he took pictures, I admired the covered porch which spanned the front of the house, the ornate columns, the full length black shuttered windows, and the cut-glass transom window fanning over the doors. When I was a little girl I used to stand on the sidewalk and wish I could see what it looked like inside. I wanted to play house on the porch and run in the yard. And now, I get to finally see inside. Who knows? This summer, I may just run in the yard.

"All finished." Ty took my hand and intertwined his fingers with mine. My business-like resolve vaporized.

When we stepped into the foyer, I caught my breath. I expected it to be lovely, but not this magnificent. The dark oak floors were so polished they reflected everything in the room. The walls were creamy white and trimmed with decorative molding from floor to ceiling. But the most elegant feature was the winding staircase. It had white risers and mahogany steps and balusters. A mahogany rail swept gracefully to the second floor and across the landing.

"Molly Kate Fairchild. This is more beautiful than I could possibly have imagined. And to think, you own it now. I can't believe it."

Molly sighed and looked around. "Me either." She placed her hand on my shoulder. "And I'm relieved you are decorating it for the wedding. I wouldn't have the first clue where to start."

Without me asking, Ty started snapping photos.

A round rosewood table stood to the left at the base of the stairs. I caressed the smooth surface and turned to Molly. "This would be a lovely place for a huge arrangement of white roses, white calla lilies, and maybe white poinsettias." I surveyed staircase. "Are you going to walk down the stairs for your wedding march?"

"Have you lost your ever-lovin mind? I'd kill myself." Molly took my hand. "Are you finished in here? I want you to see the east wing." She lifted her palms. "Doesn't that sound silly coming from me?"

Ty spoke up. "Well, now that you mention it..."

She tossed him a look. "Oh, hush up."

After a tour upstairs, we followed her into a large parlor. Adjoining the south side of the room was a double doorway opening into a large turret, a round room that appeared to have been used as a ballroom at one time. The ceiling had to be at least fourteen feet high with twelve-foot windows all around the circumference, except for one, which looked just like the other windows but was actually a door that opened to the plaza in the back. The windows were exquisitely trimmed in the most intricate molding I've ever seen.

"Molly, I have to ask. How on earth—"

"—could we afford it?"

I felt my face heat. "Well, yeah."

"Stan sold some stock which covered most of it. A developer has hounded him for over a year now wanting to buy his farm, and he is willing to pay top dollar."

"So how much acreage does Stan have?"

"A lot. Stan said it used to be a beautiful area, but when all the adjoining properties turned industrial, the quality of the land really deteriorated. The streams are dirty, and the animals are all but gone.

"The man who wants it plans to build a gated community, clean everything up, and make it a haven for young families. That was the deciding factor for Stan. He's meeting with the buyer soon. If all goes well, we'll have enough to pay off this house, buy the furniture in it, and still have a nice inheritance for his boys. A *real* nice inheritance for them."

"Wow. That's amazing."

Ty put his arm around Molly. "I know I'm just a guy and all, but in my opinion this would be the perfect room for the ceremony. Have you thought of that?"

"We wondered if this might be the best place, but we also wanted to have a room for dancing."

"As a matter of fact, you can do both." I turned to her. "Where is the reception going to be?"

"In the dining room."

"Well, while that is going on, you can hire some guys to rearrange the chairs, no problem. Is your dining room large enough for a reception?"

"I think so. Follow me."

We strolled through the parlor and passed through the foyer into a large dining room. Molly pointed to the wide window facing the west.

"We can put the cake and hors d'oeuvres there and set up round tables in the middle."

I nodded at Ty, and he started shooting. "Did you

hire a band?"

"Yes, and I'm so excited. I've arranged for the Stardust Big Band to play. My guests can dance all night long."

"Oh yeah." Ty smirked. "That's exactly what Stan will want to do."

She didn't miss a beat. "Hey, I didn't say me and Stan. Just do me a favor and lock the door when y'all leave, okay. We'll be busy."

"You got it, MK."

I thought about Momma. "Hey, is it all right to bring Momma over so she can see if the kitchen is to her liking."

"By all means. You want to see it now?"

"Sure." Molly led us to what had to equal if not surpass the kitchen at the country club. "I have a feeling it will pass Momma's muster with flying colors." I checked my watch. An hour and a half had already flown by. "Ohmigosh." I hugged Molly. I gotta run. Nathan will be here any moment."

"Oh boy." Molly shook her head. "Nathan versus Lexi. Won't this be fun to watch?"

"Loads."

Ty frowned. "Nathan?"

"A friend. Drop by later."

He reached for me, but I slipped by and dashed to the car.

Kissing the air I called over my shoulder. "See y'all later."

Twenty minutes after I walked into my house the phone rang.

"Hello Nate."

"I'm by a lake."

"Good. You are almost here. Go down Main Avenue to Washington Avenue, four lights down. Take a right on Washington, and we are on the corner of Washington and Moon Vine. It's the two-story house with a wraparound porch."

"With slaves working the cotton fields?"

"Oh, hush up, jerk."

"Kidding. Be there in a sec. Is the coffee ready?"

"It will be."

"Great. See ya."

I hung up the phone and started the coffee. In no time, Nate pulled in the driveway. I peeked out the kitchen window and noticed he had someone with him. *Oh Lord.* The last thing I needed was another houseguest. As much as I liked Nate, I wanted to wring his neck like a chicken. He got out of the car, but the person with him stayed inside. I guess he was at least going to ask permission first. Obviously he'd forgotten about Scott. His steps sounded on the porch and then the doorbell rang.

I swung the door open and there he stood in all his New York City glory—tight jeans, black pea coat, gray sweater, black and gray scarf. And whatever cologne he wore came from the gods.

"Hello, Avalee. Good to see you."

"Hi Nate. It's good to see you, and you don't smell bad either. Come on in. Coffee's ready. You might want to invite whoever is in the car, too."

"Oh, yeah, I have a little surprise for you."

"Surprise, huh?"

"Yeah, go inside and pour three cups. No peeking. Promise?"

More than a little curious, I promised and returned

to the kitchen. My back was to the door when someone called, "Girrrrlll, how much weight have you gained?"

I whirled around. "Scott!" He opened his arms in time for me to fly into them. "I can't believe it."

"Surprised?"

"Beyond surprised." I nestled into his jacket. His cologne was even more incredible than Nate's. But Scott always had impeccable taste.

Nate picked up his coffee grinning. I turned to him. "Did you have something to do with this?"

"He sure did," said Scott. "It made no sense for both of us to be driving from Memphis a day apart. Nate called and suggested we go together. So I got my special airport connection to change my ticket, no charge of course, and here I am."

Nate glanced at the smiling vegetables on Momma's kitchen walls and tried to suppress a grimace. Scott's mouth parted when he noticed the pink Depression glass in the corner hutch.

Yep, introducing these boys to the south was going to be fun. No doubt Scott would love it. Nate? I wasn't so sure.

The mudroom door slammed, and Momma called, "Avalee?"

"In the kitchen, Momma." I put my hands on Scott and Nate's shoulders. "Boys, you are in for a treat. I hope you are hungry."

Scott leaned over to Nate. "She isn't kidding. When Miss Cladie first visited Avalee in New York, she insisted I try fried green tomatoes. I drove her all over Manhattan looking for them, and we actually found some. I ate so many I made myself sick. Man, they were good."

Mom came bustling in and stopped short when she saw the boys. "Why, Scott. You came early." She strode to him and gave him a big hug. Then she looked at Nate. "And you must be Nathan." He held his hand out, which she ignored, and gave him a big hug, too.

"I see Avalee has made you coffee. How about some pecan pie to go with that?"

Nate opened his mouth, but Scott elbowed him and said, "We'd love some, Miss Cladie." He gestured to a chair. "Wouldn't we, Nate?"

He nodded. "Love some."

While we ate, Momma chatted with Scott and got caught up on his life since she saw him last. Nate listened with interest. I could see a story formulating in his head. Nothing escaped his study.

Someone knocked at the kitchen door, and before I could stand, Ty opened it. "I smell coffee."

Momma hailed him with her hand. "Come on in. I've got pie to go with that coffee."

"I knew you'd have something good to eat, and I'm starving."

"Ty, I'd like you to meet Scott."

"Ah, the roommate and best friend." He shook Scott's hand. "Glad I finally get to meet you."

"My pleasure, believe me."

Did I detect a slight blush in Ty's face? I held my hand toward Nate. "And this is Nathan Wolfe."

"Pleased to meet you." He shook Nate's hand. "I enjoy your work."

Of course this made an instant impression on Nate. "Thank you. I appreciate it."

Ty turned his back to us as he poured coffee. Scott eyed him up and down, then mouthed to me, "He's gorgeous."

I mouthed back, "And straight."

With mug in hand, Ty sat next to me. "Avalee, we need to go back to Molly Kate's. I've been looking over the pictures, and I have a few ideas I'd like to run by you."

Yeah, right. He wasn't fooling me. Mr. Nathan Wolfe had him worried. "Okay." I looked at Scott and Nathan. "Would you guys like to come?"

"Not me, sorry." Nathan set his fork on the empty plate. "I need to go over some things and get a plan of action for the next few days."

Scott stood and took the plates. "I'd love to go. Is the house nice?"

Ty peeked up at me. "Oh, you could say that."

"Momma? You need to come, too. I want you to see the kitchen."

She jumped up. "Love to. Let me get my purse." On her way out, she snatched the dishes from Scott. "You are a guest in this home. I don't want you doing the dishes." She turned to Ty. "Would you run tell Felix where I've gone?"

"Sure, Miss Cladie."

When Nathan, Ty, and Momma left the room, Scott settled back in his chair and nailed me with a look.

"Spill."

"What do you mean?"

"Oh, come on. I'm not blind. That man is hot for you."

"Scott. He's Marc's baby brother. He's twelve years younger than me."

"And your point is?"

"I'm too old for him."

"That's the stupidest thing I've ever heard you say, and you've said some doozies." He scooted closer to me. "That man has fallen for you. And I think you are falling for him."

"Oh, give me a break. You've been here less than an hour. How could you come up with such nonsense?"

"Lady, I can read you like a menu, and you are hungry. So is he. And don't give me that age thing. The only place you are old is inside." He sat back and crossed his leg over the other. "And you better do something about it."

I studied my dear friend. He was about the most handsome man I had ever seen. Dark brown hair and even darker eyes. And his expression was always a mix of sweetness and mischief. Unfortunately, his body was as toned as ever. But if Mom and I had anything to do with that, he'd pack on some pounds before he left. Lord it was good having him here.

"We're ready." Ty's gaze met mine and Scott's words, *you better do something about it,* replayed in my mind.

If only I could.

****

For supper Momma went all out. She invited Molly Kate and Stan before we left their house. Then, as soon as she got home, she called Jema and Lexi and asked them over. Of course Felix and Levi were invited, too. You'd never know she was cooking for eighty wedding guests in less than two weeks.

At the table Scott chose the chair next to Momma and asked her how she cooked each dish. I could see the menu forming in his mind for his next themed dinner party. Too bad there were no green tomatoes to be had.

Even so, he loved the fried okra. Momma told him it was *Southern popcorn.*

I kept glancing at Lexi and Nathan. Both were behaving which helped me relax a little. Jema sat next to Lexi, thank goodness. Her calm stilled Lexi's storm. Molly and Stan had their heads together making plans no doubt. Ty, Levi, and Felix discussed the greenhouse goings-on among other things men talk about.

Finally, Momma stood. "Let's have coffee and dessert in the parlor. You men go on, the girls and I will bring it to you in a minute."

In short order Lexi, Molly, and I had the table cleared and the dishes rinsed and loaded in the dishwasher while Momma and Jema made coffee and cut and plated generous slices of four-layer pecan-coconut cake.

"Hey Momma?" I nodded toward the parlor. "Make Scott's extra thick, okay?"

"Ohhh, yeah. The plan." Momma grinned and moved her knife over a quarter inch.

Scott didn't flinch when I gave him his piece. He dove right in. One would have thought it was his wedding night. He rolled his eyes upwards and groaned with pleasure.

"Miss Cladie, I must have this recipe." He lifted his fork and grinned at her. "I have a fabulous idea. Why don't we write a book together? How about *Southern Soirees* for the title? You can handle the menus and recipes, and I'll handle the decorating. How about it, darling?"

She slapped the tops of her knees and leaned forward. "Let's."

What Momma didn't understand was that Scott

wasn't kidding. I'd seen that look before. She had no idea what she was in for. Still, it *was* a good idea.

The conversation centered around Scott's proposal until Lexi spoke up.

"So, Nathan Wolfe. Exactly why are you here?"

He looked up from his plate, surprise registering on his face. He glanced around the room and cleared his throat. "Well, I suppose you've all heard about the kidnapped billionaire from Canada, Matthew Abrams?"

We all looked at him expectantly, and clueless I might add, except for Levi. His gaze stayed glued to the floor.

"Of course you haven't." Nathan's face reddened when he realized he had thought out loud. "I mean, it really isn't big news here in the States, yet."

Lexi chimed in. "I think I did hear something about that on the news awhile back."

Nathan nodded. "It's quite a mystery. Like putting together a puzzle. Nothing makes sense. For instance, Mr. Abrams is a large man who had several bodyguards. He wasn't what one would call an easy target. And yet he vanished into thin air. The bodyguards said they didn't see anything suspicious, and there was no sign of violence or forced entry at any of his homes."

"Maybe it was one of the body guards?" Lexi looked around the room. "Maybe they were bribed."

"That has been discussed. But the idea was dismissed." Nathan ran an appraising eye over Lexi. "I applaud your intuition."

Lexi actually blushed.

Levi alternately checked his watch and rubbed the back of his neck. Jema played checkers with her cake.

Something was wrong.

Nathan continued. "For weeks I've been putting together different scenarios about how the kidnapper got to him. Mr. Abrams is a renowned philanthropist, so perhaps the kidnapper earned his trust first. Maybe disguised himself or herself as someone in need? Another thing. The kidnapper left a strange note. I've read it so many times looking for clues I have it memorized. It said Mr. Abrams would be well taken care of, in fact, the kidnapper planned on returning him to his family in better shape than when he had taken him. He said the kidnapping was for his own good. He ended it with the statement that the family would just have to *trust him*."

Jema jerked her head up stared at Levi. He cleared his throat. "Miss Cladie, supper was delicious as always. But I have a busy day tomorrow. If you would all excuse me. I think I'll turn in."

He stood, nodded, and strode to the mudroom. Seconds later, the door slammed. Jema jumped up. "Thank you, Miss Cladie, I have to go, too." She waved at Nathan and Scott. "Nice to meet you boys." She hurried away, the door slamming soon after.

Scott grinned. "Well, I think I'm going to like it here in the South. It's been a while since I've been called a boy."

Nathan just stared in the direction where Levi and Jema exited. He was onto something, and I had a sick feeling he was right.

Chapter 18

JEMA
Gone

I jogged to catch up with Levi. "Wait. Please." He stopped but didn't turn around. I crossed in front of him. "We need to talk."

Never looking up, he simply said, "I know."

Taking his hand, I urged him to follow me. "We can't talk here. Let's go to my place."

He shook his head. "I don't think that's a good idea."

"Please. We need to talk." Fear stung my heart. He couldn't be the kidnapper. He just couldn't. He was too kind, too gentle, too... Nathan's words surfaced to haunt me, *perhaps the kidnapper earned his trust first. Maybe disguised himself or herself as someone in need?*

Everything in me cried no. Oh God, please, no.

He stared at me as if he could see my pain and finally said, "All right, then."

When we got to my house, he sank on the couch, and I poured two glasses of wine. He took his and focused on it like a fortune teller stares into a crystal ball.

I fortified myself with a large swig and then said, "The other day at Lifesource when that limo drove up and you left. Remember?"

He nodded and took a drink.

"The man asked me if I'd seen a Mr. Matthew Abrams."

Again, he just nodded.

"Levi? Do you know this man?"

He drank the rest of his wine. Set the glass down and drilled me with his deep brown eyes. "Do you love me?"

Well, I didn't see that coming. I stared at him.

"I must know. Could you possibly love me? Even though I'm a homeless, penniless, man with no future to speak of except working for Miss Cladie?

My heart gave me back my voice. "Yes, Levi. I can. I do."

"Then I'm going to trust you with a strict confidence. And let me preface it first by saying, things are not always as they seem." He looked away and rubbed his chin. Then turned back to me. His face was like stone. "Yes. I kidnapped Matthew Abrams."

No. I couldn't breathe. A hum buzzed in my ears.

He pulled me close and whispered, "Please, trust me. Mr. Abrams is fine. My business with him is finished, and he will soon be free. I'm going away tonight. Please don't tell anyone you know about my leaving or anything about the kidnapping. They will only make your life miserable."

"Levi? Why did you take him?"

"He asked me to."

"He what?"

Levi leaned over and kissed me before standing. "I can't say anymore. Only that I love you, Jema." After one last look, he walked out and disappeared in the dark.

I stood in a trance at the door when the phone rang. The display said Olivia. I closed the door and answered.

"Hello?"

"Hi, Mom."

The sweet voice of my youngest soothed my frazzled emotions. "Hi, baby, how are you? Everything okay?"

"Yes, great actually. Only..."

So much for soothed frazzled emotions. My stomach tightened.

"Only what?"

"Well, Amanda and I have been invited to Italy for the holidays by one of our sorority sisters. All expenses paid."

"Italy?" Lord knows I wanted to be happy for my daughters. *But Italy?* I swallowed hard and tried to sound convincing. "How exciting. Of course, Christmas won't be the same without you, but you would be crazy to pass this up."

Her voice softened. "But I'm worried about you, Mom. Spending Christmas alone."

My eyes grew hot and moist. "Oh, don't worry about me. I have Cladie Mae."

Our conversation turned to school, grades, her music, and the young man she had met. He played country and western, like her, and they were writing songs together. They even had some gigs lined up at local bars.

After we hung up, I opened a bottle of wine, poured a glass full, and proceeded to cry for hours.

The next morning I woke to someone beating on my door. I sat up and ran my hands over my face. My eyes burned from crying through the night, and my head pounded. Between self-pity and worrying about Levi, I'd gotten very little sleep. Thoughts like, what if he were caught freeing Mr. Abrams? What if Mr. Abrams didn't tell the truth? What if Levi wasn't telling the truth? What if Levi went to prison?

Whoever was on the other side of my door kept banging. "All right, all right. I'm coming." I threw on my fuzzy pink robe and slipped on my matching pink slippers. I looked like the energizer bunny, only I wasn't very energetic. Shuffling to the door, I swung it open to find Cladie on my porch all wild-eyed.

"He's gone."

I about said, "I know." But I remembered Levi's warning. So instead I played dumb. "Who?"

"Levi."

"How do you know?"

"He packed his clothes and left."

My heart sank, and I wanted to cry. If he got caught and sent to jail I'd never see him again. Cladie speared me with a look. "You know, don't you?"

"Know what? I don't know what you are talking about."

She pushed in, took me by the elbow and led me to the kitchen table. "Now you sit there, and I'll fix us some coffee." After banging every cabinet I had looking for what she needed, she brewed up Kona Blend and brought over two mugs. As she eased down in the chair, Cladie leaned forward and lowered her voice in a conspiratorial tone. "That boy didn't kidnap anyone."

But he did. I didn't think I had any more tears left, but once again they streamed down my face. She hurried to my side and gathered me up in her arms and rocked me back and forth with her cheek against my head. "There is a logical explanation for all of this mess. I don't know what it is. But that boy just doesn't strike me as a kidnapper. And if he did, well, there is a perfectly good reason."

When I'd regained composure, I said, "Cladie, I don't know what to think about anything right now."

"Well, I for one am giving him the benefit of the doubt." She cocked her head to one side and pursed her lips. "I think Nathan Wolfe had something to do with this. Everyone was fine until he started talking about that kidnapper's note. And if that Yankee comes in my kitchen asking questions, I'll give him what for."

"Same here. I don't want him getting all up in my business either." I laid my face in my hands thanking God that Cladie was convinced of Levi's innocence. When Nathan began all that nonsense, I could tell everyone swallowed his implication of Levi's guilt like a fish swallows a hook. I peered up at her and smiled. "Thank you, Cladie."

"Don't you worry, honey. Everything will work out. Just you wait and see." She slapped the table "Well. This ain't getting the baby diapered. I'd better go help Felix in the greenhouse." She rose and said, "I think he's going to miss Levi."

"Yeah. I know." I stood and hugged her. "Hey, thanks. I needed someone to talk to."

She patted my arm. "We'll stick together on this one, honey."

As she made her way across the street, I counted my blessings and thanked God for Cladie, my biggest blessing of all.

Chapter 19

LEXI
Suspicions

I stared into my makeup mirror and thought about last night. Wow. Levi and Jema sure broke up the party. The way Miss Cladie got to her feet and started clearing dishes, I could tell she was on to something, too. When she escaped to the kitchen, Scott followed her leaving me, Avalee, and Nathan alone in the room.

Awkward.

It could have been worse though. While Avalee and I chatted, Nathan sat across from us so preoccupied I don't think he even knew we were there which gave me plenty of time to give him a thorough going over. I had Googled him earlier and found out he was in his early sixties. I would have never guessed. No doubt about it, he was one fine-looking man. He still had a full head of hair with a fringe of gray at the temples. His eyebrows were a little bushier than I liked, an easy fix. I decided to suggest a trim when I got to know him better. The expression in his eyes fascinated me the most. No matter who spoke, he pierced them with his icy blue stare as if reading between the lines of what they were saying, as if trying to read their thoughts. I guess that's what makes him a *world famous* reporter.

Ack, I hated it when I reminded myself of that little

tidbit of information. Heat rose up my neck and burned my face every time I thought about it.

He had a nice jaw line even though age had softened it. And he was in great physical shape, something I noticed right away. Clearly, he was above average intelligence, which irritated me. I hate people who are always right. However, everything considered, he wasn't bad. Not bad at all.

I glanced at the clock. Shoot. If I didn't get a move on, I'd be late—again. Nathan said he wanted to drop by the office this morning. This called for me looking better than normal. No. I had to look fabulous.

By the time I finished choosing what to wear, there wasn't a single thing in my closet that remained on a hanger. I decided on my black Chico pants because they made me look slimmer, a candy apple red cowl-neck sweater for pop, a wide black belt that made my waist look thinner, and black high-heeled boots that made me look taller. I took extra pains with my hair and makeup too. After one last swipe of red lipstick, I was out the door.

On the way to work it occurred to me it really didn't matter if I was late. When I told Vince that Nathan planned on dropping by, he'd be putty in my hands. Therefore, I decided to make a quick stop at Molly Kate's shop for a latte.

When I walked in the office, Vince stared over the round rims of his glasses like a snake preparing to strike. It was hard to be intimidated when his bald head reflected the fluorescent light above him.

"Late again, Lowe."

Oh, I was so hoping he'd say that. I leaned against his door and studied my nails. "Well, I guess I could have told Nathan Wolfe I didn't have *time* for coffee and no, he couldn't possibly drop by later this morning."

"Nathan Wolfe? Coming here?"

"I believe that's what I said." Batting my eyes. "But I could call and cancel. In fact, I will as soon as I get to my office." I waggled my fingers and started down the hall.

Vince jumped up and followed me so close he nearly wore my boots. "Do that and you are fired."

He turned on his heel and ran down the hall barking orders to everyone within ear shot, "Clean this place up, look smart, look busy, get all those crappy tchotchkes off your desks, look professional, for crying out loud."

Well, that ought to keep you busy for a while. I settled at my desk and sipped my Cinnamon Dolce while the computer powered up. When I clicked on email, I sucked coffee into my lungs which sent me into a fit of coughing. *Nine hundred responses* to my last column? *No way.* I scrolled through them, scanning the first lines. Most were from men. Men! Men actually read my column? Several were from mistresses, too. I hated to admit it—again—but Nathan was right.

Ty stuck his head in the door. "Hey. What's up with Vince?"

"Nathan Wolfe is coming by."

"Oh. Great. I don't like the guy."

"And why is that?"

"The way he zeroed in on Levi, like a heat-seeking missile. No wonder the guy skipped town."

"Skipped town? Levi left?"

Ty clomped over and dropped in the seat by my

desk. "Yup. Packed up and gone."

"But Nathan hardly said a word to him."

"He could have carved marble with that stare of his. And he zeroed it fully on Levi. For some reason, Levi was in his crosshairs. I think he tried to intimidate him."

"Oh, you're imagining things."

Before Ty could answer, the phone rang.

"Hello?"

"Hi, Lexi. Nate here." I mouthed, *Nathan,* to Ty. He stood, waved, and left.

"Hi Nate."

"Mind if I drop by on my way to Jackson?"

"If you don't, I fear for my job."

"Excuse me?"

"You'll understand when you get here. Go north on Main and take a left on Martin Luther King Boulevard. The paper is on the corner of MLK and State Street."

"Okay. Be there as soon as I finish this enormous breakfast Miss Cladie has placed before me."

"Enjoy."

I hung up the phone and went to warn Vince. In all my years of knowing him, I've never seen him so frantic.

"Vince. Calm down." Sweat coursed down his face and large damp rings had formed under his arms. "Do you have another shirt in your office?"

"No, but I have a few at the dry cleaners ready for picking up."

"Thank goodness. Have someone run and get them. In the meantime freshen up. Splash your face and put on some deodorant for crying out loud. Got any?"

"Yeah, I keep a ditty bag in my desk."

"Good. As soon as your shirts get here, put one on. Nathan will be here after breakfast. You should have a good thirty minutes."

"Oh Jeez." He cast anxious glances around and zeroed in on Greg, the mailroom guy. "Greg, run down to the dry cleaners and get my shirts. There's fifty dollars in it for you if you can get back in ten minutes." Nothing more needed to be said. All we saw were the soles of Greg's shoes.

Thirty-five minutes later Nathan walked in holding his stomach. "Man. How do you tell that Cladie woman no?"

"It's a problem *and* the reason the women in this town are so, shall we say, curvaceous?"

"And just what, pray tell, do you call the men?"

"Fat."

"Why am I not surprised?"

"Mr. Wolfe. Nice of you to drop by." Vince strode toward him with his hand out and a goofy smile plastered on his face.

Nathan took his hand. "And you are?"

"Vince Marshall, editor in chief of the Moonlight Community News."

"Good to meet you." He looked around. "Quite a place you have here."

I swear I thought Vince was going to kiss the man's feet. "Would you like a tour?"

Peering at me, he covertly grinned. "No, maybe some other time. I'm on my way to Jackson to investigate a lead on a story I'm writing."

"Oh? Can you tell me about it?"

In mock alarm Nathan raised his eyebrows. "What? And have a cracker jack like you scoop me?"

A blush colored Vince's cheeks. Clearly pleased, he slid his hands in his pockets. "Well, you can't blame a guy for trying."

"But I do have an idea." Nathan put his arm around me. "Send Lexi with me. She can report highlights to you."

My mind flew back to my emails. "No, Nathan, I can't I'm—"

"—You can." Vince pointed to the door. "And you will."

Sakes. "Is it all right with you if I at least get my purse?"

He waved me off with his hand and smiled knowingly at Nathan. "Good luck. You are gonna need it."

"Oh, I'm sure I will."

I threw a smirk their way. "Careful or I'll embarrass you both in my next column." *I have nine hundred readers.*

Moments later we were speeding down Interstate 65 toward Jackson. In all my life I've never been known as a person at loss for words—until now. Sitting beside *a famous to everyone but me* journalist? Let's just say life had pushed my mute button. When I thought he was a nobody, I had no problem letting him know just what I thought. But when I found out he was Mr. CNN, Mr. FOX, MR. Every Alphabet News Station, even Mr. BBC for heaven's sake, I felt like a Mississippi hick. White trash. An idiot.

Nate glanced over and grinned. "You are quiet. I at least hoped you would have insulted me three or four times by now."

As bizarre as it seemed, his sarcasm relaxed me.

"May I remind you that I am a Southern lady, and we never insult a gentleman unless provoked? And you, sir, have not provoked me—yet." I returned his grin. "So the ball is in your court."

"I guess it will take me a while to learn how things are done in this strange culture."

"Where are you from?"

"New York City, born and bred."

"What do your parents do?"

"Both professors. How about you? Mississippi belle all your life?"

"Yes. I'm not so sure about the belle part, but Moonlight has always been my home."

"And your parents?"

"Don't ask."

"Ah. Don't you know that's like a carrot dangling before my nose?"

"No. Perhaps that is why I never made it as a reporter. Investigative that is."

"What kind of reporter do you consider yourself?"

"On life. At least, that is my passion. Maybe I'm more of an observer."

"So am I. Being observant is a must in investigative reporting. Seeing what isn't being said. Watching body language."

"Like the other night. I noticed you watching Levi. Reminded me of a hawk watching its prey. You didn't even blink."

"Levi knows what happened to Matthew Abrams. I have no doubt. I saw it in his eyes, his expression. Did you hear how his voice dropped? How he no longer made eye contact? All of a sudden he had an uncanny interest in his shoes. He began to fidget and quit eating."

Looking back, I realized Nathan was right. "I did notice but didn't think anything about it. And then he was gone the next day."

Nathan glanced over at me. "Coincidence? I don't think so."

"Well, he never would tell us where he came from or anything from his past."

"How did you meet him?"

"He was homeless. You should have seen him. The man was a mess. His hair was long, dirty, tangled. His clothes were filthy and torn. His hands were awful. All that dirt caked under his long fingernails. Blech."

"So he came to that homeless shelter, Lifesource, is it?"

"Uh huh. Jema got to know him first, and then she introduced him to us. She was, is, really drawn to him."

"Apparently Miss Cladie is too."

"Yeah, she paid for him to get his hair cut, loaned him clothes, and gave him a job. But still, I have to admit, he's a gentle, caring soul. Very quiet."

"They always are."

"They?"

"The kind who kidnap billionaires and lock them away for *their own good and the good of others.* The kind who say, 'Trust me.'"

Trust me? Levi tells Jema that all the time. A shiver ran across my shoulders and forced an involuntary swallow. "What do you hope to find in Jackson?"

"It just so happens some washers and dryers, as well as plumbing supplies, were recently donated to Lifesource. They were purchased in Jackson. The money to pay for them came from a bank account in Canada." Nathan glanced at me and lifted one brow. "Don't you find that odd?"

"Odd? In what way?"

"You really wouldn't make a good investigative reporter would you?"

Ouch. "Depends. It just so happens crime doesn't interest me."

"Cheating husbands do?"

"Yes. Relationships are my area. Now let's get back to yours. Crime. So what did you find so odd?"

"Mr. Abrams is from Canada. I think this guy, Levi, has a Robin Hood complex. And he feels perfectly justified stealing from Mr. Abrams."

Of course. It all made sense. Perfect sense. *Poor Jema.* "Do you think he has hurt Mr. Abrams?"

"Who knows? These kinds of people are unpredictable. But, if your friend thinks she is in love with this guy, you need to talk to her. That said, I don't think you will see this Levi character again, under his own free will, anyway. I intend to find him."

"So what's the plan when we get to Jackson?"

"We'll go to an industrial laundry equipment distributor where the mystery philanthropist purchased the equipment, ask who gave the order, who signed the check or get the credit card information, see what address was given for the receipt. Any information helps."

"What if they won't show you?"

"I have my bases covered. All the official-looking papers."

"Official-looking?"

"It's my turn to say, don't ask."

"Ooooh, I see."

When we arrived in Jackson, we made several stops. To Nathan's utter amazement, he learned Southerners loved to talk about anything and everything. No one, I mean no one, was close-mouthed about the mysterious orders for the washers and dryers or plumbing supplies. Even the delivery companies spilled all they knew. He never had to use his *official looking* papers.

Perhaps it is because these folks recognized him, unlike *moi.*

Store after store, business after business, the story was always the same. A woman ordered the equipment, gave the delivery instructions, and wired the money. When asked where to send the receipt, she said there was no need. All clean with no hint of who could have been behind the purchase.

By the end of the day, cool, confident, perfectly coiffed Nathan had raked his fingers through his hair so much it fell across his forehead. We were about to leave the Plumber's Pal Supply when I noticed the sales clerk lean against the counter, knit her brows, and chew the end of her pencil. Nathan looked her way and waved. "Well, thanks anyway."

I touched Nathan's arm. "Just a minute." Then I ambled over and leaned next to her. "It's strange that whoever purchased such a large order didn't want a receipt, isn't it?"

"Yes ma'am. It sure is."

Nathan dropped one eyebrow and faced us.

The salesclerk took her pencil out of her mouth and pointed at me. "I thought the same thing, and I said as much to that woman. And you know what she said? She said her boss instructed her to say he trusted us."

Both Nathan and I yanked our heads around and stared at each other.

She continued, "But that isn't all. Just the other day, a man in a long black limousine came here asking the same questions that you two are asking. He showed me a picture and asked me if I'd seen the man in the photo."

Nathan took over. "Did he say why he was looking for the man?"

"No."

"Did he mention the man's name?"

"He told me the name, but I can't remember what it was."

"Matthew Abrams?"

She waggled her pencil at Nathan. "Yes sir. That's what it was all right." She thought a moment. "And he sounded strange. Had a funny accent. She stuck the pencil behind her ear. "I don't mean to sound rude, but he sounded like you, sir."

At this I bit my tongue to keep from laughing out loud. He gave me a wry look then turned his attention back to her. "No offense taken. And thank you. You've been a lot of help."

Once we were in the car, Nathan asked, "Okay, how did you know to keep talking to her?"

"Just seeing what wasn't being said. Watching body language, you know, investigative stuff like that."

"Okay, I deserved that. How about a drink and some supper before we head back? Maybe we can connect the dots."

"Sounds lovely."

I could really get into this investigative stuff. And

if I saved Jema from this impostor, all the better.

Over a few drinks, we discussed our suspicions of Levi and how the evidence had coalesced into his obvious guilt as a kidnapper or possibly worse, a psychopathic murder.

Then we moved on to my article. To my utter surprise, he'd been following me. And those nine hundred men? He had put something in his column challenging men to read my column and answer me. I wanted to get angry with him, but between the twenty-five dollar an ounce bourbon drinks he kept ordering and the fact I was getting national attention, I found it in my heart to forgive him.

We ate a nice supper and then drank coffee. Lots of coffee before we felt safe enough to drive. It was a fabulous evening, and I had to admit he wasn't all that bad. In fact, he was kind of nice in a rude sort of way. I guessed it took all kinds. Right then and there I made it my goal for the word *y'all* to roll off his tongue like it was his mother language.

The next morning when the alarm clock rang at six, I got out of bed and emailed Vince informing him I wouldn't be in to work because Nate and I didn't get home until after two in the morning. I could get used to this. It was like having a permission form from the principal. He'd forgive anything as long as Nathan's name was attached.

My real reason for staying home, however, was to get to Jema before she left for work. I prayed all morning, *"God, please help her to see reason. Please."*

I downed two cups of coffee, pulled on my sweats, and jogged to her house. The steel-gray sky threatened snow. A rarity in Moonlight. Another thing to worry about.

Please hold off until after the wedding, okay?

When I came to her door, I rang the bell. No one answered. Then I started beating on it. No response. The wind blew icy daggers through me. I hugged myself and pounded again. *Where was she? Surely not at work this early? The shelter?*

"Lexi?" Jema stood on Miss Cladie's porch.

"Hey, I came over for coffee. We need to talk."

"Come on over here. I'm helping Cladie with the reception food."

"No. I need to talk to you alone. Please. I'm skipping work. It's that important."

She wrinkled her forehead and said, "Okay, just a sec. Go on in. I'll tell Cladie."

I hurried inside and started the coffee, all the while rehearsing what I would say and how to phrase it in a delicate and diplomatic way."

"Whoa, it's cold out there." Jema draped her coat on the back of a chair. "Okay, here I am." She took the cup I handed her. "What's all this about?"

"Oh Jema, Levi is a psychopathic kidnapper and murderer. Nathan and I investigated him yesterday. I'm so sorry."

She stared at me and sat down. "What?"

So much for delicacy.

Over coffee I related all Nate and I had learned. Her face remained relaxed, no sign of distress. Odd. I'd be over the moon. When I finished she smiled and shook her head. "No."

"No? What do you mean *no*?"

With a tenderness one uses with a cranky child, she put her hand on mine and smiled that huge, beautiful smile. "That isn't Levi. I can't explain it, but while I don't know his history, I know his soul. Whatever has happened, I'm sure of this, he's a good man."

I wanted to slap sense into her. "Jema!"

She patted my hand. "Stop. Don't go there. I won't hear it. And for Molly Kate's sake, we must forget all of this. I won't have her special day ruined because of such nonsense."

Jema had a point, to a certain degree. I didn't want this investigation to detract from Molly's wedding either.

If Jema wanted to be a fool... No. I couldn't let her destroy her life.

Even so, we women of Washington Avenue would deal with her after Molly left on her honeymoon, make no mistake about it. So I patted her hand right back. "You're right. Let's protect her day at all costs."

But what price would our dear Jema pay?

Chapter 20

MOLLY KATE
Attacked

Martini Monday! No better time to show the girls the wedding dress Carli and I found in Memphis. While I made cheese straws, I pictured their shocked expressions. Would it be the crimson red fabric? The beading and sequins? Maybe the strapless bodice? Most likely it would be the figure hugging lines that revealed every lovely bump and bulge of my bountiful frame.

Whatever. I simply didn't care what anyone thought. I'm a full figured gal, and I love it. Even more important, Stan loves my fat. Besides, if I lived in the sixteenth century, I would have been a sex symbol.

Last week the girls and I chose their dresses— strapless hunter green velvet gowns with green satin sashes. Of course, they all looked amazing, but *if they* had lived in the sixteenth century, they would have been pitied for their figures. *Ha!*

The only thing that bothered me about tonight was Avalee's insisting Scott come. So strange. Why in the world would a man want to have martinis with a bunch of women discussing a wedding? Sure, they are best friends, former roommates no less. Something has to be going on. I don't care what Avalee says about their relationship being strictly platonic. That boy's way too handsome. Maybe they were rekindling the fire? If so, I felt for poor Ty.

The doorbell rang, and I nearly jumped out of my apron. Before I answered, I slipped the straws into the oven and wiped my hands on a dishtowel. It rang again, and Avalee called through the door. "Hurry up. It's freezing out here."

"I'm coming." *Sakes alive why don't you just walk in like you always do?* When I got to the door, I realized it was still locked. *Well no wonder.* I swung the door open. "Come in before you catch your death. Sorry about the locked door. I've been so busy today, I haven't even gone outside to get the paper."

Scott grinned. "You girls call this cold? Come see me in the city and let's take a walk down Rector Street and get blasted by the wind tunnels. Then you will experience cold."

Avalee flipped her hand up. "And when you call it hot in August there, come here. Hell is just around the corner."

"Yup." I took their coats. "As my father-in-law used to say, 'Everything is relative.' Avalee, honey, why don't you mix us up a martini, and I'll get the cheese straws out to cool and crisp up. Oh, and make mine with gin." I turned to Scott. "How do you want yours?"

"Vodka."

"Did you hear that Avalee?"

"Yeah, I know how he likes them."

Of course you do. She wasn't fooling me one little bit.

"Mmmm, cheese straws huh? Smells delish." Scott followed me to the kitchen. "What's in them?"

I lifted the cooking stone from the oven and set it on the stovetop. "Oh, we Southerners have all kinds of recipes for them."

Avalee chimed in from the living room, "And we all think ours is best."

"Think?" I smirked at Scott and answered back, "I *know* mine are the best." I scooped one up with the spatula and put it on a napkin, then handed it to him.

He took a bite, closed his eyes, and inhaled. "Oh my, I'm having an out-of-body experience." He pointed to the stone. "What did you say were in those?"

"I didn't, *but*, if you'll include me in your book, I'll tell."

"Done. So tell me."

"Flour, butter, cheese, and lots of cayenne pepper. Some people put spices, but I like to keep it simple and let the cheese do the talking."

"I taste cheddar."

"Sharp cheddar. None of that wimpy mild stuff. And I add Gruyère for its nutty, sweet flavor."

Avalee eased in the kitchen balancing three drinks. "I hope you don't mind us coming early, but we wanted to discuss your bridal bouquet. Scott had some concerns.

"Concerns?" I sipped my Rangpur gin martini. I loved the hint of citrus.

"Well..." Scott glanced at Avalee and she nodded. "What you've described has a lot going on. Red roses, white poinsettias, holly berries and magnolia leaves, calla lilies and baby's breath. Honey, you will need a sling to help you carry it. It'll be so big no one will see *you*."

I waved him off. "Oh pshaw. The gaudier the

better.'"

"I get that. My boyfriend says the same thing. We argue all the time about how to decorate our apartment."

"*Boyfriend?*" I shot a look at Avalee. Then back at Scott. "You? You're...?"

"Gay? Yeah, you didn't know?" Scott grinned at Avalee. "I thought you had told your friends. Or did you want them to think we were living in sin?"

"It just never occurred to me to say anything." Ava looked at me with a quizzical expression. "You okay?"

"I'm fine." But I wasn't. More like tongue-tied, embarrassed, at a total loss for words. "It's just that … well, I've never met a homosexual before." My face burned. *Shut up, Molly Kate, for heaven's sakes.*

Scott touched my arm. "It's all right. Being gay isn't contagious. You're safe."

His remark struck me as funny, and I got the giggles. *Those* were contagious. We all laughed till we were dabbing our eyes with our sleeves.

"Well now, at least *that* mystery is cleared up."

Avalee frowned. "What mystery?"

"How you could live with such a good-looking man without, well, you know."

Scott started laughing again. "Molly Kate, you and I are going to be great friends. I can tell already."

"Good." I wrapped my arm around his and lead him to the couch. "Let's get to business. So what do you suggest?"

"How about a delicate balance of white rose buds, white Calla Lilies, with pops of red holly berries and green holly leaves?"

"Sounds pretty. It will look beautiful against my

dress."

Avalee raised her eyebrows. "You bought one? I want to see it."

"When the girls get here. I'll model it."

The words had no sooner left my mouth than Jema and Lexi rushed in with their bags and plates. Lexi set her Grey Goose on the bar and rubbed her hands together. "It's freezing out there."

Jema took her platter to the kitchen. Once again, like a starving puppy, Scott followed. "What did *you* bring?"

She lifted the foil. "Fried up some dill pickles and made hot crab dip."

"Fried pickles?" Scott's look of wonderment could have easily matched a child seeing Santa Claus land on his roof.

"Try some." She held the platter up.

He took one and popped it in his mouth. While he chewed, a slight shiver shook through his shoulders. "That's *incredible*. The marriage of flaky fried goodness and tangy pickle ought to be illegal." He took a couple more.

Since everyone had arrived, I decided it was time for the fashion show. "Y'all have your drinks. I'm going to put on my wedding dress and model it for you."

Lexi looked up while pouring her martini. "When did you get it?"

"Avalee will fill you in. And be careful, you're missing your glass."

"Oh, shoot." Lexi grabbed a napkin and mopped up her spill. "What a waste."

I motioned to Jema. "Come help me?"

"Sure thing."

When we were in my room, I closed the door and pulled the dress out of the closet. Jema's eyes widened.

"Oh, my word. Molly Kate. It's beautiful. It's... positively wicked. I love it."

"Wait until you see it on."

It took a while to wiggle it on and awhile longer for Jema to zip it up. I had a vague understanding how Marilyn Monroe must have felt when she was sewn into her dress before singing for the president. Thank goodness for the thigh-high slit on the side or I wouldn't be able to walk at all. After positioning *the twins* in the strapless, beaded bodice, I made a slow turn for Jema. "Well?"

"All I have to say is you better not let Stan see you in it until the wedding or he just may want to elope. You're stunning."

"Let's go show the girls."

"And Scott."

"And Scott. Oh, FYI, he's gay. In case you didn't know. I made an idiot out of myself when I found out."

Jema frowned. "No, I didn't know."

I nodded. "Yep."

"That's too bad for women everywhere. He sure is fine looking."

"Yea, I know."

When I made my entrance, all talking stopped. Just as I had hoped. "Didn't think an ample woman like me had the nerve, did you?"

Lexi was the first to find her voice. "Hoooneeey, do you ever have some pumpkins on *your* porch. Wow."

Avalee walked around me taking it all in. "You are

gorgeous. I'll bet Stan has never had a Christmas gift wrapped up so pretty."

Scott delivered the best compliment of all when he said, "Lady, I'm rethinking my orientation."

I raised my empty martini glass. "Here, here! High praise indeed!"

"A toast to the bride-to-be." Jema passed out flutes of champagne.

We all hoisted our glasses and then drank. While everyone laughed and talked, I surveyed the room. This would be the last time we'd meet like this in my house on Washington Avenue. A lot of sweet memories lingered here. In a few days, I'd live in my new home on Nightingale. It felt so bittersweet. The page in my life was about to turn, but I had no regrets. Fools refuse to move forward into the future. And I'm no fool.

****

The move to our new home was a simple matter of packing up my clothes, my cat, the things I couldn't bring myself to leave, and walking out the door. Since I didn't need the furniture, I left everything for Carli. After all, her life began on Washington Avenue, and all her childhood memories were made in this house.

After I'd cleared out my stuff, we met in *her* new home and walked through it room by room, reminiscing, weeping, laughing. When we finished, I gave her the keys.

"Here, baby. From your momma and daddy."

She took the keys and held them to her heart. "Thank you, Mom." Then she lifted her face. "Thanks, Dad."

No more duplex living for her. She was now a homeowner, and her girls had rooms of their own.

As if I hadn't been blessed enough already, I was overjoyed how Carli and Stan had bonded on the spot. He had always wanted a daughter. She needed a father, and her girls needed a grandfather. It was all so right. I hoped Stan's sons and I would bond like Stan and Carli.

In no time, Gypsy and I had settled, more like nestled, into our new home. As strange as it sounded, it seemed as if the house was pleased to have residents once again. Gypsy spent most of her time exploring interesting nooks and crannies. Me? I loved reading in the sunroom that connected our house to what would eventually be the Norton Mansion B&B. Stan and I had discussed other names for the business, such as Montgomery House or Moonlight B&B, but I felt we should preserve the historical integrity of the mansion. And I think Mr. and Mrs. Norton, God rest their souls, would approve. And if by chance any of the Norton family came by, I hoped they would appreciate it, too. We also decided to keep the Norton family portraits on the walls. Apparently, the paintings were either too large for the homes of the remaining family members, or they didn't fit the family's decorating schemes. It seemed like such a shame to put them in storage where they'd be forgotten.

After Stan and I returned from our honeymoon, I intended on researching the Nortons and have their historical information available for our guests. Who knows? I may even invent a ghost. I heard haunted rooms always stay full.

For the past few weeks, Avalee and Scott practically lived at the house, sketching and planning. To be honest, I was glad for the company. Overwhelmed didn't begin to describe me, and they kept me organized. In five days I would be married in a virtual fairy tale. Scott bought Christmas trees for every room. We all decorated them together while eating cookies, drinking eggnog, and listening to Bing Crosby. Garland graced every doorframe and flowed down the banister. But what made it a real fairyland were the thousands of tiny white lights. When the rooms were dark, it looked like brilliant stars sparkled everywhere.

I spent my days roaming from room to room imagining my life with Stan. How I wished he were with me instead of in Salina finalizing the sale of his farm. I picked Gypsy up and rubbed my cheek against her soft fur.

"I'm ready for daddy to come home. How about you?"

"Mrrr?"

"I'll take that as a yes."

I put my cat-child down and decided to make a cup of tea. When I passed through the foyer I heard footsteps thump across the porch, and then the doorbell rang. Who could that be? I wasn't expecting anyone?

When I opened the door, I couldn't believe my eyes. It was as if I had gone back in time. There stood the Stan I knew years ago. This *had* to be his son.

"Yes? May I help you?"

"I'm looking for a Mrs. Fairchild."

"I'm Mrs. Fairchild."

"Do you have a daughter named Molly Kate?"

"No. I am Molly Kate."

The man stepped back with a quizzical expression, then studied me from head to foot. His mouth hardened in a thin line, and he shook his head.

"You must be Stan's son. You look just like him."

"I am. Stanley Jr."

I stuck out my hand. "I'm so glad to finally meet you."

He stepped back and clenched his hands against his sides. "Mrs. Fairchild. This is no social call. I need to speak with you."

Alarm raced through me. My heart slammed so hard I could hear it. I gripped the door to steady myself. "Stan? Has something happened? Is he all right?"

"Something has happened all right, and no. In my opinion he isn't all right. You have a lot to do with that."

Cold wind lifted my hair and whipped it in my face. Just what was he saying? "It's chilly out here. Come in and let's talk." He stepped into the foyer. "Make yourself comfortable in the parlor, and I'll bring some coffee to warm us up."

"No ma'am. I'll not go another step in this godforsaken house."

"I beg your pardon?" This boy began to frighten me.

"Look. I don't know how you did it, but my father has sold his land and his farm and bought this monstrosity. For who? *You*? A stranger he met on the Internet? I at least expected some voluptuous twenty-year-old. Not someone so," he twisted his mouth in disgust, "so, matronly. How did you do it? Are you blackmailing him?"

By now the man's face flamed red. His blue eyes took on an iridescent glow. Sweat beaded his brow and wisps of hair stuck to his forehead.

"My dad and mom were married forty years. Did you hear that? *Forty years*. He loved my mom. There has never, *ever,* been any other woman in his life. They built their farm together." He pointed his finger in my face. "It was supposed to be my brother's and my inheritance. I find it strange that in a few months' time he sells it all for a woman he barely knows. And why? It can't be your looks. It clearly has to be something else."

I knew I should say something in my defense, tell him I knew his dad before his mother knew him. But I was so dumbfounded I just stood there speechless.

Like a gathering storm his anger grew. He flailed his arms and spewed obscenities. His lips turned back over his teeth in a snarl, and he stepped closer and closer, invading my personal space. "I promise you this." He pressed his finger in my chest. "I will find out."

The room took on a surreal appearance. Stanley Jr.'s voice sounded distant. Once again I heard my heart's erratic beats. Tiny lights flashed before my eyes, and I flailed for the stair rail.

He turned and stomped to the door. Before he left, he gripped the knob and looked over his shoulder. "I'll make you another promise. If you marry my father, he will never see his sons or his grandchildren ever again." After a hard glare, he turned and slammed the door behind him.

My back hurt, I couldn't catch my breath. I wanted to throw up. God, help me.

Chapter 21

AVALEE
Last Word

I started out the kitchen door on my way to pick up a few things for Momma at the Piggly Wiggly when the phone rang. Never fails. "Hello?"

"Help me...please."

The breathless whisper made it hard to recognize the voice on the other end, but it sounded like...

"Molly Kate?"

"Call 911."

Panic seized me by the throat, and I screamed into the phone, "Molly? What's wrong?" The line went dead.

Momma ran into the kitchen. "Good Lord, what's wrong? What's happened?"

"I don't know. Call 911, and tell them to get to the Norton place. Something has happened to Molly Kate. I'm going over there right now."

Mom grabbed the phone and started punching. I flew out the door, jumped in the car, and roared toward Molly's. When I turned down Leslie Lane, I noticed a man standing on the corner, staring at her house. The ambulance had already arrived. I dashed up the walk and ran inside. Molly was on the stretcher mumbling answers to the EMT's questions. They put an oxygen mask on her face, kicked the gurney wheels up, and rushed her toward the ambulance.

I reached for one of the EMT's arms. "What happened? What's wrong with her?"

Without looking back he yelled. "Possible heart attack."

"Heart attack?" I watched from the doorway, frozen to the spot, helpless, as they slipped Molly into the ambulance and sped away. The man who watched from the corner approached me, clearly distressed.

"What happened to that lady?"

"Heart attack, they think." Fear buckled my knees. My body wracked and I cried out, "Oh, dear God. Please don't take her. Please."

He knelt beside me. "You know her pretty well?"

Tears blurred my vision, but I could swear I had seen this man before. "I've known her all my life. There isn't a kinder, more giving, loving, honest, or harder working person in the world. I'd be lost without her."

He ran his hand over his face. "Damn." And then he stood and left.

How strange.

Finally I got my emotions under control enough to call Stan. When he answered, I whispered a prayer of thanks. "Hi, Stan. Listen, honey, I have some bad news."

"Molly? Has something happened to her? What? *What?*"

The level of panic in his voice made it hard for me to keep my composure. Tears forced their way to my eyes and my voice cracked. "We think she's had a heart attack. They are taking her to the hospital."

"Oh God, help me. I'm almost home. I'll meet you

there." He hung up.

I jumped in my car, threw it in reverse, and spun onto the street, straightened it out, and then pressed the accelerator, daring a policeman to stop me. This was an emergency.

By the time I arrived at the ER, they had already taken Molly Kate in for tests. In the far corner of the waiting room, I noticed that man again.

This was getting weird. What did he have to do with Molly Kate? While trying to determine if I needed to approach him myself or get security, Carli, Jema, and Lexi ran in.

Carli's face was streaked with tears. "Where's Mom?"

"How is she?" Jema threw her purse in a chair. "Miss Cladie just called. Is she okay?"

Lexi slumped in a chrome and black vinyl seat and laid her head in her hands. "She has to be. She just has to be."

The man in the corner leaned over and rested his arms on his knees, hung his head, and then I noticed his shoulders shaking. I made up my mind to go speak to him, but then Stan ran in. "Where is she? Where's Molly? Please tell me she is still with us." He bent over and braced himself with his hands on his thighs trying to catch his breath between sobs.

I never could bear hearing a man cry, much less completely break down. I hurried over to him with Jema and Lexi close behind. We enveloped him in a hug.

"Yes," I whispered. "She's in for tests. All we can do is wait."

We led him to a chair. After a while, he gained

control and reached in his pocket for a handkerchief. When he lifted his bloodshot eyes, he noticed the man in the corner staring at him.

Stan froze. Then said, "Stanley?"

The man in the corner looked away.

Stan lurched forward and strode to him. "Stanley? What are you doing here?" His mouth hardened, and he fisted the handkerchief in a ball. "*You* are responsible for this, aren't you?"

The man never looked up. "I didn't know she'd have a heart attack."

Stan's cheek twitched, and his eyes narrowed. In one swift fluid movement he seized Stanley by his collar and yanked him up out of the chair. "I told you to stay away from her."

"Dad, stop. You're choking me."

"I told you to *stay away.* Now look at what you've done."

Stanley began to weep and he pressed against his father. "Not here, Dad. Let's go outside before someone calls security."

"No. I have nothing to say to you. Do you hear me? *Nothing.* Now get out of here before I do something we'll both regret."

"I'm sorry. I didn't know."

"There is a lot you don't know." Stan released his hold, then slung his finger toward the sliding glass doors. "Get out."

Stanley kept his gaze on the ground as he strode away.

When the emergency room doors closed, Stan slumped into a chair and scrubbed his face with his hands. We surrounded him like mother hens, crooning and petting. That was all we knew to do.

In what seemed like forever, the doctor finally came in. We jumped to our feet and charged him. Holding his hands in self-defense he said, "She's fine. She will be anyway."

Stan leaned against the wall. "Oh, God, thank you."

The doctor gestured to the chairs. Let's sit down, and I'll explain what happened.

We moved like zombies to the seats.

"Mrs. Fairchild told me she's been under stress lately. And even though it has been for a happy occasion, it is still a strain. And given the shock of the verbal attack she received this afternoon, it simply pushed her over the edge."

"Verbal attack?" I stared at the doctor. Lexi, Jema, and I turned to Stan. "Is that the reason you were so angry at your son? He attacked her?"

Stan's face steeled. "I have no doubt." He pinched the bridge of his nose and then asked the doctor. "What about Molly Kate? Did she have a heart attack?"

"No. She had what we call a stress cardiomyopathy. For several days she has probably had surges in her adrenaline and today's event, for lack of a better way to put it, *stunned* her heart. We will keep her here a couple of days. And she should be as good as new."

"Is...?" Stan flushed. "Is it still all right for us to marry on Saturday?"

"I don't see why not. But try and protect her from stress. Make sure she gets a lot of rest."

He hung his head, breathed out, then looked back at the doctor. "When can I see her?"

"You can see her now." The doctor stood. "But don't stay too long. She needs to rest."

Stan nodded and motioned for Carli. They followed the doc out of the room. When they were out of sight, Jema, Lexi, and I stared at each other, took each other's hands and laced our fingers together. Life was so unsure. No one is guaranteed another hour—another second. I resolved that from now on everyone I loved would know it.

Chapter 22

MOLLY KATE
Understanding

Carli came in with the nurse and rushed to my side. "Mom, how do you feel?"

"I'm fine baby. Don't worry."

She smiled through tears. "You'll do anything for attention, won't you?"

"You know me well, dear."

The nurse uncapped a tube connected to my IV bag. Carli watched her. "What's that?"

"Something to help your mother rest. Don't stay too long, all right?"

"I won't." Carli leaned over and kissed my cheek. "Stan is in the hall, falling apart I might add. I'll go get him before you drift off. I love you."

"Love you too, baby."

The monitors beeped and whooshed while I thought about my *encounter* with Stan's son. I wondered how he'd react to his son's behavior. Or if he'd react? What if he just blew it off? Could I live with that? On the other hand, what if he was livid? Ready to disown him? Could I live with that? And what about this son? There had to be more to his outrage than money. Something deep down in the boy troubled him, I felt it. If money were the reason for his outburst, which would amount to nothing more than unadulterated greed, then his son's behavior was truly tragic. Especially for Stan. But there was pain in his eyes. Yes, there was more to this story. A lot more.

The door cracked, and Stan peeped in. "Molly Kate? Honey? Are you awake?"

"Hi, babe." The poor man looked like he'd wrestled with an alligator and lost.

He rushed in and leaned over the bed kissing me over and over. His red-rimmed eyes filling. "I thought I had lost you." He picked up my hand and kissed it. "I'm so sorry about my son. He had no right…"

"Stan. It's okay. I'm okay."

"He will never—"

"—No, Stan. Don't make any decisions now. Not while you are upset." I started feeling woozy. "We do need to talk about your Stanley, but later, okay? The nurse put something in my IV, and I'm getting so sleepy."

"Good. You need your rest." He stood and began to fuss with my covers. "I'll stay right here."

"No, hon. Go find your boy. Talk to him. I have an inkling there is more to this outburst than our marrying. Some kind of root is feeding his anger. What happened today is only the fruit."

"I don't know if I can talk to him right now."

My eyelids grew heavy, but I managed to murmur, "You can. I know you can." Sleep pulled me toward a deep, peaceful hole, and I gave in to it.

****

Soft light filtered through my fluttering eyes. *Where am I?* This wasn't my room. And what did I smell? Kinda antiseptic-like.

Stan took my hand. "Hi, baby. How do you feel?"

It all came back to me. I was in the hospital with a stunned heart. "Good, I think." Shifting in the bed, I tried to sit up. "When can I go home? There's so much to do."

"The doc says you have to stay a couple of days so they can watch you."

"A couple? But the wedding is in a three days. There's no time. Besides, I don't like it here. The beds are uncomfortable, and the food is awful."

"What's wrong with it?"

"There isn't enough salt and fat in it."

"I can take care of that. I'll see what I can sneak in."

"Good." I grinned. "You don't want me losing weight. My dress won't fit as good."

"Don't worry, babe. I plan to have you out of your dress as soon as decently possible."

"Can we get married right now then?"

He smiled. "You *are* feeling better."

I sensed a change in him. He seemed at peace, and it made me wonder if he'd worked things out with his son. "Did you talk to Stanley?"

His expression softened. Another good sign.

"Yes. We spent the afternoon together. And you were right. There is a lot going wrong in his life, and our marriage was the proverbial straw. I'm just sorry he took it out on you."

He sighed and leaned back in his chair. "I should have known something like this would happen. When I went home to meet with the developer and work a deal on the property, I decided to call Stanley and tell him all my news. Knowing him and his easy-going ways, I expected him to say, 'that's great, Dad.' So I told him about selling the farm, about us getting married, and that we'd bought a house." Stan stared out the window and shrugged. "All hell broke loose instead. You would have thought I had sacrificed his oldest child. He started yelling so loud and talking so fast I couldn't get a word in edgewise." He turned his attention back to me. "You know, Molly Kate, neither of my boys have hardly stepped foot on the farm since their mother died. Thanksgiving and Christmas were about it. Sometimes not even then. They were never interested in the changes I wanted to make or offered to help out in any way. So, I said to him, 'If this outburst is about the money, you needn't worry. I've already made provisions for a generous inheritance for both you and your brother.' He wasn't satisfied. Then he started in on you. He wanted to know about you, how old you were, if we were sleeping together, and if you were pregnant."

I burst out laughing. "Oh babe, I know it wasn't funny at the time, but pregnant?" The very image made it hard to suppress my laughter.

"Yep. Pregnant. He said I was acting like an old fool, and he would do everything in his power to stop me from making the biggest mistake of my life."

"Well, that explains it."

"What?"

"His surprise when he saw a fat old woman named Molly Kate Fairchild. He was flabbergasted at first. But it didn't take long for him recover and think of new threats."

"The way he was acting on the phone, I had a feeling something like this would happen, so I warned him to leave you out of this, and if he disrespected you in any way, there would be no inheritance."

"But you can't do that."

"*Oh, I could.* But I won't. Molly Kate, you were right. His behavior today was so unlike him. After we had a couple of beers, he told me his wife had left him for an older man, a *wealthy* older man, I might add. She even left the kids."

"Left her own children?"

He nodded. "Then a few days later, I told him I was selling the farm and getting married. To his way of thinking, he was getting it from both ends, an older man stealing his wife, a younger woman stealing his father and inheritance."

I took Stan's hand. "Poor guy. I can see why he reacted the way he did."

"And babe, he is so ashamed. His anger and hurt fueled his words, but when he saw the medics carrying you out of the house, he told me he thought of his mother and how he would have beat anyone to a pulp if they had talked to his mother the way he had talked to you."

"Well, then, there's hope yet."

His brow creased and he pushed his smile up one cheek. "What are you hoping?"

"That one day he will love me like a mother."

"Molly, I don't know of anyone who couldn't love you." He placed his hands on either side of my face, "I sure do," and then he kissed me.

My soul did cartwheels. *Saturday couldn't come soon enough.*

Chapter 23

THE WEDDING
Ever After

Molly
For my wedding day, the good Lord blessed me with sunny blue skies, fifty-degree temperatures, and the promise of a starlit night for the evening reception. Poor Stan worried over me and treated me as if I were a delicate China doll. I loved it. However, I warned him he better get over this fear of my fragility by bedtime, because I expected action. *Lots* of action. In fact, I had him get some of those pills that, well, you know.

The house looked exquisite. My newest best friend, Scott, had the Norton House B&B looking like a Christmas feature in *Southern Living Magazine*. Imagine that? Him being a Yankee and all. He had this Southern thing down. Even better? According to Avalee's triumphant report, he had gained ten pounds since coming to Moonlight. A new Cladie Mae record.

The grandfather clock chimed one. The girls would arrive soon to dress and help me get ready for my absolute last wedding. The ceremony was set to start at five, giving us plenty of time to primp and preen. I hurried to the kitchen and made mimosas. By the time they were ready, the girls arrived.

"Hey y'all! I'm in the kitchen." When they paraded

in, I held out the tray of drinks. "Let the fun begin!"

"Woohoo!" Lexi took one in each hand.

We left the B&B and went to the pool house to begin our beauty treatments. While I was in the hospital, Scott and Avalee had decided the pool house would be the best place for the wedding party to dress. Later I found out why. As a surprise they had transformed our bedroom into a sexy boudoir for our first night before leaving on our honeymoon the next day.

After our first mimosa, we gave each other mani/pedis. While our polish dried, we drank another. Then we put on our makeup and styled our hair. Jema fixed Avalee's, Lexi's, and my hair in a chignon and fastened tiny baby's breath springs along the side. Since Jema's was short, I curled hers into soft curlicues. Then I pulled one side up, fastening it with a comb and stuck in some baby's breath.

We stood together in front of the mirror admiring ourselves and each other. Avalee's blond frosted hair, my black, Lexi's red, and Jema's honey-brown. We looked like those boxed dye models along the hair products aisle.

"Girls, we are gorgeous. Now for the icing on the cake, let's get dressed."

"Not yet, girlfriend." Lexi picked up bronzing powder and a blush brush.

I held my hand up. "Now Lex, I don't want to look like a geisha gal. I think I have plenty of blush."

An impish smile crossed her lips. "Oh, this isn't for your cheeks."

Ava frowned. "What then?"

"Body makeup. Now y'all turn around." We

followed her orders and she proceeded to put makeup on our breasts.

"What on earth, Lexi?" I started giggling. The mimosas had kicked in.

"I saw this somewhere in Google land." She brushed blush along our cleavage and used a pearlescent powder along the top of our bosoms. I have to admit, the effect was amazing. I couldn't wait to see Stan's expression.

We got dressed and hurried back to the mirror to admire ourselves—again. Especially our cleavage.

"I can't believe this." Jema sighed. "Too bad there isn't anyone to appreciate your magic Lexi."

"Oh, there is bound to be some single men tonight who will admire your charms." Lexi gave Jema a side hug. "I just feel it."

A tap sounded on the door then it opened a crack. "Hi ladies. It's Scott. Everyone decent?"

"Come in, sweetie," we all said in unison.

He sashayed in with the most beautiful bouquet I had ever seen. My eyes misted again.

"Now, honey, you can't cry." He pulled a hanky from his vest. "You'll mess up your makeup." While he daubed the corners of my eyes, tears rolled down his cheeks. Taking my hand, he twirled me around. "My word. I've never seen a more beautiful bride."

"Even though I weigh over two hundred pounds?"

"Lady, I've learned a valuable lesson here in the South. Beauty is in the soul. And if it comes with curves like yours, that's a bonus."

I couldn't resist. "So no more hounding Avalee?"

He crossed his heart. "I promise."

Avalee blew me a kiss. "Thanks, MK."

Music from the stringed quartet floated from the house across the lawn. A signal the guests were being seated. Scott kissed me on the cheek, handed the girls their single calla lily, and left.

I smiled at my friends—my sisters by choice—and tried to speak, but my voice came out in a whisper. "I love you all so very much."

The air thickened with emotion. Leave it to Lexi to shake it up. She lifted her arms and shook her hips.

"Come on, sisters. It's show time."

The seats for eighty guests had been arranged so there was an aisle down the middle. Scott stood at the back orchestrating our entrance. When the stringed quartet played Pachelbel's Canon in D major, he signaled the girls one by one to begin their way to the front in the traditional step-pause march. It took forever. This bride wanted her groom.

While I watched this impossibly slow processional, I noticed two men standing with Stan and squinted to see who it could possibly be. Stan hadn't said anything about groomsmen.

Stanly, Jr.! And I guessed the second man was his son as well. Happy tears filled my eyes, and I blinked them back. Scott kissed my cheek and waved a hanky reminding me about my makeup. I nodded and lifted the one he gave me.

The music swelled. Finally, my turn. I drifted down the aisle never taking my gaze off my love. His expression drank me in, making me feel like the most beautiful woman on earth. From the moment I took his arm, all I could see, all I could feel, all I could hear, was Stan.

****

Jema

By the time Molly Kate had walked down the aisle and wrapped her arm around Stan's, I was a wreck and cried like a baby. Thank goodness the rivulets running down my cheeks looked like happy tears. And for the most part they were, but not entirely. I also wept for Levi, for what I thought we had. I hadn't heard a word from him. Fear tormented me. Either he'd left the country, or maybe he was in jail. I missed him. I missed what might have been. As soon as a socially respectable amount of time had passed, I planned on going home and crying into my pillow all night—again.

After Molly Kate and Stan said their vows, we wandered to the dining room for hors d'oeuvres, champagne toasts, and cake. While Stanley, Jr. made his toast to the bride and groom, I happened to glance out the window. In the twilight dimness I noticed a black car pull onto the circular driveway.

Wait. It wasn't just a black car. It was that limousine.

Oh no. Not that rude man. What is he doing here?

My heart raced. There was no way I was going to let him interfere with the Molly Kate's special day.

I eased out the front door just in time to see the driver open the passenger door. A well-dressed man stepped out. It wasn't the same man as before. It was hard to see in the duskiness, but I recognized this man's gait even though I couldn't make out his face.

All the way to the first step, he watched me with his dark, soulful eyes.

Oh, my...It's—

My hand involuntarily clasped against my mouth. Hot tears filled my eyes.

"Levi?"

He reached out and took me in his arms. "Jema."

I lifted my mouth to his and let all the relief from my pain, fear, and hope respond to his kiss.

It was all surreal. He was here, holding me, kissing me. I surveyed him from head to toe. His hair fell in short salt and pepper curls, and he wore an expensive looking tux.

"Levi, what happened?"

"Is there someplace where we can talk?"

I thought of the library behind the stairs. "Yes, follow me."

Thankfully, it was Avalee's turn to toast the bride, and all eyes were on her. We snuck past the dining room unnoticed and eased into the library.

The blaze in the fireplace and the tiny white lights on the Christmas tree cast a soft glow against the dark mahogany paneling.

Levi led me to a leather chair. "Please. Sit."

I lowered onto the cushion, and he kneeled beside me. He studied my face without saying a word.

Finally he said, "I am Matthew Levi Abrams."

Did I hear him right? "You are...? Mr. Abrams?"

"I am." He continued to watch me as if to discern my feelings.

Confusion swarmed in my head like bees without a queen. "I don't understand?"

He took my hand. "Let me try to explain." After taking a deep breath, he began. "My family is one of the wealthiest in Canada." He let his words sink in for a moment. "Jema, I married young. It wasn't a marriage, really. More like a business arrangement of sorts. Because of our passion—our lust—I believed myself in love with her and gave in to the wishes of her father and mine. Even though my wife was a kind woman, neither of us really loved the other. We had nothing in common, not even children. She lived her life, and I lived mine. When she died a few years ago, I wanted to marry again, but this time for love. However, being as wealthy as I am, I can never be sure anyone loves me for me." He grimaced. "I can't even be sure anyone really likes me apart from my wealth."

Poor dear. I'd always envied the rich. I had never thought about how lonely it could be for them. How shallow relationships could be. I reached for his hand and squeezed it.

He lifted my hand to his lips and kissed it before continuing. "So I came up with a scheme of masquerading myself as someone who had nothing. A dirty homeless man. I wrote the ransom note Mr. Wolfe referred to at Miss Cladie's, to throw off my bodyguards. But I also wanted to tell the truth. So I said I had taken Mr. Abrams and would return him a better man."

The fire popped, and sparks shot onto the marble hearth. Levi, rather, Matthew, rose and stepped on them, then stared at the dancing flames, gathering his thoughts before continuing. "And, I believe, that is exactly what I did. While living in the camps among the homeless, I learned about the suffering of others. I experienced a compassion I never knew existed. At Miss Cladie's, I learned how to work with my hands." He turned and gazed at me. "But best of all, I found someone who loved me, even though I had nothing to give. Someone who loved me when I was a nobody. I found a priceless jewel, far beyond my wildest hopes. I found you."

I stood and went to him. He took me in his arms, and I nuzzled into his embrace. All my sorrow, fear, and hurt melted away in the warmth of his strong arms.

"I was so afraid you'd gone." I looked up at him. "I realized I could never love anyone again after you."

"Nor I you. The moment I met you, I knew you were different." Levi knelt down, took a tiny box from his pocket, and opened it. The largest diamond solitaire I'd ever seen sparkled in the firelight. "Jema, you said you loved me and would be willing to marry me when you thought me poor. Are you still willing to risk a life with me as a wealthy man?"

It took all my strength to remain standing. I felt faint. Could this really be happening? *To me?*

"Yes, a million times yes. I will take you as the man I love, no matter what you do or do not have."

"You have just made me a truly rich man." He stood and said, "Before I kiss you—good and proper—I want to give you a wedding gift."

His cologne, his touch, filled my senses. What did he say? "A wedding gift?"

From the same pocket he pulled out an envelope and handed it to me. I slipped open the flap and gasped. Inside were two tickets—*to Italy.*

"For our honeymoon. We will tour all of Italy, and when you have seen the entire country, I want you to choose your favorite city because I am going to buy you a villa there."

"Wha…?" I put my hands to my head to stop the swimming.

"Then you can go anytime you want and call it home." He pulled me close, then kissed me, as he put it, good and proper.

****

Lexi

After the toasts someone pointed out the limo in the driveway. I walked to the window and stared out. Nathan joined me. "I'd say whoever that is arrived a little more than fashionably late, even for the South, eh, Lexi?"

"Very late. But I didn't see anyone get out. Did you?"

"No."

Molly Kate and Stan moved beside us. She took my arm, "Who is that?"

"I have no idea." I surveyed the room. "There's Avalee over there talking to Ty. Have you seen Jema?"

"No."

Things started to churn in my mind. I seemed to remember something about a limo at Lifesource, a rude man and how he upset Jema. A sick feeling washed over me. Oh, no. No.

"What? What's wrong?"

"Jema. That man in the limo at Lifesource. Something bad has happened. Oh, Lord help us. We have to find her."

Just as those words left my mouth, Jema walked in with an incredibly well-dressed man who looked a lot like, like...? Nah. Couldn't be.

Jema glowed. "Everyone, I have an announcement to make."

Well, she definitely had everyone's attention, especially mine.

"I would like to introduce you all to my fiancé."

Molly Kate, Avalee, and I moved closer, leaned

forward, and stared. He looked so familiar.

"Some of you already know him as Levi Smith. But his real name is Matthew Abrams. Matthew *Levi* Abrams."

Nathan snapped his head around and blurted, "What?"

Miss Cladie whooped, ran over, and took them both into a bear hug. "I knew you were a fine man the minute I clapped eyes on you."

The room erupted into applause. I grasped MK's and Avalee's hands. We looked from one to another, still stunned. But when she held out her arms we ran to her laughing, crying, and dying to ask a million questions. At least I was. When we all calmed down, she gave us her huge million dollar, rather, her billion dollar smile.

Stan waved his arms. "This calls for more celebration." He signaled for the attendants to serve another round of champagne. We toasted the newly engaged couple, all the while I was dying to hear the details. I knew Nathan positively itched to get the scoop.

All in good time, Nathan. All in good time.

I took his hand and consoled. "I'll have what you want tomorrow night. My place?"

"The story? Details?"

I nodded.

"Promise."

"Yes."

A devilish grin spread across his face. "But that isn't all I want."

A shiver ran through me. It wasn't all I wanted either.

****

Avalee

After Stan toasted the newly engaged couple, Ty took my hand, leaned over, and whispered. "Unbelievable, isn't it?"

I nodded and remembered the vow I made to myself at the hospital. "Ty, we need to talk."

He frowned. "Is there a problem?"

"It's complicated."

I signaled for him to follow me and led him to the library behind the stairs. I liked this room because it was quiet. It smelled of leather and dusty books. Scott had decorated the Christmas tree in a Dickens theme. Little ghosts of Christmas past, present, and future hung on the branches amid snowflakes, crutches, holly berries, gold chains, geese, skates, and little books. It was all so whimsical.

I paced the room, wringing my hands. Ty leaned against the chair and crossed his arms. "What's all this about?"

"Ty, there is something I have to tell you, and I'm afraid it will change things between us."

His eyes darkened.

"Just promise me you will hear me out."

He dipped his head. "Oookay?"

I took a deep breath and let it out in a long, slow sigh. Searching his face, tears filled my eyes and spilled onto my cheeks. "Tyler, I am responsible for your brother's death. I guess you could say, I killed him."

Ty drew his eyebrow together. "I don't understand. He died alone in a car accident. How can you blame that on yourself?"

Painful memories rose in my mind, and I closed

my eyes against them. Finally I found my voice. "It was a week before the wedding." Heat crawled up my neck, and I fixed my gaze on the fire. "This may be TMI, but, I was late for my period which had never happened. I was never late. You could have set your watch by my cycle. So, I bought one of those pregnancy tests from the drug store and planned to check the next day." I glanced at him then back to the safety of the cavorting flames. "Back in those days, the home tests were only accurate when taken first thing in the morning."

Ty's face remained expressionless.

I pressed on. "The evening Marc died, his fraternity brothers had given him a bachelor's party. When it was over, he drove to my sorority house to say goodnight. I could tell he was pretty tipsy and in an upbeat mood, so I decided it was a good time to tell him my suspicions. Just as I thought, he took it well. He said, 'No problem, Ava.' I remember feeling so relieved. But then he said, 'you can't be *that* pregnant. So wait until after the honeymoon to get your abortion.'"

I swiped tears from my eyes. "I was stunned. That was the last thing I expected Marc to say. Abortion? Abortion wasn't even on my radar, and I told him so. He tried to explain how we were young and had plenty of time for children. He said while he was in medical school and I was working, there wasn't enough time to devote to a baby. How it wouldn't be fair to the child or us."

Ty walked to the window and shoved his hands in his pockets while staring out. I hated upsetting him, but I had to finish.

"We argued. I kept insisting I wouldn't kill our

baby, but he kept pressing for abortion. Finally, I threw my ring at him and told him I couldn't marry a man who was so selfish that he'd actually put his personal desires over a human life. He picked it up and left. The last thing I heard from him were his tires squealing out of the parking lot. Later I received the call telling me he had died in a crash."

Hesitantly, I lifted my eyes to Tyler's. "The next morning the test read negative. Two weeks later I started my period. The doctor said stress and excitement sometimes caused a woman to miss her cycle."

The weight of my guilt and grief made me fold into myself. I sank to the floor and sobbed. "If only I hadn't said anything. If only I had waited until the next morning. Marc would be alive."

Ty strode over and gathered me in his arms. "Avalee? Listen to me. Marc's death *wasn't* your fault. *Not at all*. He was drunk and angry. You were honest and stood up for what you believe. Marc's death was his own fault."

I gazed up at him. "But, if I had handled it differently..."

"We will never know, will we? Alcohol and cars are never a good idea." He tightened his arms around me. "Let it go. You didn't kill Marc. And if he were able to say anything to you, he'd ask you to forgive him."

"Do *you* forgive me Ty?" I needed to hear him say it.

"What is there to forgive?"

"Just say it, please."

"Okay, I forgive you for being a loving woman

who was shocked and momentarily displayed anger. I forgive you for not knowing my drunk brother would get in his car and drive like a bat out of hell until he ran into a tree." He put his finger under my chin and lifted my face to his. "There. Better?"

"Yes." And it was. I looked deep in his eyes and admitted. "Even if there hadn't been an accident, I don't think I could have married him. I didn't know who he was after all. I thought I did. But I really didn't."

Ty watched me a moment, hesitated, and then said, "Could you love me?"

Since I was being honest, I couldn't stop now. "Yes."

His dimples deepened. "Good. Because I've fallen in love with you." He sat in the chair, pulled me on his lap and took my hands. "I don't have a three-carat diamond, and I cannot buy you a mansion. But I can give you a lifetime of love and devotion. I will idolize you, as you deserve. Avalee, would you take a chance on me? Would you marry me?"

His voice was gentle, his face more handsome than any man I'd ever seen. But it was his heart that had me from the beginning. These past months he'd put me before himself, my needs were above his. He'd been so persistent, yet patient. Did the years between us really make a difference? No. They didn't.

"Yes, Ty. I would be honored."

He pulled me close. His kisses promised many evenings filled with love, lovemaking, and life building.

With a gleam in his eye, he said, "Come on. It's the night for announcing good news." He kissed me again. "And ours is the best."

I followed him and imagined my momma's face. While the guests mingled in the ballroom around the bar and refreshments, the musicians warmed up. Ty jumped on the stage and grabbed the mic.

"Hey folks. Can I have your attention?" All chatter and laughing stopped. "What a night. Right?"

Everyone applauded. Stan twirled Molly Kate and Levi, I mean Matthew, bowed to Jema.

Ty held his hand out. "Avalee? Could you join me up here?" Scott nudged Nathan, wearing a Cheshire cat, *I knew it,* smile. Lexi let out an ear-piercing squeal, and Jema folded her hands under her chin. Molly Kate hugged Stan and stared at the stage. Ty let a few seconds pass for dramatic pause. "Just a few minutes ago, I asked this amazing woman to be my bride. And she said YES!"

Momma threw her hands in the air and bustled toward the stage holding her arms open. Ty and I hopped off the stage and gathered her in our arms. Jema, Lexi, and Molly Kate encircled us and joined the hug. Arms, kisses, and tears swarmed Ty and me.

What a night, indeed.

I gazed up at my husband-to-be, then at my precious Momma and friends who were as dear to me as sisters. We were the women of Washington Avenue, and our lives were so intertwined it was hard to separate where one story began and the other ended. I liked it that way.

The town slogan was right after all: Moonlight, Mississippi was where my romantic dreams came true.

And the stories, the dreams, continue…

A word about the author...

Although Linda Apple lives with her husband in the hills of Northwest Arkansas, her roots run deep in the South. Originally a Mississippi gal, her stories grow from childhood memories of sleepy Southern towns, conversations around her grandmother's decadent meals, and all the rich, diverse personalities she has had the privilege to know.

The Women of Washington Avenue, her first mainstream novel, is a tribute to the kindred souls and friendships of Southern women.

More information about Linda Apple and her upcoming projects can be found on her website:
www.lindaapple.com

Thank you for purchasing
this publication of The Wild Rose Press, Inc.

If you enjoyed the story, we would appreciate
your letting others know by leaving a review.

For other wonderful stories,
please visit our on-line bookstore at
www.thewildrosepress.com.

For questions or more information
contact us at
info@thewildrosepress.com.

The Wild Rose Press, Inc.
www.thewildrosepress.com

Stay current with The Wild Rose Press, Inc.

Like us on Facebook
https://www.facebook.com/TheWildRosePress

And Follow us on Twitter

https://twitter.com/WildRosePress

www.ingramcontent.com/pod-product-compliance
Lightning Source LLC
Chambersburg PA
CBHW070846260626
47170CB00007B/2522